T0007486

THE LAWS OF
MAGIC

Praise for M. Ullrich

What the Heart Remembers Most

"Ms. Ullrich has written a beautiful romance with this book that delves into how a loving couple can end up almost destroying their love through neglect and lack of communication. This is an angst ridden story that will pull at your heartstrings so hard you may hear them protest the harsh treatment, but don't let that stop you from reading this book. It is beautifully written with characters you can easily connect with because they are so human."—*Rainbow Reflections*

"[T]his is an emotional roller coaster, full of angst and drama… but the characters were so lovable and vulnerable that it made it easy to get into. Ms. Ullrich takes her time to develop the story, with small details that seemed apparently unimportant but later gained crucial relevance."—*LezReviewBooks*

"*What the Heart Remembers Most* is a romance that tears through the readers' hearts. It is a reevaluation of what is important in life. As we experience the traumatic recovery of Gretchen along with all the characters, we feel the desperation and tension and love. We live it all through with Jax and Gretchen, and upon finishing, dare to believe in forevers again."—*Hsinju's Lit Log*

Top of Her Game

"[T]his is a beautiful sports-related romance that I thoroughly enjoyed."—*Rainbow Reflections*

Pretending in Paradise

"*Pretending in Paradise* has real depth while still maintaining the lightness and sexiness of a true romance novel and it is this unique mix that really makes M. Ullrich's books the ones to look out for when you're on the search for the next steamy romance read."—*Curve*

Against All Odds

"*Against All Odds* by Kris Bryant, Maggie Cummings, and M. Ullrich is an emotional and captivating story about being able to face a tragedy head-on and move on with your life, learning to appreciate the simple things we take for granted and finding love where you least expect it."—*The Lesbian Review*

"I started reading the book trying to dissect the writing and ended up forgetting all about the fact that three people were involved in writing it because the story just grabbed me by the ears and dragged me along for the ride...[A] really great romantic suspense that manages both parts of the equation perfectly. This is a book you won't be able to put down." —*C-Spot Reviews*

Love at Last Call

Love at Last Call is "a very well written slow-burn romance. Another great book by M. Ullrich."—*LezReviewBooks*

"[I]f you enjoy opposites attract romances—especially ones set in bars—you'll love this book! I'll definitely be looking up the rest of the author's work!"—*Llama Reads Books*

Love at Last Call is "exciting, addictive (I was up all night reading it) and still gave me all the major swoon moments I've come to love from this author. Can I give it more than five stars?"—*Les Rêveur*

"This book was like a well-crafted cocktail—not too sweet, not too bitter, and left me with a warm feeling in my body."—*Love in Panels*

"*Love at Last Call* is M. Ullrich's fifth full-length novel and it's truly excellent. The writing is smooth and engaging, with perfect pacing and a plot that's sure to please fans of contemporary romance. If you're looking for a book to sink into, have some fun, and get away from it all, you'll want to pick this one up."—*Lambda Literary*

Time Will Tell

"I adored the romance in this. I got emotional at times and felt like they fit together very well. They really brought out the best in each other and they had a lot of chemistry. I really did care whether or not they were together in the end…It was a very enjoyable read and definitely one I'd recommend."—*Cats and Paperbacks*

"M. Ullrich just keeps knocking them out of the park and I think she's currently the one to watch in lesbian romantic fiction."—*Les Rêveur*

"*Time Will Tell* is not your run of the mill romance. I found it dark, intense, unexpected. It is also beautifully romantic and sexy and tells of a love that is for all time. I really enjoyed it."—*Kitty Kat's Book Review Blog*

Fake It till You Make It

"M. Ullrich's books have a uniqueness that we don't always see in this particular genre. Her stories go a bit outside the box and they do it in the best possible way. *Fake It till You Make It* is no exception."—*The Romantic Reader Blog*

"M. Ullrich's *Fake It till You Make It* just clarifies why she is one of my favorite authors. The storyline was tight, the characters brought emotion and made me feel like I was living the story with them, and best of all, I had fun reading every word."—*Les Rêveur*

Life in Death

"M. Ullrich sent me on an emotional roller coaster…But most of all I felt absolute joy knowing that in times of darkness you can still love the one you're meant to be with. It was a story of hope, tragedy, and above all, love."—*Les Rêveur*

Life in Death "is a well written book, the characters have depth and are complex, they become friends and you cannot help but hope that Marty and Suzanne can find a way back to each other. There aren't many books that I know from one read that I will want to read time and time again, but this is one of them."—*Sapphic Reviews*

"This story pulls at your heartstrings in so many ways that I had to give it five stars."—*The Key to My Happiness*

Fortunate Sum

"M. Ullrich has written one book. That one book is *Fortunate Sum*. For this to be Ullrich's first book, well, that is just stunning. Stunning in the fact that this book is so very good, it was a fantastic read."—*The Romantic Reader Blog*

By the Author

Fortunate Sum

Life in Death

Fake It till You Make It

Time Will Tell

Love at Last Call

Pretending in Paradise

Top of Her Game

What the Heart Remembers Most

Holiday Wishes & Mistletoe Kisses

The Laws of Magic

Against All Odds
(with Kris Bryant and Maggie Cummings)

The Boss of Her: Office Romance Novellas
(with Julie Cannon and Aurora Rey)

Visit us at www.boldstrokesbooks.com

THE LAWS OF MAGIC

by

M. Ullrich

2022

THE LAWS OF MAGIC

© 2022 By M. Ullrich. All Rights Reserved.

ISBN 13: 978-1-63679-222-4

This Trade Paperback Original Is Published By
Bold Strokes Books, Inc.
P.O. Box 249
Valley Falls, NY 12185

First Edition: October 2022

THIS IS A WORK OF FICTION. NAMES, CHARACTERS, PLACES, AND INCIDENTS ARE THE PRODUCT OF THE AUTHOR'S IMAGINATION OR ARE USED FICTITIOUSLY. ANY RESEMBLANCE TO ACTUAL PERSONS, LIVING OR DEAD, BUSINESS ESTABLISHMENTS, EVENTS, OR LOCALES IS ENTIRELY COINCIDENTAL.

THIS BOOK, OR PARTS THEREOF, MAY NOT BE REPRODUCED IN ANY FORM WITHOUT PERMISSION.

CREDITS
Editors: Jerry L. Wheeler and Ruth Sternglantz
Production Design: Stacia Seaman
Cover Design by Inkspiral Design

Acknowledgments

I signed a contract for my very first novel back in 2014, and in 2016 *Fortunate Sum* was born. I had no idea where life was going to take me over the next six years or who I would meet along the way, but boy howdy what a wild ride it has been.

As usual, Radclyffe and Sandy deserve a hundred thank yous for welcoming me into the Bold Strokes team and for allowing me to keep creating time and time again. Jerry Wheeler, my amazing and brilliant editor, I cannot thank you enough for everything you've taught me and the support you have shown. I'm also grateful for the authors I've met and learned from and was lucky enough to call my friends.

Lyndsey, how can I ever thank you enough for the inspiration and encouragement you've given? This story would've never been if it wasn't for you; you're my witch and my twin flame. But it also helped that you rolled over one night and said, "Write your next book about a witch." You know I can never say no to you. Thank you for listening to me vent and helping with story ideas, but most of all thank you for putting a spell on those rocks.

Last but certainly not least and perhaps the most important thank you of them all, my readers. Thank you, each and every one of you, for looking forward to and consuming these little worlds I created with characters who mean so much to me. Thank you, thank you, thank you! I wouldn't be here today without you all. I'm not sure if/when I'll write another book, but in case this is my last, I want to say: every review, every message of excitement, and every time I got to meet a reader meant the world to me. Thank you.

Now buckle up, buttercups, you're in for a bumpy ride.

For Lyndsey:
83/88

THE ISLAND AND THE MOON

*O*nce upon a time there was a flourishing Island floating in the heart of the sea. Though her surface thrived, the Island's greatest pleasure was basking in the Moon's glow every night. For the Island and the Moon were soul mates, separated at one time but destined to meet again. The Island would wait and wait for the Moon to appear and finally come close enough to kiss. The moment the Moon touched the horizon, the Island knew she was falling in love.

CHAPTER ONE

The sun shone brightly through the haze of a sticky summer morning. Summers in Bender, Massachusetts, were unpredictable in heat, humidity, and rainfall but could always be counted on for beauty. Isla Hoffman stared out at the lush trees lining the parking lot. The strip mall housed several half-vacant stores, with Isla's pride and joy sitting at one end. Hoffman's Apothecary was coming up on its eighth anniversary and stood stronger than ever.

With great pleasure, Isla flipped the switch to turn on the purple *Open* sign in the window. The interior was calming with natural wood counters and floors, and sage-green walls lined with jars and plants. She adjusted a small display of crystals on a table beside the door. The smooth surface of a polished amazonite felt cool to her touch.

"Today is going to be a good day," Isla said. She went behind the counter where an intricate teapot sat on a burner. Herbal teas were one of the apothecary's specialties, and while some of the hot water came from a carafe, the majority of the recipes required a more delicate pour. She began humming as she gathered ingredients, ignoring the movement beside her. "Don't even think about ruining my mood."

"I'm offended," Daria said in a deep, sultry voice.

Isla stopped working and greeted her with a genuine smile and small tilt of her head. "Good morning, Daria. Happy Thursday."

Daria Kane exuded darkness from her jet-black hair and black wardrobe to her stoic appearance. That was one of the reasons Isla had hired her. Daria narrowed her eyes as she looked at Isla. "Happy Thursday. Why does your hair look different?"

Isla started to worry. Daria was her most trusted friend and confidant, and the one person who would always tell her the honest truth. Brutal or otherwise. "I cut two inches off myself last night." She fingered the ends of her light brown hair, lazily playing with the loose curl. "I needed a small change."

"I'm off for two days, and you go making crazy decisions without me."

Daria went silent, causing a flutter of nerves to erupt in Isla's stomach. Maybe the at-home trim was a mistake.

"I absolutely love it," Daria said. "Your curls came back to life."

Isla relaxed her shoulders and released a breath. "I thought so, too. I can't do a thing with it in this humidity, so I might as well work with these curls and waves."

Daria nodded. "Speaking of hot and steamy, is this tea for your lover?" Isla made a small choking sound and rolled her eyes. "Officer Good-Looking?"

"Okay, all right, that's enough." Isla kept her head down to hide her warming cheeks. Her reaction never changed no matter how many times her staff teased her. She concentrated on the vanilla bean between her fingertips. She laid it on a wooden cutting board and sliced it down the center. The vanilla must always be fresh.

The bell above the door chimed. "Hello, everyone."

"Hello, Christopher." Isla began grating fresh ginger.

Daria leaned in close, the kind of close meant to annoy, and spoke right into Isla's ear. "You should add some clove."

"Shut up."

"Ooh, is this for Patrolwoman Hot Stuff?" Christopher dropped their messenger bag behind the counter and craned over Isla's free shoulder to watch.

Isla felt like a mother with attention-hungry children. "Will you two please stop? Doing this every time I bring Lu a cup of tea is getting to be a bit much." She added cardamom, lemon balm, and crushed green tea leaves to a small square of cotton fabric. After drawing the edges together and securing it with a thin piece of string, she dropped the sachet into a paper cup adorned with the shop name and gingerly poured boiling water over it, circling the teapot three times clockwise and three times counter. "Now we wait five minutes."

Isla turned around to find both Daria and Christopher staring at her. She placed the cup down on the corrugated rubber surface they worked on for drink preparation and crossed her arms. "Don't you two have something better to do? Like work?" Christopher and Daria looked at one another, and Christopher started whistling a familiar tune.

Daria pressed her palms together and brought her hands to her cheek. "Isla and Lu sittin' in a tree—"

"You know what? I think this has steeped long enough," Isla said, picking up the tea and walking quickly to the door.

"*K-I-S-S-I-N-G!*"

Isla let the door slam behind her. The temperature was climbing, near eighty-five already. The strong sun felt hot against the skin of her shoulders, left bare by her black tank top. She scanned the parking lot and spotted the patrol car with very little effort. Was her heart speeding up?

"Must be the heat," she said quietly, walking across the blacktop. By the time she made it to the car, her smile was too big for her own good. Isla tapped on the driver's side window and waited. She watched Lu toss a small notebook onto the passenger seat and crank down her window. Isla knew the owners of the strip mall weren't millionaires, but to think they hired a security company that couldn't afford a car with power windows blew her mind. Once the window was fully down, Isla prepared herself for her most favorite assault of the day: Lu's vibrant blue eyes.

Lu looked up and smiled. "Good morning, Isla," she said, squinting one eye against the brightness of the day. "How are you?"

"I'm doing very well." Isla wanted to ask Lu how she was doing or at the very least speak a little more, but she was distracted by Lu's appearance. "You cut your hair. I cut my hair, too."

Lu raised her eyebrows. "Uh yeah. It was time for a summer cut."

Isla didn't know what to say. Lu's thick dark hair no longer curled around her ears or fell on her forehead the way it had since Lu began patrolling her parking lot three months ago. The sides were tightly shaved and faded from bottom to top, leaving a few inches to style back and away from her face. Lu's *stunning* face. Isla had never seen such a stunningly butch woman before. The lips she stared at began moving.

"Isla?"

"Hm?" Isla snapped her attention back to Lu's eyes, now filled with humor. She had to say something. "Your face."

"My face?"

"Your hair is very complementary to your face. Drink your tea before it gets cold." Isla turned and walked briskly back to the safety of her apothecary. "*Your face,*" she said, mocking herself as she opened the door. "What is wrong with you?" She shut the door and saw everyone looking at her, employees and customers alike. "It's another hot one." Isla turned away and went straight for a display of bath salts and herbal additives.

Isla took pride in how she ran her business. The shop was clean, neat, and easy to navigate, and her inventory skills were impeccable. Every item was stocked and in place, much to her chagrin at the moment.

"Didn't go well?"

Isla jumped. Daria had an infuriating knack for sneaking up on people. "I brought her the tea, and I came back."

"Then why are the tips of your ears red?"

"I'm hot."

"Isla?"

Isla shifted every wooden scoop delicately placed in loose bath salt containers, making sure they'd all match. Anything to avoid looking at Daria, because the moment she looked into Daria's dark eyes, she'd start talking, and talking was what always got her into trouble. She kept her head down and said, "I have an appointment with Peter this morning at ten."

"He canceled."

Isla looked at Daria, completely shocked. "Peter never misses an appointment. He can't."

Daria smirked. "He didn't. Now tell me what happened that has you all flustered."

Isla wanted to be mad she'd fallen for one of Daria's tricks, but she should know better by now. They'd been friends for years. Isla knew Daria played dirty, and now she had to spill the beans. She supposed that's what happened when you had the ability to glamour anyone you met.

Isla was unable to look away from Daria's gaze, even after she shrugged. "I brought her the tea, then I noticed she got a haircut, and I complimented it."

"Sounds okay to me."

Isla tried to keep the story at that, but she felt the truth bubbling up in her throat. "I started it by announcing I had cut my hair, too."

"Oh. Well, that's not terrible—"

"I *stared*. For a long time without speaking."

"Isla…" Daria's tone dripped with sympathy so thick it nudged the line of pity.

"I blame you two," Isla said, waving her index finger between Daria and Christopher. "You've manufactured some fantastical crush, and it's gotten into my head." A young woman browsing elixirs raised one eyebrow but had enough manners to not look at Isla.

Christopher raised their hands in defense. Large silver rings adorned every other finger, and their fingernails were painted with a matte black polish. "I have a customer to assist." They walked away and left Isla and Daria alone to duke it out. A common, smart decision.

Daria never got flustered, a quality Isla was often jealous of. "We manufactured nothing," she said coolly.

"If you say something enough times, it'll sound true even when it's not."

"That's manifesting, and it's true."

"No, it's not."

"You don't have a crush on the attractive security guard outside?"

Isla opened her mouth. She had a million colorful denials locked and ready to fly, but a harsh laugh came out. "You're my best friend. You should believe me immediately."

"I always believe you. I trust you more than any other person on this earth, mostly because you can't lie anyway, but still."

Isla rolled her eyes. "Thank you. That means a lot."

"So if you looked me in the eyes and told me you don't have a crush on Lu, I would believe you."

The staredown began.

Isla focused on the hint of gold surrounding Daria's pupils. Pupils that would be swallowed by darkness without their halo. She thought of her feelings toward Lu and tried to find a loophole that could get her out of her present predicament. Did she have a crush? What was a crush? As a thirty-six-year-old grown woman, was she even capable of a crush? "Aren't crushes for schoolgirls?"

"Deflection is for adults."

"Ooh," Christopher said from across the shop.

"Fine. If you say it's a crush, then it's a crush. Either way, it doesn't matter, and we all should get back to work." Isla crossed her arms over her chest.

"Or..." Daria pursed her lips and tilted her head in implication.

"No."

"You could..."

"Absolutely not."

"Ask Lu *out* for tea instead of *bringing* her a cup."

"It won't happen because it can't."

"Why not?"

Isla sighed. She had explained herself countless times over the years, but no one seemed to believe her. Or take her seriously. "You know why."

"Oh, come on," Daria said softly. "You made a mistake twenty years ago. You have to let that go and stop walking around like you're cursed."

"Aren't I?" Isla said, waiting. For what? She was unsure. Maybe she wanted to hear something she hadn't considered, something new that'd give her lonely heart some hope. "I can't trust myself to fall in love." She shook her head and looked away from Daria. "Sure sounds like a curse to me."

Daria placed her hand on Isla's shoulder, not quite an awkward pat but not committing to an encouraging squeeze either. "You have to let it go."

"I have to be careful. Not just for me, but for this," she said, motioning to her apothecary. "We're doing important work here."

"Are you happy, though?"

Isla smiled. "My purpose is helping people, and I get to do that every day."

"I want you to be happy, but I'm afraid you won't find that here and with one-night stands or an occasional day with a succubus."

Isla felt her ears warm. "I *am* happy. Now I need to prep for my appointment with Peter. We can't have his feet turning back to hooves, now can we?" She started for her office, but Daria stopped her. She wouldn't turn around, but she listened.

"Even the most powerful witches deserve to live for themselves."

Isla walked away then, thinking of all the ways she truly was happy. "Happy enough," she whispered, going into her office.

CHAPTER TWO

L u Cadman slowed her patrol car as she approached the farthest corner of the parking lot near the dumpsters. She collected various fast-food bags and Little Debbie wrappers from around the car. She shouldn't be eating this kind of junk. She knew better, but with a McDonald's less than a mile in one direction and Wendy's in the other, convenience often won. She stretched to get a few empty water bottles and coffee cups from the passenger-side floor.

She stopped before stepping out of the car to throw away the ridiculous amount of garbage she had accumulated and looked at the cup in the holder. She emptied her hands into the dumpster and came back for the cup. Softly, she smoothed her index finger over the apothecary's name. She smelled the contents, just as she did every other time Isla brought her tea. Lu tossed it into the dumpster.

She was only supposed to work this location for a month, but she'd grown more attached to the town, this strip mall, and that apothecary as the days went on. She adjusted her belt and made sure her standard blue button-up was still tucked in. Thank God security uniforms came in short sleeves because the air-conditioning in her car was spotty at best and the summer heat was unrelenting. Lu should have been used to extreme weather after several tours in various desert and arctic lands, but time was starting to catch up to her. As forty approached, Lu started to notice her resistance and stamina faltering. Great.

Patrolling the grounds of Bender's one and only strip mall brought very little excitement. Aside from loitering and the occasional rambunctious teenager smoking and throwing butts where they shouldn't, this town hadn't proved to be as interesting as Lu was promised.

"Bump in the night, my ass," she said. She continued her usual path back to the center of the parking lot. Hoffman's Apothecary was by far the most visited store, sitting at one end of the strip, with a pizzeria on the other. In between were two vacancies, a Stop and Go that stayed in business thanks to regular lottery players, and a struggling dance studio. Judging by the lack of cars in the lot, Lu gave the studio a month at most. She grabbed her notebook and reclined her seat a bit. The last incident Lu had documented was from three days ago when a homeless man was rummaging through dumpsters. She bought him two slices of pizza and explained he couldn't hang around the businesses. No harm, no foul. But according to her notes, she de-escalated an altercation between him and the pizzeria owner, Pat.

As of late, Lu found herself padding her notes more and more. Her boss wanted proof she was needed and that resources were being spent in the proper locations. She couldn't admit her post was a waste, and she didn't dare explore why. Motion caught her eye. A middle-aged man walked with a limp toward the apothecary. Lu tried to determine whether he had an injury to his right or left leg—maybe it was both. He opened the door, and Isla greeted him immediately.

Her smile was bright and genuine, soft in every way Lu had started to expect. She couldn't look away as the two shared a quick hug. She recognized him as a customer, but he wasn't a daily visitor. She flipped her notebook back a few weeks and continued searching. Sure enough, he'd been in one month ago exactly. Coincidence? Maybe. Noteworthy? Probably not. Lu rested her head back and sighed. She was tired and hungry again, but it was still too early for many options to be open. She'd have to settle for water and a protein bar. Unless...

Lu stepped into Hoffman's Apothecary and froze, becoming instantly aware of the mistake she had made. A woman in all black stopped what she was doing and shot Lu an amused smile.

"Can I help you?" she asked with an obvious amount of humor in her tone.

Lu couldn't retreat now—she had come too far. "I...um..." She cleared her throat and found the strength in her words again. "I was wondering if you carried any snacks."

"Snacks?"

"Yeah. Snacks." *This is fun.* "I'm hungry, and it's too early to leave for lunch. I wanted something more substantial than my usual oatmeal cream pie from next door, and considering the tea selection, I figured I might be able to find something here." Lu took a deep breath and barely resisted a facepalm.

The woman stepped closer, looking Lu up and down along the way before she reached out her hand. "Daria. I can't believe it's taken this long for us to meet."

Lu wasn't sure why they had to meet at all, but she returned the handshake regardless. "Lu."

Another employee slid up next to Lu. "I'm Christopher. Your haircut really *does* look great on you."

Lu tried her best to school her reaction, but her mouth dropped open anyway. Did Isla really talk about her that much? "Thank you. About those snacks?"

"No. I'm sorry," Daria said, her apology sounding deeply genuine.

"I could think of one snack for her to eat," Christopher mumbled, only to be elbowed by Daria.

"I keep telling Isla we should at least offer muffins at the tea bar, but she won't listen. I'm sure she'd be kicking herself now."

Lu nodded and looked between Daria and Christopher. "Got it. Thank you for the help."

Daria's voice nearly purred. "Anytime, darling."

Lu could hear them whispering and giggling as she left the store. *Note to self: stick to Little Debbie.* She sat back in her car and opened her peanut butter protein bar, considering all the ways she did not like how that visit made her feel. What did Isla say about her? Did she talk about her often? What did it mean?

She stared off into the distance, at no fixed point in particular but in the direction of Isla's shop. She could go back in and ask to speak with Isla. That'd be a surefire way to get to the bottom of what was going on. Lu stopped chewing. But she couldn't purposely seek out Isla, no way, because then she'd be expected to speak in real, coherent sentences, and Lu did not believe that was possible. Not when Isla looked at her with such softness. Lu choked on her own spit. After she gulped some water to calm down, she looked up through watery eyes to see the limping man leaving the apothecary. He was no longer limping. Lu leaned forward and narrowed her eyes.

"Oh, Isla. What are you up to?"

❖

"Peter is good as new, and he promised me his wife would stop by with some of her infamous pierogis next week." Isla emphasized her statement by drumming her fingers on the countertop. "You all are welcome to some." Her announcement went unacknowledged as Daria finished a customer's tea and Christopher looked out the window.

"Have a great day," Daria said, handing the tea to a lovely woman wearing a mint-green sundress. She waited until the customer was out the door before showing her excitement. "Did you ask for double this time and admit you never share fairly?"

Isla looked at her, brows raised and mouth agape. "I do *too* share."

"Share *fairly*."

Isla let out a long breath as she tried to think of a retort, but she couldn't argue. "I'll do better." Both Daria and Christopher looked at her like she'd finally figured out how to lie. "I promise. Anyway, while I was with Peter, I was thinking we could figure out a way to broaden our salve and ointment selection in the storefront. I'd like to make things more convenient for some of my clients who have a hard time coming to me. Especially in the daylight, if you know what I mean."

"Oh, please," Christopher grumbled, leaning back against the counter. "Ivan and his crew can come out during the day. Vampires are seriously dramatic."

Isla chuckled. "I'm going to tell him you said that."

"No! You can't. He'll make me pay full price for my drinks."

"We'll see."

"How do you think we can do that when Peter's needs aren't exactly the same as Jane Doe's eczema?" Daria made a good point. "And we're pretty space limited."

"I'm not completely sure yet, but it's something I'd like to brainstorm with you two." Isla could tell Daria and Christopher weren't completely sold on the idea. "Daria, you are a problem-solving witch. Your brain works in a way mine never could. And Christopher, you're a warlock whose creativity knows no bounds."

"I prefer witch," Christopher said. "Warlock never felt right." They picked a fuzz from their tunic shirt. The eggplant color enhanced their olive complexion beautifully.

Isla smiled. She had watched Christopher grow over the years, both in their powers as well as their personality. "I have two brilliant witches and my grandmother's book. I feel like we can do anything."

"Don't forget, we also have you."

"I'm only as good as my coven."

"Stop minimizing yourself," Daria said firmly. "You're the most powerful witch around, and your crusade to help those like us is admirable. Your grandmother would be very proud of you."

Isla fought back tears. Daria wasn't one for warm and fuzzy moments, and she must've made herself uncomfortable because she immediately changed the subject and went in an unexpected direction.

"Lu was looking for you."

Isla went from choking back tears to just choking. "Looking for me? Why me?"

"Well, technically she was looking for a snack."

"A snack?"

"She was hungry."

"And she came here for a snack?"

"Mm-hmm."

"Here?"

"Yes, darling. Here."

Isla placed her hand to her forehead. "I'm confused."

Christopher pushed off the counter when the door chimed. "So were we, but then it became pretty obvious she was looking for an excuse to see you."

"No way. After how many months of sitting outside? She's never once come in here, and whenever I go out to her, she barely says more than hello and how are you. She must've been desperate." Isla looked out the window at the idling patrol car.

"Desperate for you," Daria said, followed by a deep chuckle. "I'm going to play around with the ointments. Maybe I can expand the space."

Isla didn't reply, nor did she look away. She squared her footing and channeled her focus into watching the slight motion within Lu's car. If she could shut out the noise around her, she might be able to pick up on Lu's energy. She leaned slightly, shifting her body forward and closing her eyes. Nothing was coming through, which was strange. Even if she couldn't pick up energies from her target, her surroundings should offer something. The muscle in the arch of her foot began tightening, and it cramped before Isla could straighten her stance. The pain hit her so suddenly that she sucked in a breath and opened her eyes.

"Ow, ow, ow." She hobbled back to sit on a stool behind the

counter. "Ow!" She slipped off her ballet flat and started rubbing circles into the arch of her foot. Christopher looked over with concern. "I'm fine," she said, "but I should take this damn charley horse as a sign to stay right here and mind my own business."

"*Or*," Christopher said, dragging out the word, "it's a sign to get moving and go talk to Lu. What if she's the love of your life?"

"She's not."

"How do you know?"

"I just do."

"Like how you know her exact schedule? Which spots she likes to park in?" Christopher put their hand on their hips. "I bet you even know what color underwear she's wearing."

"Christopher," Isla chastised. She looked around even though she already knew there were no customers. "Her schedule is nearly the same as ours, and there's a very distinct pattern to the spots—" Isla held up her hands. "You know what? I don't have to explain myself to you or anyone. I can't have that kind of distraction, and that's that."

Daria came back to the front of the store. "What if she's good for you and not a distraction?"

Isla smiled in spite of her ire. Lu would probably be good for any woman who'd love her back. "I wouldn't be good for her, and I've accepted that. You should, too."

"Let's imagine for a moment that you didn't have to worry about a thing. You're free to fall in love with whoever strikes your fancy. What would you do?"

"I can't imagine that life." Isla turned away from Daria and looked up at the large painting hanging behind the counter, a crescent moon glowing above a small island floating in colorful waters. "Plus, she's normal."

"Nobody's normal," Christopher said.

"You know what I mean. She's a regular, everyday human. She wouldn't understand our world."

"How do you know?" Daria asked.

"I see it when I look at her. She has very honest eyes, soft and open. Like you can really see the person she is when she looks at you." She turned to look at Daria and added, "I see it when I look at her."

Daria smirked. "I meant, how do you know she wouldn't understand our world?"

"We work here to help so many of us hide, and the ones of us who choose not to hide?" Isla said, shrugging. "Nobody believes they exist." Isla lowered her head and walked toward the back. "I don't see me winning. She'd either prefer we hide or not believe a word I say."

Christopher sidled up next to Daria. "She has a point."

Daria watched Isla until she disappeared into her office. "Sounds more like a problem."

CHAPTER THREE

"Hey, boss. This is unit sixty-six calling in the end of her shift," Lu said directly into her CB radio. She waited for confirmation.

The radio crackled to life. "Anything to report?"

Lu considered lying. She moved the microphone back and forth in front of her mouth as she fabricated incident after incident in her head. She sighed and gave up. "Nothing here."

"Is it even worth me having you out there, Cadman?"

She wanted to be honest, but before she could open her mouth, she spotted Isla switching off the *Open* sign in the apothecary's door. Lu pressed the radio's button and said, "Not really sure, yet. If I don't witness anything noteworthy by the end of the summer, I say it's time to move me." A beat of silence followed.

"Roger that."

Lu mounted the microphone back onto the base and laid her head back. "End of the summer," she said resolutely. Sticking around only prolonged the inevitable. She wasn't needed here in Bender, and staying for the sole purpose of seeing Isla was unprofessional and unlike her. Her skills and training could be helpful elsewhere. Plus, Lu hadn't even managed to get to know Isla beyond quick small talk in the mornings. She looked at the apothecary again and noticed all the lights were out. Lu allowed herself to consider getting to know Isla. Why not? If it went badly, she could leave town. If it went well, she could try for a more permanent job in the area. She smiled at the thought.

What if she doesn't even like you? Lu wanted to swat away the intrusive thought. Lu wasn't exactly a top scholar, but she wasn't clueless when it came to women. Even if on purely a physical level, Isla was interested in Lu. She would start slow and small, maybe an innocent question in the morning about Isla's weekend plans or the story of opening the apothecary. Lu simply wanted a little more insight into this woman who had captivated her from her very first day on the job.

Lu put the car in drive and started home. The cramped two-bedroom condo she rented was cozy, which was the only positive word she could use to describe it. The soldier in her kept it clean and clutter-free, but with the limited space, even her daily necessities seemed too big. Ten minutes later, Lu pulled into her designated spot and cut the engine. As she stood at her front door, she noticed a small spider making a home around the weathered black address numbers. Turned out forty-four was a good enough home for the two of them.

Inside, the decor was simple, streamlined, and immaculate. Anyone who stepped into Lu's condo could guess she was ex-military, or at the very least a minimalist with a hatred for disorder. She walked along the foyer and hung up her keys on their hook. Lu went about putting away her workbag and shedding her uniform. She grabbed tomorrow's identical look from the closet and laid it out on a brown leather chair in her bedroom. Only then did her six-year-old bloodhound come shuffling around the corner.

"Hey, Samson," Lu said, smiling. She crouched to scratch the top of his wrinkly head. He yawned. "Long night, fella?" She stood, and Samson followed her movement. She laughed at his droopy eyes. "You may not be a good guard dog, but you're the best at everything else you do. Come on, I'll put a towel on the bathroom floor for you."

After a quick shower with Samson at her side, Lu sat on the couch in her boxers and sports bra. She allowed herself one hour of mindless television a night, a way to decompress but also process. Every night, without fail, she'd think about Isla. And every night, without fail, she'd smile. Her phone rang and tore her from her thoughts.

Lu slid her thumb across the screen. "Hey, sis." She lowered the TV volume.

"Your niece won't stop asking for you. Will you please talk to her so she'll leave me alone?"

Lu looked at the small digital clock next to her TV. "It's after ten."

"There's no real schedule to these monsters, and anyone who says there is, is a liar. Please. Put me out of my misery."

"You know, Kayla, if anyone heard you talk like this, they'd think you hate your child."

"I love my child. I would die for her, but that doesn't mean I like her all the time."

Lu covered her face with her hand. "Please tell me she's not right next to you."

"Oh my God, no. Do you really think I'm that awful? She's in the bath."

"Unattended?" Lu said, horrified.

"She's four years old, Lu. Bathing unsupervised in six inches of water is no more dangerous than the way she decided to go down the stairs this morning."

"I don't even want to know."

"I'm putting you on speaker while I dry her."

"Lulu!"

"Hi, Lilly. What are you up to?" Lu ran her fingers over Samson's ear aimlessly.

"I just got out of the bath. I want to watch *Frozen*."

Kayla's groan was audible, making Lu laugh.

"What did you do today?"

"I went to school and played with Tristan."

"That sounds fun. What did you learn?"

"Colors," Lilly said very loudly for no apparent reason.

"She sort of learned her colors," Kayla said. "She still thinks red is purple."

"Colors can be tricky." Lu chuckled. "Are you excited to come to my house soon?"

"Yes!"

Kayla grunted. "Stop moving. I can't get your underwear on."

"She can bathe unsupervised, but you have to put her underwear on?"

"Here's a fun fact about kids, sis," Kayla said drolly. It always annoyed Lu when her family treated her differently for not having or wanting kids. She barely spoke to her parents, but when she did, they always treated her like her life wasn't as important as Kayla's. "They go through phases, and right now Lilly is going through a terrible panty-hating phase. If I don't put them on her myself and then make sure her pants are on, she'll pull them right off and hide them."

"Hide them?"

"I've found more underwear in my couch this week than you did during your twenties."

Lu thought about her wild years for a moment and smiled. "That's a lot of panties."

"Ew," Kayla said with a laugh. "Speaking of, you've been in Massachusetts for a while now. Seeing anyone yet?"

Lu shook her head before realizing Kayla couldn't see her. "No way. Dating would be too complicated right now. What about you? Will things work out with Steve?"

"No way. He hates how involved Lilly's father is, and that, to me, means he's incapable of putting Lilly first."

"Toss him to the curb," Lu said, motioning with her thumb.

"Lulu?"

"Yes, Lill?"

"Can I see Sa'son?"

Lu's heart swelled. Lilly's inability to say the *m* in Samson's name was one of the last traces of her tiny-human days. Now Lilly spoke in complete sentences, and most of her words were fairly clear. Kids really did grow up too fast.

"Sure thing," Lu said, hitting the FaceTime icon and turning the camera around. Lilly's chubby cheeks appeared on the screen, and she started giggling instantly. "You'll get to see your best friend really soon."

"Promise?"

"Promise. But first, you have to be good for your mom and go to bed." Lu turned the camera around and gave Lilly her best assertive gaze. "Will you do that for me?"

Lilly's pout was severe. "Yeah."

"Good night, Lilly."

"Good night, Lulu."

"Hang up on me." The phone screen disappeared immediately. "Damn, kid." Lu laughed. She scratched Samson's chin and said, "Are you excited to see your cousin?" Samson snored louder. "I knew you would be." She turned the TV back up and got lost in another episode of *Hoarders*.

The next morning came with too many obstacles. Lu woke up cranky and achy on her couch, uncharacteristically late. After rushing to get herself ready and Samson fed, she forgot her phone at home and had to turn back halfway through her drive. She didn't arrive at the shopping plaza until well after eight. She put the car in park and sat back with a grunt. Lu knew early morning anxiety would sour anyone's mood, but her mood felt impossible to shake even once she was settled. The most painful part of her entire morning was not having enough time to get coffee.

Lu wasn't exactly a coffee snob, but she did have standards. Fast-food coffee was acceptable, but she avoided gas station coffee at all costs, and the convenience store in the strip mall was a last resort. If Isla's apothecary was open, she'd even settle for one of those funky teas over bitter regular, old decaf, and watery French vanilla, but it wasn't. She looked around before getting out of the car and walking up to the Stop and Go—it opened at eight, so at least the coffee was fresh. She filled the largest paper cup they had and kept it black, never trusting the pint of half-and-half that sat in a bucket of ice, all day, every day. She put a five on the counter in front of the owner and nodded.

"Just this, Ray."

"Oh wow. No doughnuts this morning? Are you feeling okay?"

Lu dropped her head in shame. "I'm fine. Thank you." She took her change and left the store without another word. Once she was seated back in her car, she took a sip of her coffee and cringed. "In what world is *that* coffee? Jesus." She drank more.

The morning moved slowly, and Lu didn't see Isla once. Lu didn't necessarily see Isla every morning, but she saw her most, and looking for her had turned into a habit. Lu moved her car to a shaded part of the parking lot in an attempt to avoid the noon sun. She was grateful the almost empty strip mall had such lush landscaping.

She turned up the air-conditioning and opened the weather app on her phone. The high for the day was forecast to be a staggering ninety degrees, well above the eighty-degree average. Lu unbuttoned her uniform shirt and pulled it from her damp body. She tossed it on the passenger seat and grabbed a magazine from the floor to fan herself. It shouldn't be this hot. She turned the AC up as far as it would go and pointed the vents to blow directly on her face. She closed her eyes and waited for cool relief to come, only to feel the air grow hotter.

"No," she said, reaching desperately for the climate control. "No, no, no. Please no." Her dash confirmed what she feared. The patrol car was running hot, and her AC had finally kicked the bucket. "Great. This is a great day."

CHAPTER FOUR

Isla felt her cheeks grow warmer and warmer, both from smiling nonstop and from bashfulness. "I am very happy for you, Maribel."

"I'm telling you, whatever you put in that passion elixir revived Henry's drive. It's like we're newlyweds again." Maribel started to fan herself. She looked around before continuing. "I couldn't walk straight for a whole day."

"Wow."

"Isla is the best for a reason," Daria said, nudging Isla.

Isla held her side and could feel the heat emanating from her skin through her thin cotton tank. "I'm really glad it worked for you."

Maribel clearly wanted everyone to know just how well it was working. "He gets home from work, and almost immediately I'm on my back. He was always a man of few words, but now he's a man of all action. I swear I can still feel him, hours later."

"On your skin or inside?" Daria asked.

"Daria," Isla said firmly. Embarrassment washed over her and heat rushed to her ears.

Maribel placed her hand on Isla's forearm. "It's okay, Isla. I don't mind." She looked at Daria and smirked. "Outside, inside, and every inch in between. The thing about being married to a"—she paused to look around—"werewolf is once a month you are guaranteed the most carnal, raw ride of your life. But it's much less intense now since we started suppressing that side of ourselves."

"I'm sorry—"

"No, Isla, do not apologize. You're helping us so much. It's the only way we can live our lives as teachers and parents. We've been married for eighty-four years. We're bound to hit a few dry spells."

Isla knew better than to feel bad for helping someone, but guilt still crept in from time to time. She smiled stiffly. "Just let me know when you need a refill."

"You'll be hearing from me soon. Our anniversary is coming up." Maribel winked before sashaying out the door, her long black braid brushing over her curvy behind.

Isla stared at the closed door.

"You okay, hon? You're very flushed." Daria's voice cut through the thick silence. She reached out to touch Isla's cheek.

"I'm fine," Isla said, swatting away Daria's hand. "I'm just a little…" Isla motioned her hands up and down.

"Turned-on? Horny?"

Isla widened her eyes. "Daria. Jesus."

"What? We're all adults with adult feelings and adult body parts that tingle when we focus on specific feelings. I know I'm tingling."

Isla pressed her thighs together. "It's been a while since I've seen anyone, which means my tensions are running high."

"You need to go out and get—"

The door chimed, and in walked Lu, looking very different than her normally polished self. She stood just inside the store, her crisp white T-shirt tight across her chest. A darkened V of sweat ran down from the neckline. Lu's eyes, made even bluer by her red cheeks, went right to Isla and never wavered.

"Laid," Daria said quietly. She cleared her throat and walked off, nearly colliding with a table along her way.

Isla looked at Lu, blinked, and blinked some more. She knew she needed to speak, but her throat was dry, and she couldn't trust her mouth to *not* say what she was thinking. "Hi," she said, but the one word sounded more like a scratchy exhale.

"Hi, um…" Lu looked down at herself. "I'm sorry to barge in looking like this."

Isla considered this permission to let her eyes wander. She noticed Lu's dirty hands and dark smudges extending up her forearm. Lu had a number of veins popping along the way, which complemented the apparent strength of her body.

Isla tried her best to focus and say something, anything coherent. "You're a mess."

"Yeah. Shit. I shouldn't have come in here." Lu turned back to the door.

"No!" Isla shouted. She covered her mouth in shock over her outburst. "I just meant you don't look like you normally do."

Lu's worried expression smoothed into a crooked smile. Her forehead had a few deep wrinkles that grew as her eyebrows rose. "Clean?"

Isla giggled, a God's honest giggle like a little girl. "Yeah. Clean."

"The air-conditioning broke in my car, and under some butch delusion I thought I would try to fix it."

"No go?"

Lu shook her head. "I tried fixing my own car, and all I got was this dirty T-shirt."

Isla looked at Lu's shirt and focused, again, on the way it hugged her chest. But this time she also noticed how snug the short sleeves were around her biceps. *Speak, Isla.* "The shirt didn't get that dirty." Silence fell, and she looked up at Lu's face again.

"It was a joke. You know? Like the *I climbed Mt. Everest and all I got was this lousy T-shirt* shirt?"

Isla forced a laugh. "Oh. Sorry." She wrapped a loose curl around her index finger and said with a self-deprecating laugh, "The blond is natural."

"You wear it well." Lu's eyes widened. "Anyway, I'm waiting to hear back from the mechanic down the street. I have to get a rough estimate for my boss before any repairs are approved. I won't stay long."

"You need air-conditioning."

"Don't I know it," Lu said. She swiped at her forehead. "That's why I'm in here. Do you mind if I hang out for a bit and soak up the cool air? It was like an oven in that car."

Isla tried to tamp down her excitement. "I don't mind at all, but I can probably do better than sheltering you from the heat. Go out to your car, and I'll meet you in one minute."

Lu looked at her skeptically. "Okay?" She left but not eagerly.

Isla hung her head. "*Sheltering you from the heat?* Isla, what is wrong with you?" She wanted to smack herself. Instead, she rubbed her hands together and squared her shoulders. She left the shop, instantly breathless from the heat. She shielded her eyes from the sun and started for Lu's car.

"Why are we out here if the air-conditioning is in there?" Lu said, pointing to the apothecary.

Isla smiled, feeling a tad cocky and even a little more underestimated. "I think I can fix it." Disbelief was written across Lu's face. "Actually, I know I can."

"All right," Lu said, digging into her pockets and tossing Isla the car keys.

She fumbled the keys and winced when they hit the ground. She picked them up as gracefully as she could and walked them back over to Lu. "Get in and pop the hood, then start it when I tell you to."

"Yes, ma'am."

Isla had to press her thighs together again. Maribel's story had really gotten to her. She bit her lip to keep from dropping her mouth open at the beautiful yet unwelcome thought of Lu saying that to her in the bedroom. The sound of the hood popping brought her back to safe and boring reality. She propped it open with the hood stand. Isla had no clue what she was looking at, aside from the easily recognizable well for windshield washer fluid and cap where you'd pour motor oil.

"Do you need me to do anything?" Lu said from the driver's seat.

"No. It'll take me a minute or so. Stay there and wait for my signal." Isla ran the fingertips of her right hand over the housing of the motor while she rested her left hand on the battery. Isla closed her eyes and focused her energy on the car. "Cool the air, cool the room, fix the broken, and run like new," she said in a low, even voice. Her fingers began tingling and grew cold. "Cool the air, cool the room, fix the broken, and run like new."

"Did you say something?"

She opened her eyes. "Start the car." She didn't move her hand as the engine roared to life. Her fingers grew colder and colder still, nearing a point of pain. "Come on, come on." Isla took a deep breath, broadening her diaphragm and channeling the energy through her body and back to the car.

"It's working," Lu said in a shout.

Isla pulled away and shook off the currents still running through her. She dropped the hood back down and smiled through the windshield at Lu's shocked expression. She wiped her hands on her black linen pants and waited awkwardly for Lu to speak or move.

Eventually, Lu turned off the car and got out. She walked to Isla slowly and shook her head. "How did you do that? Are you secretly a mechanic?"

"It runs in the family."

"Thank you," Lu said, extending her hand.

Isla looked at Lu's hand, big and welcoming, and hesitated before taking it. She gave Lu's hand a brief shake, going breathless at a late tremor. She signaled back to the store and said, "I need to get back."

Lu rubbed her palm and looked at Isla quizzically. "Have lunch with me?"

"What?"

"As thanks." Lu scratched at the back of her neck, and Isla tried to keep from staring at her bicep as it flexed. "I'd like to buy you lunch as a thank-you. You saved me from heat exhaustion and spared me from a lecture about expenses from my very cheap boss."

Isla knew better than to accept, but she also knew she needed to eat. "Okay."

"Great." Lu's excitement was apparent. "Shall we go now?"

"Now?"

"Yeah, it's"—Lu looked at her watch—"after one o'clock now."

"Oh. Wow. Okay." Isla looked over her shoulder to the apothecary. "I have to get my phone and my purse. I'll be right back." She heard Lu speak after turning away but didn't stay to hear whatever it was she said about cooling off the car. She rested her back against the door once she got back to the store. "Shit."

"What did you do?" Christopher said.

Isla looked at Christopher but didn't really see them. She stared through them and off into the distance. What had she just agreed to?

"Isla? Honey?" Christopher approached slowly. "What happened with lover B-O-I?"

Isla blinked away her stupor, and she forced a smile. "I'll be out of the store for a little bit."

"Are you okay?"

Isla couldn't look at Christopher. "I'm having lunch with Lu?"

"Are you asking me or telling me?" Christopher threw their long black scarf over their shoulder. "Because if you're asking, the answer is absolutely yes."

Daria sauntered over. "I think you meant abso-fucking-lutely yes."

"I shouldn't."

Christopher held up their hand. "You should."

"And you will," Daria said.

Isla nodded and squared her shoulders, movements that would normally accompany confidence, but her stomach churned with worry.

CHAPTER FIVE

L u should've kept looking. She should've ventured outside of her safe two-mile radius and picked a nicer place for lunch. But they settled into a booth at Chili's instead. The menus and table were clean, and at least they got unlimited chips and salsa. She reached for a chip and started eating immediately. Her first nervous habit.

She chewed and swallowed. "I was surprised when I saw a Chili's. Bender is small and doesn't have much. It's not really a place I'd put a corporate chain restaurant, but if I did, I'd probably go with a Panera or Red Lobster." Lu grabbed another chip and drowned it in salsa. Eating helped control nervous habit number two: talking.

Isla covered her smile with her hand. She tilted her head and said, "You'd put a Red Lobster in a small town in a state known for their great seafood?"

Lu stopped chewing. "I guess there's no hiding I'm not from around here." Lu watched as Isla shifted in her booth and ran her hand up her bare arm to the mandala tattoo on her shoulder. "Are you cold?"

"No. I'm fine."

"I like your tattoo," she said, hoping to keep the conversation neutral and comfortable. "I've been wanting to tell you that since we met."

"Thank you." Isla looked at her shoulder and traced the pattern. "I know this brilliant Buddhist artist who designed it. I keep thinking about getting another one, but I kind of like this being my only one."

"I have a few," she said, pointing to her uniform, "but for professional reasons, I get them where I can keep them covered."

Isla took a few gulps of water. "So, where are you from?"

"Well." She raised an eyebrow and considered whether or not she should be playful. She could only get into so much trouble over lunch. "Wanna guess?"

Isla leaned forward and placed her elbows on the table. Her loose magenta tank fell into a V on her chest, tantalizing Lu with a hint of cleavage. "I won't guess a Southern state because you don't have the accent, but you're not a New Englander either. Can I get a hint?"

"No."

"Will you tell me how you take your coffee?"

"My coffee?"

"Yes, your coffee. How do you take it?" Isla sat back and crossed her arms. The ends of her loose curls touched her upper arms and looked so soft, Lu's fingers begged to touch her.

Lu cleared her throat. "Depends on the coffee, but my favorite is home-brewed in a French press. A tablespoon of sugar and some vanilla creamer that'll make my coffee taste more like dessert. Big bonus if I can have a fresh-baked banana muffin with it." Lu remembered her morning coffee that day and shivered. "But I can drink it black when necessary."

"Tristate area."

Lu was taken aback. "How did you do that?"

"You can tell a lot about a person by how they take their coffee."

"Really?" She sat in disbelief.

"No," Isla said, laughing and licking her full, angular lips. "But I can tell a lot about a person by how they say *coffee*."

She had finally caught on. "Interesting detective work."

"Are we ready to order?" their waitress said, appearing out of nowhere.

Lu looked at Isla. "Are you ready? I always get the same thing."

"I've never been here," Isla said shyly and picked up the menu.

The waitress put her notepad back into her apron. "I'll give you two a few minutes."

Lu and Isla discussed different food options, and Isla confessed to being a vegetarian.

"Is going out to eat hard for a vegetarian?" Lu asked, genuinely curious. She ate more chips while Isla answered.

"Not really, but it can be when I'm with a group of carnivores and we're trying to pick a place to go. Many places have vegetarian options, and I'm not talking salads only," Isla said with raised brows. "But there are still a good number of places that don't. So I have to look at menus beforehand to see if I can order anything. Sometimes this annoys people."

"Well, that's rude." She didn't like Isla's defeated shrug. "I guess I'm lucky Chili's has a few good dishes for you."

"I think I'm luckier you didn't pick Red Lobster. I'm allergic to shellfish."

"Guess I won't show you my clam farm then." Lu wished she could take it back immediately. She hung her head. "That was the worst joke I've ever told, and it sounds like the worst lesbian pickup line ever used, too." She noticed the way Isla's laughter faltered and she shifted again. "I'm sorry, did I make you uncomfortable?"

"What? Why? How would you make me—" Isla's mouth fell open. "Oh my God, no. You didn't make me uncomfortable. It's very obvious you're a lesbian." Isla covered her mouth. "That's not what I mean."

Lu bit the inside of her cheek to keep from laughing. "So it's not obvious I'm a lesbian? Is it the hair?"

"Lu, please."

"The way I walk?"

"Stop." Isla covered her face with her hands.

Lu felt a little flutter in her chest and chose to ignore the warmth she felt from Isla's adorable nature. "Okay, okay. I'm done." She reached across the table and gently grabbed Isla's wrist. Her skin was sinfully soft and smooth. Lu waited to see her hazel eyes again before explaining herself. "I was worried you thought it really was a pickup line. I didn't mean for it to sound like that." She missed the touch when Isla pulled back.

"It's okay. Even if you were hitting on me, I probably wouldn't have picked up on it. A woman asked me out once, and I was shocked. She told me she'd been sending me signals for a month. I was oblivious."

Lu swallowed hard at the mention of a woman in Isla's romantic past. She shouldn't have felt hopeful, but she did, and she started laughing uncontrollably. Nervous habit number three.

"What's so funny?"

"You caught me by surprise. It's just not that obvious you're a lesbian."

"Because I'm not."

Lu wanted to shove her foot in her mouth and all the way down her throat. "I'm sorry."

"We sure are apologizing a lot, and this is only the first time we've ever really talked."

"I'm sorry," Lu said without thinking.

Isla's smile was small and soft. "I identify as pansexual. I'm attracted to spirits and hearts and energy, not bodies or gender." As Isla spoke, she appeared confident again, an air she hadn't carried since fixing the air-conditioning. "That's not entirely true. I'm usually attracted to the body, too."

"It's kind of important."

Isla grabbed her wrapped silverware from the tabletop and pulled the paper ring off. She laid the napkin across her lap. Isla looked up at her through her long lashes and said, "I shared something about myself—now it's your turn."

"We already established I'm a lesbian." She couldn't control her smile when Isla laughed. "What do you want to know?"

"Anything, really. We've known each other for what? Four months now? We don't really know each other, though. Tell me something about your home life. Pets? Do you live close? Where in the tristate area are you from?"

Lu opened her mouth only to be stopped by the waitress.

"Are we ready?" She put her pen to paper.

Lu glanced at her name tag and put on her most charming smile. "Annie, I am really sorry. We've been chatting this whole time. Can we get an awesome blossom and guacamole for the table? I promise we'll be ready to order by the time you come back."

Annie's smile could not have gotten any brighter. "Sure thing." She walked away with an extra sway in her step.

Lu's gaze did not follow her. "We should look at the menu."

"Does that happen everywhere you go?"

"What?"

"Women melting."

She knew what Isla was getting at, but admitting it would not make her look good. "I don't know what you're talking about."

"You know exactly what I'm talking about. You smile, you sweet talk, and then they melt."

"There's no melting and no sweet talking. I felt bad we were taking this long, and I apologized for it. Speaking of, you still haven't decided." She flipped open a menu and pointed. "They have black bean fajitas, and it comes with avocado. Sounds delicious."

"Are you in a relationship with anyone?"

Lu was caught so off guard only a small choke came out of her open mouth. "I'm not, no."

"That fits."

"What do you mean?"

"You're too charming to be in a relationship."

She focused on the insult instead of acknowledging Isla saying she was charming. "The reason I am not in a relationship has nothing to do with my behavior."

"Then what's your reason?" Isla's smugness was oddly attractive.

She took a slow sip of water to buy some time. She wasn't about to hand Isla all the control. "I have a bloodhound named Samson, I live on the border of Bender and Peabody, and I'm from New York. Queens, if you must know."

"One awesome blossom and a bowl of fresh guacamole. I got you an extra basket of chips, too." Annie winked before pulling out her notepad again. "Now, I do believe you promised to be ready for me."

She sucked her lips between her teeth and hummed. "I'll have the queso burger, cooked medium. Thank you." She handed back the menu, her eyes never leaving Isla's smirk.

Isla didn't look at Annie either. "Black bean fajitas, please. Extra avocado."

"Coming right up," Annie said, her enthusiastic chirp sounding out of place. She left, and Lu breathed a fraction more easily.

Desperate to erase the last thirty seconds of her life, Lu asked the first question that came to mind. "Are you in a relationship with anyone?"

Isla outright laughed. "No. I'm not looking for a relationship."

She fought to hide her disappointment. "Now, if I was like you and judged a book by its relationship status, I'd probably say something like you're not looking because you expect them to find you."

Isla sat back, looking aghast. "You are very, very wrong. I can't even tell you how wrong you are—*that's* how wrong you are."

She started to laugh. Isla was getting cuter by the second, but also more unattainable. "See? It doesn't feel good when someone does it to you, does it?"

Isla rolled her eyes. "Fine. You're right." She folded her hands on the tabletop. "Our lunch went from all apologies to insults."

"Aren't you glad you fixed my car?" Lu started chewing her straw, desperate for a way to release a sudden swell of nervous energy. She didn't like the silence that fell, neither awkward nor comfortable, but tense enough to eat away at their connection. "I'm divorced," she said suddenly, surprising both herself and Isla.

"Oh. I'm sorry."

"We're back to apologizing? Really?" She waited for some smart remark from Isla, but nothing came. "It was finalized a year ago, and then I moved out here for work not too long after. I haven't been ready. I don't know when or even if I'll be ready."

Isla's smile was gentle and sympathetic. She took a chip and swirled it through the guacamole before eating it in one big bite. She covered her mouth with her hand, but the guacamole at the corner of her mouth was still visible. She mumbled something.

"What was that?" Lu said with a short laugh.

Isla motioned to her mouth like she couldn't chew fast enough. "That's good," she said after swallowing. "I know it sounds clichéd, but I care too much about my shop and my work. I don't have any time or attention to spare."

Lu couldn't possibly agree any less with Isla, but that didn't mean she couldn't understand. "I don't think that's clichéd at all. You give the big thing in your life all your attention. If anything, I think it's great that you recognize it, and you're doing a kindness to whomever you would date. No one wants to play second fiddle to either another person or a job."

"Exactly. Thank you."

"Do you really think you can control it, though?" Lu said, her tone more taunting than intended.

"Control what?"

"Falling in love."

"Queso burger?" A young man, no more than twenty, stood beside their table and held a plate.

Lu raised her hand. She salivated at the food being placed in front of her.

"Fajitas?"

"Thank you," Isla said.

Once they were alone, Lu considered dropping the conversation altogether and changing to safer topics like politics or religion. "Your fajitas look good."

"It's not about control, it's about being open to receiving love. I'm not open."

Lu put her hands up in surrender. "Okay."

"There's nothing wrong with being a serial singleton."

"Serial singleton?"

"Like serial monogamist but single."

"Oh. Clever."

"Not everyone has to be in a relationship or want one."

Lu's head was spinning. "I never said there was anything wrong with it. It's a little surprising because you look like you'd be more romantic."

"Maybe you look like you wouldn't be romantic at all."

Lu recoiled. "Maybe you're right." She looked to her burger for relief from this now suddenly painful conversation. She cut it in half like she had to kill it first and started eating without a break. The sooner this meal was over, the better.

Lunch continued in silence, and Lu practically jumped for the check once it hit the table. They made it back to the shopping plaza in one piece and didn't bother to share a good-bye. Lu sat and stewed in her patrol car, replaying the conversation over and over in her head, but was left with only one question every time: Why did Isla saying she didn't look romantic bother her so much?

CHAPTER SIX

Isla rushed about and tackled all the finishing touches. Her apartment was clean but a little cluttered. Stacks of books sat in one corner, and a pile of blankets took up an ottoman next to her small green velour couch. Exactly six candles were lit, her sheer purple scarf was over the lamp, and her favorite patchouli incense was smoking away on the antique coffee table. The mood was set just in time for the knock at the door.

"Thank you for coming on such short notice," Isla said, shutting the door behind her guest and locking it with a flick of her wrist.

"I'm surprised you even called. How long has it been?"

"Christmastime, when the weather was cold, but you kept me warm." Isla leaned back against the door.

"We were definitely more than warm." They both chuckled. "But what I'm even more curious about is this meeting. You usually give me a few days' notice."

"I'm sorry," Isla said, feeling herself blush. "I was so frustrated today, I didn't know what to do with myself, and then it dawned on me. Call Rumi."

Rumi's scarlet lips turned up at the corners. She tossed her long black hair over one shoulder and gave Isla a look of pure seduction. In the summertime, Rumi's wardrobe was usually minimal and attractive, with a strapless romper at the heart of tonight's outfit. A whole lot of her dark skin was left bare in the most tantalizing way. Rumi exuded sex appeal.

Not much of a surprise for a succubus.

"I hope I'm not stealing you away from some hopeless man's dreams."

"Oh, sweetie," Rumi said, slowly approaching Isla, "those are the myths. Being a real-life succubus isn't about torturing someone in their nightmares—it's about liberating them in their wakefulness." Rumi lowered the top of her romper and revealed her naked breasts.

Isla stared unabashedly. "You're perfect."

"I'm whatever you want me to be," Rumi said, leaning in and capturing her lips in a kiss.

Isla moaned and took Rumi's face in her hands. Nothing compared to the energy exchange with a succubus. Desire reached new extremes, passion ran so hot her breath ceased, and every inch of her body grew incredibly sensitive. One little touch from Rumi made her clit quiver.

"How do you do that?" Isla said, sighing deeply when Rumi dragged her fingernails down the back of her neck.

Rumi ran the tip of her tongue along Isla's throat. "Everything you feel right now," she said as she caressed the inside of Isla's thigh, "is because of you."

Isla laughed and closed her eyes. Rumi's touch felt like fire through her tight yoga pants. "I am absolutely sure this is all you."

"Remember, I feed off energy. But in your case, I feed off your magic." Rumi cupped her through her pants. "What you're feeling is your power."

Isla felt weak.

"What do you want?" Rumi asked.

She sighed, her mind immediately betraying her by flashing an image of Lu, sweaty and disheveled. "Fast and hard."

"Wow," Rumi said. She placed her hand over the center of Isla's chest. "I don't know what I'm feeling, but something's different."

Isla came out of her sexual daze. "What do you mean?"

"When we're together, everything I absorb comes from your sex and your magic."

"Well, yeah." Isla tried to laugh. For some reason she started to grow uncomfortable.

Rumi shook her head. "I'll put it into terms that'll make sense to you. Picture your chakras."

She closed her eyes again, this time relieved to avoid Rumi's gaze. "Okay."

"They're all glowing—all seven are lighting up like a Christmas tree. When we're together, only the chakras necessary for sex and arousal light up. You don't need your crown or third eye. Your brain essentially turns off because your body is in charge. Same goes for your heart and root chakras."

"I'm all orange and yellow.".

"Yes. The two chakras responsible for pleasure and sex are blazing. But tonight, your solar plexus and sacral chakras are not in charge."

Isla opened her eyes and was very confused. "Which one is?"

"Your fourth chakra."

"My heart? No. No way."

"Yes way," Rumi said with a hesitant smile. "And judging by the very perplexed look on your face, I probably shouldn't tell you this next part."

"What?" Her stomach sank.

"You've never been more powerful. I can taste and feel it."

"That's not my heart." Isla slipped out from between Rumi and the door.

"I'm pretty sure—"

"You know what you felt, but I know me." She regretted the bite in her tone, but who did Rumi think she was? She started fluffing the throw pillows on her couch and kept her eyes on her task. "I don't think having company tonight was a good idea."

"*Right*," Rumi said, elongating the short word. "Guess I'll get going. Call me sometime when it is a good idea."

She kept silent as she watched Rumi leave. Once the door shut, she let out a long breath and ran her fingers through her hair. Scratching at her scalp and a pint of frozen yogurt would be the only pleasures she'd be experiencing that night.

❖

Isla wasn't sure if she should keep the small jars of pink Himalayan salt in the bath section or the edible section. Perhaps both. She started picking up a few jars and turned around to find Daria and Christopher behind her, both looking mad.

"Good morning?" Isla walked between them to get to the spice section.

"Are you asking?" Christopher quipped.

"Judging by your faces, yes."

Daria crossed her arms. "We're not very happy."

"That much is obvious."

"What is going on with you?" Daria said.

"Nothing." Isla began rearranging a display of dried ginger and red peppercorns.

"Look," Daria said, placing her hand on Isla's to still her, "you've been really quiet lately, and quiet isn't one of your many personality traits."

Isla wondered how many people were going to read her in twenty-four hours. "I'm fine. I have a lot on my mind."

"I know we tease you a lot, probably too much." Christopher shrugged slightly. "But we didn't realize you were going to shut us out."

"Shut you out? I didn't shut you out."

"You went out to lunch with Lu, and when you got back you locked yourself in your office. We didn't hear a peep from you for hours, and then you just left. You barely said good-bye." Daria's tone was uncharacteristically wounded.

She dropped her shoulders in guilt. "I'm sorry. Lunch was..." Isla thought of her conversation with Lu and winced.

Christopher waved their hand in front of Isla's face. "What? Lunch was what?"

"Weird. And then I got back late and had to prep for Ezekiel's appointment."

"What about running out of here?"

She began fidgeting but wouldn't look away from Daria's prying eyes. She had nothing to be ashamed of. "I called Rumi."

Daria rolled her eyes so hard her entire head moved.

"Why do you hate Rumi?" Isla said.

Christopher laughed. "I love it. It's like someone hating Christmas. Or chocolate."

"Don't compare Rumi to chocolate."

"I would," Isla smirked. "She's delicious."

Christopher made an O with his mouth. "Spicy chocolate, I bet."

"You know it." She gave Christopher a high five.

"You two are disgusting, and I would be walking away right now if I wasn't curious about what made your lunch date weird."

Isla surrendered. "We talked about me being a vegetarian, and then she was flirting with the waitress."

"Lu flirted with the waitress while she was on a date with you?" Daria said, obviously horrified.

"Okay, maybe she wasn't flirting. She was being *very* charming." She wanted to kick herself for feeling the need to defend Lu. Why couldn't she let her friends dislike Lu?

Daria pointed at her and said, "Charming is not flirting."

"Be on my side," Isla said flatly. She took a deep breath, and Daria held up her hands. "This led to a conversation about relationships."

"Oh boy." Christopher pulled a face. "That's a hot topic for you."

"I told her I don't want a relationship because I'm focused on myself and my business. She doesn't believe you can control love like that."

"Because you can't," Daria said.

Isla looked at her. "My. Side."

"And then what?" Christopher looked thoroughly enthralled, like all they were missing was some popcorn to munch on.

She dropped her head back and let out a groan. "She told me, and I quote, that I look *more romantic than that*. I can't believe her."

Daria looked at her like she made no sense. "You *are* more romantic than that."

Isla waved her off. "I'm not romantic." Daria grabbed her and dragged her to the office.

"What's that if it's not romantic?" Daria said, pointing to a large painting hanging behind her desk. It depicted a small island surrounded by choppy waters. The moon glowed in the sky above, its bright ring of light nearly touching the top of the island's trees.

"That's sentimental. Not romantic."

"The moon and an island falling in love every night and waiting for each other every day. Mother Earth's soul mates. I think that's what you called them when you explained it to me."

Isla refused to budge. "My grandmother told me that story and had this made for me. That's sentimental, Daria. Anyway, Lu is divorced. Let's focus on that."

"Divorced and single?" Christopher said. "Because that's what really matters."

Daria raised her hand to silence Christopher. "How did the conversation end?"

Isla looked everywhere but back at Daria because she didn't want to answer the question. She should demand they get back to work and not speak of this again, but she ended up looking into Daria's damn entrancing eyes.

"I told her she looks like she wouldn't be romantic at all," Isla said, blurting it out before she could stop herself. Shame washed over her like a heatwave.

"Isla Hoffman, why would you say something like that?" Daria looked at Christopher for support, but they just stood with their mouth hanging open in shock.

"I was mad!"

"Do you even believe that?"

"I don't know." Isla turned and slumped with her back against the counter. "No, but in the moment I did."

"You have to apologize," Christopher said.

"No, I don't."

Daria smiled so stiffly it looked painful. "Yes, you do. Come on." Daria took Isla's hand and led her to the door.

Isla put her hand on the doorknob, but before opening the door, she looked for Lu's car and was surprised to see a much fresher cruiser sitting in the lot. She squinted to see the figure behind the wheel.

"That's not Lu," she said, disappointed. Daria and Christopher came up to stand at her sides. "What if she quit?" Panic started to set in.

Christopher looked at her. "Because you insulted her in Chili's? I doubt it."

"You're right. What if she asked to be transferred?"

Daria put her hand on Isla's shoulder and said, "I highly doubt that."

"Yeah. I doubt it, too." She tried her best to mirror Daria's confidence.

She couldn't shake the feeling something wasn't right. One minute she was having lunch with Lu, a woman she could not get off her mind, and then Lu disappeared after a rough conversation? Isla believed in many things, but coincidence wasn't one of them.

CHAPTER SEVEN

An entire week passed before Isla accepted the truth: Lu was gone. Even Daria and Christopher kept their comments to a minimum, including their pep talks about Lu coming back. And truth be told, Isla hated the way Lu's departure affected her. Every time she brewed a cup of tea, she'd think about Lu. She'd drive past Chili's and think of Lu. She couldn't even look in the parking lot without thinking about Lu and the way she'd get butterflies at the sight of the patrol car. How dared someone to have such a hold over her?

"Gabriella is coming in at two, and I suspect I'll need an hour with her, give or take. I'll be in my office until then," Isla said listlessly. Any spark, spunk, or fun she normally carried with her was dormant. Isla refused to accept it was gone altogether, but she also didn't know when she'd ever return to normal.

Daria was hot on Isla's heels. "Can I get you anything?"

"I'm okay. Thank you." Isla smiled softly. Daria had been caring and gentle with her since Lu had disappeared.

"Have you eaten?"

"I had a muffin and a shake when I got in."

"Would you like me to grab you a matcha latte?"

Isla considered the offer. She did love her matcha lattes, probably even more than any other treat she could have, but not even her favorite drink could spark joy in her. "No, thank you." She focused on the order forms in front of her. She needed to restock on rare herbs. "How are we on anise hyssop?"

"We're fine, but you're not. I really wish you'd talk to me about it."

She would if she could, but she didn't know how to explain

herself. "I'm really okay, aside from being slightly behind on ordering this week."

"We're not running low on anything important."

"Everything in this store is important," Isla snapped. She sat behind her desk and took a calming breath. "I'm sorry."

"Don't apologize—just admit you're not okay."

She pinched the bridge of her nose. "I'm struggling, and I don't understand it. I haven't talked to you about it because I wouldn't even know how to explain it. Lu is gone and I'm—"

"Sad?"

"No."

"Heartbroken?"

She looked at Daria with zero amusement. "No. It's like my energy is down. I have no desire to do much of anything except work, and even that is very matter-of-fact for me. Take this appointment with Gabriella, for example. I love when she comes in. We talk about plants and gardening, and she tells me the latest fairy gossip. But the best part is getting to reminisce about our grandmothers' friendship."

"Maybe this meeting is exactly what you need, then."

"Maybe," Isla said, tapping her pen. What she really needed was to talk to her grandmother. Celeste was the only person who could guide and teach Isla and keep her on track. "I just want to take a bath."

Daria leaned her head against the doorframe. "Why don't you take tomorrow off. You don't have any appointments scheduled, and you know we'll call you if we need you. Your apartment is right upstairs, so it's not like you'll be far."

"I can't…"

"When was the last time you had a day off?"

"New Year's." Isla vividly remembered her slow, mildly hungover morning, and she also remembered the private workshop on new moons and manifestation she'd held that evening. "Sort of."

"Take the day. Please."

She breathed deeply to quell her stubbornness. She imagined what she would do with a day to herself. She'd probably plan the next few months of events and begin holiday preparations. But working from home still counted as a day off, right?

"You're right. I think I'll take the—" A sharp pain tore through her feet. She slumped forward onto her desk and gripped her right foot.

Daria rushed to her side. "What's the matter? Are you okay?"

"I'm fine," Isla said through her clenched teeth. "Must've been a cramp or something." She rubbed the arch of her foot.

"You should take it as a sign that you need to rest."

"Oh sure, I bet." Isla chuckled. "Painful feet mean...something else." Isla racked her brain for the memory as she alternated massaging each foot. "My grandmother would always say it."

"Was there anything Grandma Celeste didn't know about?"

"She knew everything, but what was the thing about the feet? Itchy hands, itchy feet? Painful hands, light on your feet? No."

"Head, shoulders, knees, and toes?" Daria said.

"I got it! *Ache in the hand, you're keeping trouble at bay. Pains in the foot...*" Isla felt nauseous.

"What? Pains in the foot...what?"

"Danger's on the way." Isla looked at Daria as her tension level ratcheted up. "What if it's Lu? What if something happened to Lu, and that's why she's gone?"

"Slow down," Daria said, turning her chair and placing her hands on Isla's shoulders. "Why do you think Lu's in danger?"

"My grandmother always said foot pain meant danger, and you said yourself that Celeste knew everything, and this isn't the first time I've had foot pain recently." Isla was talking fast now. "Lu has been gone for a week, and they hurt last week. Even though things ended awkwardly at Chili's, I'd still expect her to say something if she was leaving this job." She inhaled. "Lu is missing, my feet hurt, and I don't believe in coincidences."

"You're making yourself sick."

"Maybe, but I won't be able to stop until I have some answers." Isla stood abruptly, causing Daria to stumble back a step. She marched out of her office and straight for the door. She didn't care about the light drizzle that hit her bare arms or what the humidity would do to her loose curls. All Isla cared about was getting to the patrol car as quickly as possible. She stepped up to the driver's side and knocked on the window. The middle-aged man behind the wheel nearly spilled his drink.

He rolled down the window. "Can I help you, miss?"

"Where's Lu?" she said, leaving no room for pleasantries or soft excuses. If something happened, Isla wanted to know. No. Isla *needed* to know.

The security guy looked at her strangely. "Who are you?"

"Isla. I own that apothecary," she said, pointing to her store. "Where's Lu?"

"She's on vacation."

Isla's determination deflated. "What?"

"She's on vacation and will be back tomorrow. Are you guys friends or something? Should I let her know you're looking for her?"

Isla stared at his thinning hair as she thought. "No."

"No, you're not friends or no you don't want me to let her know you were looking for her?"

"No—I mean, yes. We *are* friends, and no, you don't have to tell her anything. Thank you." Isla tapped the side of the car and stepped away.

❖

McCafferty watched until she went inside the apothecary. He sighed and checked the rest of the parking lot. "You are supposed to report anything weird." He picked up his radio and said, "McCafferty to home base." In an instant, another voice crackled to life.

"What's up, McCafferty?"

"I'm sitting in this parking lot, and I'm bored out of my mind."

"So you called in for small talk?"

"No. I'm sitting here when, all of a sudden, the chick that owns the apothecary is banging on my window asking for Lu." Silence stretched on, which led McCafferty to believe he was right for being suspicious.

"Did she say what she wanted?"

"Just Lu."

"I'll let the boss know."

McCafferty replaced his radio and sat back. He strained to watch for any movement through the apothecary's big windows. "And here I thought the only thing interesting about this strip mall was the pizza place."

❖

"I cannot believe you convinced me to do this." Lu sipped at her IPA and stirred onions as they sautéed in a frying pan.

"I was reading an article about how long-distance relationships survive, and the idea of virtually cooking together really appealed to me. Plus, I think your cooking skills could use improvement."

"And how do you think I'm doing?" Lu picked up her phone and switched the camera around to focus on her food.

"Don't let them get too brown. You'll ruin everything."

Lu rolled her eyes before placing her phone back on its little perch beside the stove. She looked right into the camera and said, "I don't think the article was meant for sisters who live less than two hours apart. Especially when one sister is such an ass."

"Don't talk about yourself like that." Kayla stuck out her tongue. "You know this is a cute idea, and we both know improving your cooking skills could potentially land you a girlfriend. Then I won't have to worry about you so much."

"I hardly think a frittata is the key to my relationship woes."

"You do realize in order to have relationship woes, you have to try to have a relationship."

"Mm-hmm." Lu drank her beer and looked away from the camera. No one needed to know about Isla or the failure of their lunch date. Not that it was even a date. Lu focused on the lightly browned onions sizzling away before her. "When do you know they're caramelized enough?"

"I'll file that deflection away for later." Kayla looked down, seemingly at the food she was also cooking. "They get very brown and really soft."

"I think they're almost there." Lu cringed at one or two completely black onions clinging to the side of the pan. "When does Lilly get back from her father's?"

"Ken is keeping her for another two days. Apparently, his girlfriend's family is here from Virginia, and he wants Lilly to spend time with them all." Kayla gagged.

Lu laughed at her dramatic sister. "I think that's really sweet."

"Yeah, yeah. Add in your peppers."

Lu did as instructed. "All I'm saying is it's nice to see Ken growing up. When Lilly was born, he was a mess and no good for either of you. I know it sucks not having Lilly sometimes, and it probably isn't all that great to see Ken flourishing the way he is."

"Excuse me?" Kayla held up her wooden spoon. The lighting from over the stove highlighted her flyaway hairs. She looked like a maniac. "What is this that you're saying to me?"

Lu wished she could take it all back. "Right now, I mean, you're healing after a breakup with a guy who seemed great on paper but wasn't good for you, and Ken finally has his ducks in a row, and he's in a healthy relationship."

"We don't know it's healthy. For all we do know she's a controlling nag who won't let him watch the games every Sunday."

Lu clenched her jaw and took a deep breath to control the next words out of her mouth. The last thing she wanted to do was point out how Kayla gave Ken a hard time every Sunday during the game. She cleared her throat. "Maybe. Anything is possible, but I'm happy for him. He's doing good, and that means Lilly's life will be fuller."

"You always had a soft spot for Ken, and I hate it."

"You don't hate it."

"Add the zucchini. Yes, I do."

Lu dumped the matchstick-cut zucchini into the pan and shrugged. "Would you ever get back with him?"

Kayla nearly spit out her wine. "I don't know how we got on this subject, but we are definitely done with it now."

Lu held up her beer and said, "A deflection I will file away for later."

"I hate you—I know that much."

Lu laughed so loudly Samson perked up from where he was snoring on the sofa.

CHAPTER EIGHT

Isla lay restless. Lu was back at work, and the first few days passed in a sort of odd standoff between them, neither one making the first move to talk to the other. But that didn't mean Isla refrained from peeking out the window compulsively to see Lu with her own eyes. Isla sank her teeth into business-owner duties more than ever to keep herself busy during the day, but nighttime posed other challenges. No matter how much paperwork or how many order forms and client files she brought home, Isla couldn't escape the constant thoughts of impending danger and Lu's sudden disappearance.

Yes, all signs pointed to coincidence, but she wasn't about to quiet her gut instinct now. As she lay in bed and stared at the glow her salt lamp cast across the ceiling, she forced her thoughts to business and the upcoming events. Her slow season hit at the end of summer and again during March, and she had to come up with something to alleviate at least one of the droughts. A thought occurred to her. She sat up straight and grabbed her phone from the nightstand. She dialed Daria's number and bounced her leg as the phone rang.

Isla didn't allow Daria more than a quick hello before saying, "Summerfest."

"Isla? It's after eleven at night."

"Oh," she said, looking at the clock. "I'm sorry. Were you sleeping?"

"Of course not, but you did scare the bejeezus out of me."

"I had an idea. We should get a booth for Summerfest this year."

"You always say our target demographic wouldn't be interested in visiting a festival."

"Then we'll cater to the rest of the people. We'll get a stand and sell crystals, bath oils and salts, teas, and even some salves and balms.

We can do demonstrations, too. I think it'll be a great way to make a little more cash and advertise to the rest of the town what we have to offer. Not everyone is comfortable coming in off the street."

"Because a witch owns it, and witches are scary."

Isla chuckled. "Exactly. So, what do you say? Are you in?"

"Of course I'm in. If for no other reason than you're my boss. You tell me to be somewhere, and I'll do it for the pay."

"Ouch," Isla said with her hand over her heart, "is that the only reason?"

"Heck, no. I love you and I love festivals. But for real, though, I expect you to feed me festival food all day on the company card."

"Deal. Great. Okay, you go back to enjoying your night and doing whatever unsavory thing it is you're doing, and I'll see you in the morning." She hung up and fell back onto her pillows with a grin. A new project was exactly what she needed, and it worked better than counting sheep to put her to sleep.

Even the birds were chirping a new melody come morning. Isla was up and out of bed earlier than usual, and a thought dawned on her on her way to work. Instead of opening the shop well before the nine o'clock posted on the door, she decided to go for a walk instead. Not many people were out, save for morning commuters and a pair of joggers. The sun and sky were bright and starting to warm the earth, but a strong breeze added a welcome chill. Isla breathed deeply every few steps and felt the fresh air fill her body and fuel her spirit. Her happiness was genuine. Fall would be here soon enough.

She arrived at the nearby park, an open green space by the bay where they hosted Summerfest every year. Sitting on a bench facing the water, she took in the air and the peace and couldn't remember how she'd reasoned away participating in the festival. She'd made excuses every year, and now they all seemed ridiculous. Isla accepted this new project with excitement and enthusiasm and saw it as an opportunity to further grow the business. No small feat.

Isla slipped off her flats and sank her bare feet into the grass. She stretched her toes and let the earth press into her skin. She felt connected, sure, and grounded in life. Isla closed her eyes and continued to breathe slowly, noting the sounds around her, the feelings growing in her chest, and every point along her body nature touched. She counted to ten and opened her eyes. The smile she wore was one of gratitude.

❖

Lu shuffled into the bathroom and hissed when her feet touched the cold tile. She looked at herself in the mirror, one eye open, and sighed. She had forty minutes to get herself together and in the car. Mornings were getting harder and harder. In the Air Force, Lu had lived many different schedules, but now—as a thirty-nine-year-old civilian—she didn't even want to know the world before six.

She stripped off her tee and boxers before turning the shower water on to an ungodly temperature. The best way to wake up was a hot shower and even hotter coffee. Lu went about brushing her teeth and gathering a towel. She stepped into the near-scalding water and let the heat wake her up inch by inch. Her shoulders were stiff from her latest workout, and her bad ankle was crying. Lu rolled her ankle and winced. Her body wasn't what it used to be. She scrubbed her skin with her favorite Moroccan mint bodywash, indulgently fresh in scent but also incredibly moisturizing. She washed from top to bottom and back up again, around her full breasts and down the center of her flat abdomen.

Lu raised an eyebrow and considered the time. She allowed her left hand to wander lower to her mound and ran her fingers through her rough curls. Lu touched herself slowly, and much to her dismay, her body barely reacted. She pulled away her hand with a huff and went back to business. Her libido seemed to have taken a vacation of late. She wasn't sure if it was the new job, her age, or exhaustion taking its toll, but she'd be lying if she said it didn't bother her.

Lu stepped out of the shower, greeted by Samson's expectant stare. His eyes might have been slightly obscured by his heavy brow, but his message was still clear. Lu laughed.

"I'll get you your breakfast in a minute. I have to get ready for the job that pays for your food and the orthopedic bed that helps your achy joints." Lu wrapped the towel around her body and crouched down to take Samson's face in her hands. "And those treats you deserve for being an actual angel on earth." She kissed his nose and received a slow lick in return. "Okay, okay. You convinced me. I'll feed you first."

Lu spent the next twenty minutes racing around to take care of Samson and get ready on time. Her job allowed her the leisure of running a few minutes late, but that didn't mean Lu liked it. By the time she was in the car and on her way to her favorite Dunkin', she knew she'd be cutting it close. She hated the anxiety accompanying tardiness.

Why are you even rushing? Lu rolled to a stop. She watched a guy cut his lawn. To see Isla? Really? A honk from the car behind her alerted Lu to the green light. She continued driving with all her focus on the road. Well, maybe not *all* her focus. She thought about Isla and the quiet days that had passed since she got back. She didn't feel she should be the one to give in and talk to Isla, and it seemed as though Isla felt the same. She gripped the steering wheel tighter.

She pulled up to the strip mall minutes before eight, and even as she tried to resist, her eyes went immediately to the apothecary. Everything was dark, an odd occurrence at this time. Lu always caught Isla opening or already open for business. Her natural instinct was to go on high alert. Lu didn't handle out of the norm very well. Call it paranoia or call it soldier's intuition, either way she felt uneasy. She parked in a spot with a clear view of Hoffman's Apothecary and its big windows. Over the months, she had learned Isla lived upstairs from the apothecary, but the apartment windows facing the parking lot always had closed curtains. Lu sat up straighter and drank her coffee, eyes trained on the shop, waiting for any signs of movement. At eight fifteen, someone knocked against her window.

Lu jumped and went so rigid she started to crush her coffee cup. She rolled down her window and smiled up at Isla. "Thanks for waking me up."

"No problem at all," Isla said with a grin full of amusement. Lu's worries about seeing Isla again faded away. "How was your vacation?"

"My vacation…" Lu didn't quite know how to describe a trip that wasn't at all for pleasure. "Wasn't really a vacation. It was more of a training opportunity."

"Oh. I'm sorry. The guy who took your place—"

"If you see McCafferty anywhere, don't believe a word he says."

"Is he a liar?"

"No, he's a fool." Lu's chest warmed as Isla threw her head back and laughed. Lu missed her smile. She cleared her throat. "How was it without me? Did I miss anything exciting?"

Isla shook her head. "Look, I really have to open the store, but I wanted to apologize really quick."

"What for?"

"Lunch."

"I'm the one who proposed Chili's."

"Lu," Isla said softly, and Lu went mushy inside. "I'm sorry for getting so defensive. A lot of people tease me for choosing my business over relationships. It's a sensitive subject for me, and I fired off at the wrong person. You."

"We're all good." Lu looked into Isla's eyes and accepted that Isla was only going to become more appealing as time passed. After all, what's more attractive than someone admitting when they were wrong and apologizing for their behavior? Lu's own experience with women had rarely seen such a thing.

Isla shook her head. "Um, would you like a tea?"

"I have this," Lu said, holding up her large coffee, "but thank you."

"If you change your mind, you know where to find me."

"I do—" Lu's phone started ringing, the *Austin Powers* theme sounding loud in the moment. She looked at the screen and hated how poorly life could be timed. "I have to take this. It's my boss."

Isla held up her hands. "I have to open the shop anyway. Have a good day."

"You, too." Lu slid her finger across the screen. "Hello?" She listened for her boss while watching Isla walk to her shop.

"Cadman. I'm calling for an update."

Lu was surprised, which worried her. Her boss was given nightly updates at the end of her shift. He had never called her like this. "Of course, sir. I don't have much to report at the moment since I was away last week, but everything is status quo here."

"Nothing to report?"

"No, sir."

"Nothing about that shop owner you've been cozying up to?"

Lu was taken aback. "Excuse me?"

"McCafferty reported a woman, a female business owner from the mall, coming to check on you when you weren't there."

Lu lowered her head and pinched the bridge of her nose. "I get tea from her often. She was just curious, I guess."

"McCafferty seems to believe there's more to it."

"Pardon my language, sir, but McCafferty wouldn't know his ass from his elbow."

"And yet, he's the only one who has given me an actual report since we've been surveilling that property."

Lu clenched her jaw to remain composed. Firing back at her superiors wasn't her style. "I get tea from her shop, and we get along. She keeps me in the strip mall gossip loop, too." Lu wondered when she had become such a good liar.

"Your choice of company is very interesting to me."

Lu's nerves were fraying. "What are you getting at, sir?"

"Do I have any reason to question your ability to do your job?"

"No, sir." Lu rested her head back when he hung up without another word.

She knew from day one getting close to Isla was a bad idea, but what was she supposed to do? Isla was friendly and treated Lu like a real person trapped in a car for hours a day. No one else in the strip mall cared about her. Pat from the pizza place was pleasant, but he only cared when Lu walked in and spent money. Isla never asked for a penny toward the many teas she'd made. Lu danced with the dangerous decision to get to know Isla better, and maybe this was a sign to keep her distance.

"Second sign," she said, reminding herself of their disastrous lunch. Lu slouched in resignation and continued drinking her coffee, now as cold as her attitude.

CHAPTER NINE

O kay, team, we have three weeks to prepare for our inaugural
Summerfest." Isla rubbed her hands together excitedly. She'd
spent the morning and greater part of the afternoon making calls and
filling out online forms to make sure it wasn't too late for Hoffman's
to participate. "I just got off the phone with the festival's organizer and
secured a large space with a covering, just in case it rains." She waited
for praise, but none came. "Guys, this is great news."

"It is," Christopher said flatly, "but do we know who our neighbors
will be? I'd hate to be stuck between a pickle stand and a flag vendor."

Isla looked at them oddly. "Why a flag vendor?"

"Incessant flapping." They looked disgusted by the thought.

"Okay. What about you, Daria? Where's your enthusiasm?"

"I *am* looking forward to it—I'm just really tired today." As if
staged, Daria added a yawn.

"Late night?" Isla said with a raised brow.

Daria shook her head. "I couldn't sleep last night. I've had this
splitting headache that just won't go away."

"For how long?" Isla approached Daria and brought her hands up
to her head. She pressed her fingertips to Daria's temples and gently
massaged. She closed her eyes and let herself absorb Daria's energy,
but something felt clogged. "Let me in."

"I'm not keeping you out."

"Then why can't I feel more?"

"I thought you don't read people anymore," Christopher said.
Their usual sharpness was absent, making it obvious even they were
slightly worried.

"I don't, but that doesn't mean I can't."

Christopher shrugged. "Maybe you're rusty."

Isla shot them a glare. "When did the headache start?"

Daria rolled her neck. "Sometime yesterday afternoon. I made some peppermint ginger tea, but it didn't help. I popped two ibuprofen when I got home. Don't judge me," she said, pointing at Isla.

"I support pharmaceuticals when necessary."

"Well, this was necessary, but it only kind of helped. When the headache would fade in one spot, it would reappear in another. I started with a migraine roller and targeted massages, but I just felt like I was chasing it around my head. Once it settled in my neck, I just gave up and lay in bed."

Isla felt nauseous. "Daria, I have to ask you something, and I need you to think really hard."

"Thinking is painful."

"Please. Did your headache start before or after I went outside looking for Lu?"

Daria rubbed her forehead and covered her eyes, a clear sign she wasn't feeling well. Daria wouldn't normally risk her impeccable eye makeup.

Christopher looked at her in shock. "Do you think your dreamboat has something to do with this?"

"She's not my dreamboat, and no, I don't think she has anything to do with this. I'm just trying to get an idea of the timeline."

Daria uncovered her eyes and said, "There is no timeline. It's just a headache."

"I got the pains in my feet, and then you have a never-ending headache? Come on, I'm sure even you see the correlation." She looked from Daria to Christopher. "Christopher, have you noticed anything weird? Are you feeling anything new?"

They looked thrown by being put on the spot. "Uh, no? I don't think so?"

Isla held their shoulders and looked into their dark eyes. "No new aches or pains? Indigestion? Constipation?"

"No," Christopher said, taking Isla's hands from their shoulders, "I'm all good."

"Maybe because you're the newest and the youngest one here. They don't see you as a threat."

"I'm totally a threat."

"We know that," Isla said.

Daria raised her hand. "Or maybe there's nothing going on besides

Isla standing too much in flat shoes and me being dehydrated or stressed or one of the other thousands of headache-inducing things." She caught her breath. "You're going to drive yourself crazy."

"Or I'm going to save us." She walked behind the counter.

"From what?" Daria turned to follow but stumbled. "Whoa. Got a little dizzy."

"You need to go upstairs and lie down. Now."

"No way. I've been wanting us to do Summerfest for years, and now we finally are. I'm not missing preparations."

"You can brainstorm from my bed. I am not taking no for an answer." Isla crossed her arms, daring Daria to test her stubbornness.

"I'll make you a tea."

"I've tried tea."

"With butterbur?" Isla knew the answer. "I'll make it and walk you up."

Isla made the tea in minutes, thanks to her special ability to heat water quickly. She walked Daria up to her apartment and settled her into her king-size bed. After a bit of pillow rearranging, Daria was comfortable.

"If you need anything, I'll be right downstairs."

Daria smirked. "Is this all a trick just to get me into your bed?"

"Careful with your jokes. I'm going to assume you're all better and make you get back to work." Isla laughed when Daria feigned sleeping. "Seriously, get some rest. I'll come check on you soon."

Isla let herself out, but the moment Daria could no longer see her, she began to rush. She ran down the stairs and reentered the apothecary to find a line of customers waiting. She assisted those in need as professionally and politely as possible while subtly trying to rush them out. The sun was setting by the time Isla was alone with Christopher.

"We're done. We're closing for the day, and we need to cleanse this place."

Christopher looked skeptical. "Do you really think something's going on?"

"Yes. I don't know what, and I don't know how I know, but I do. I feel it." She was ready to argue any bit of reasoning Christopher threw at her, but none came.

"Okay. What do you need me to do?"

"You believe me?"

"I don't know what to believe, but I do remember the very first bit of advice you gave me when I started here."

Isla smiled. "Always trust your *intuwitchin*."

"Always." Christopher grinned. "Now let's get to work."

❖

Lu lost yet another game of solitaire and tossed her phone onto the passenger seat. She blamed hunger for her inability to concentrate. Her stomach growled, telling her she was right. She weighed her meal options as if they weren't the same choices she faced every workday, and as if she wasn't going to settle for pizza. Again. She cast one last glance at the apothecary before getting out of the car and stretching her legs. Walking up to the front of the strip mall, she patrolled under the shade of the small overhang. This gave her the opportunity to peek into each store and see if anything was going on inside. But she avoided the apothecary, not really needing to be seen by Isla. A light flickered overhead. She waved to Ray inside the convenience store as she passed by, and the next light flickered, too. Lu looked back over her shoulder. All the lights were shining steadily now. She was probably seeing things.

When she walked into the pizza place, Pat greeted her right away.

"Hey, Pat. How are things?"

"Busy, not busy, and then busy again," he said, flipping his hands back and forth. He said the same thing every time Lu stopped in. "What can I get you tonight?"

"Did you change your mind about the buffalo chicken pizza yet?"

He cringed and waved her off. "I keep telling you, that's not real pizza."

A small group of teens shouted from the back of the pizzeria's small dining area. "Hey, Pat. What's wrong with your TV? We can't see the game no more."

"The Sox are losing. That's all you need to know."

Lu leaned forward to see around the beverage fridge. The TV was flickering in and out of picture. Was there supposed to be an electrical surge or storm in the area tonight?

"Lu? What're you having?"

"Has your TV been acting up all day?" she said.

"No. It's probably the channel cutting out. Kids today are spoiled with technology. They don't know how to handle one little inconvenience. Plain? Pepperoni?"

Lu kept looking at the fuzzy screen. "Yeah."

"Yeah what?"

Lu turned back to Pat. "Yeah, one of each please. And a Dr Pepper."

Five minutes later she walked back to her car across the parking lot, instead of under the lights. Lu carried her plate with two slices in her left hand and her soda in the other and walked as quickly as she could without risking her dinner. She needed to get back to her phone to research why the electricity was funky in the area. A distant squawking stopped her in her tracks as a crow swooped down and knocked the pizza from her hand. She ran the remaining distance to her car.

"What the fuck," she said, breathing heavily and rapidly. "What the actual *fuck* was that?" She looked up through her windshield to see if she could spot her feathered assailant, but something else caught her eye. A large, dusty handprint was smack-dab in the middle of the glass. She looked around frantically, but no one else was in the parking lot.

She grabbed her phone from the seat and slowly exited her car. She leaned over, careful not to disturb anything, and she took pictures of the print. Whoever left this mark had very, very big hands. A motion out of the corner of her eye grabbed her attention. The apothecary's open sign switched off. As much as Lu had been trying to keep her distance, Isla might have seen something that could clue her in to what the hell was going on.

Lu jogged to the door and turned the knob. The open sign was off, but the door opened. She stepped into the store and heard Isla, but she was nowhere to be seen. Lu checked around displays on her way to the counter. She could smell something burning, but no alarms were going off.

Isla popped up from behind the counter. "Ahhh!"

Lu jumped back. "Shit. Sorry."

"We're closed," Isla said firmly.

"The door was open."

"What's going on?" Christopher turned the corner too sharply and whacked their knee on the wall. "Ow." They gripped their knee and bent over.

"We're closing early because I'm not feeling well."

"Okay," Lu said, but her attention was on Christopher. "Do you think he's really hurt?"

"They," Christopher said in a low, pained voice.

Lu looked to Isla in confusion.

Isla rolled her eyes. "They-them."

"Oh. My bad. Are they really hurt? Should we help them?" Lu

started to walk over to Christopher only to be stopped by their hand in the air.

"I'm fine."

"Do you need something?" Isla said.

"I, uh, no. I guess not." Lu understood not feeling well, but she didn't understand why Isla had to be short and curt with her. "I hope you feel better." Lu walked right out the door without looking back.

Christopher hobbled to stand beside Isla behind the counter. "That was a bit uncalled for."

"We need to focus," Isla said, believing her own words but also never taking her eyes from the door. Her chest felt tight from sending Lu away. "Did you see her arms?"

"Muscular."

"No." Isla looked at Christopher in disbelief. "She had goose bumps like she was cold. It's seventy in here."

"Maybe she caught a chill from your attitude."

Isla concentrated on the task at hand. "We're smudging this place from top to bottom with our grandmother's sage and palo santo. The doorways will be lined with salt, and I want to move the planters by the door."

"Which planters?"

"The ones with the fresh rosemary and lavender. Then you'll go home, lock your doors, and come right back here in the morning. Understood?" She wanted to insist Christopher stay with her and Daria in the apartment, but maybe moving them away for the night was safer.

Christopher saluted her. "Yes, ma'am."

Isla took a deep breath and tried to calm herself. "I know I may seem like I'm a bit extreme, but leading a coven, even one as small as ours, is a lot of responsibility. I can't have anything happen to you two."

Christopher visibly relaxed. "I know. Now let's cleanse and protect the shit out of this place."

They got to work and didn't stop until every inch of the space had been smudged properly. Isla said a quick good night to Christopher and waited for them to get in their car before heading up to her apartment. She was happy to find Daria right where she left her, snoring away.

"At least I don't need to use a mirror to check her breathing," Isla mumbled to herself. She walked quietly around her small apartment, gathering a few ingredients and her grandmother's book from its pedestal in the living room. The spare bedroom had been converted into a space for magic and meditation. With a large bay window offering an unobstructed view of the night sky, Isla could center and relax. She felt most herself and most connected to her abilities and her grandmother there. She felt the many dents on the leather-bound book in her hands.

"I need your help, now more than ever, Grandmother." She looked out the window at the clear, starry sky. "You taught me to trust my feelings, and that's what I'm doing."

She grabbed a small metal pot, dark and charred from years of spells, and placed it on a hanger. Next, she took her mortar and pestle and filled the bowl with orris root. She crushed the root using a specific rhythm, three times clockwise and one time counter. Once the root was ground down, she placed it into the pot in a small pile. She added a piece of sandalwood, frankincense powder, a small bit of moss, and a sprinkle of oregano. She took out a long match and struck it.

She looked directly into the flame and recited, "Danger is knocking, but I will not let you in. Show me your face before the fight begins." She lit the contents of the pot, and after the sandalwood ignited, she blew it out and fanned the embers to encourage everything to burn. She hadn't tried to scry in a long time, but she knew this was the only way to get some answers.

Isla closed her eyes and repeated, "He who hides in the shadows is the coward. He who hides in the shadows is the coward." Colors came alive behind her eyes. She inhaled and focused on the scent of sandalwood to stay grounded on earth. Although a scry began in one's mind, the danger of getting lost was still great. Within the swirling colors, a figure became clear. Someone large and broad—but before the person's face came into view, everything went black. Isla felt a sharp pain between her eyes, and she collapsed.

CHAPTER TEN

"She has another think coming if she thinks she can just waltz up to me with a tea and sweet smile today like nothing happened." Lu tucked her shirt in forcefully. "I'm gonna tell her I don't appreciate her hot and cold attitude." She looked down at Samson. "After all, I'm just some security guard to her, right?" Samson perked one ear up. "I know, I know. I'm not just some security guard." She crouched down and scratched his head. "Thanks for listening, bud."

Lu gathered the rest of her stuff and headed out to work. The entire drive, she considered every scenario she could find herself in with Isla and prepared a wicked response to every single one. She was going to keep to herself unless Isla had an emergency, but she changed her mind drastically by the time she parked. She went from cursing Isla to worrying about her. She didn't really know Isla, but this didn't seem like normal behavior for her, and it didn't sit right with Lu. She took pride in her ability to judge someone's character, and from the first time she met Isla, Lu had sensed her warmth and welcoming spirit. She'd felt Isla's kindness well before she felt the obvious spark between them.

She needed to check herself. *Keep drinking your coffee.* She chose to park in front of a vacant store, right over where she had dropped her pizza the night before. She wanted a view of each storefront equally and the paths between them, and that included the open parking space as well.

After spending an hour online in various weather forums and on different science pages, she found no evidence of natural causes for last night's electrical phenomenon. No storm was rolling around within twenty miles. Lu was stumped, making the situation all the more urgent and frustrating for her. The handprint was still faint on the windshield, and Lu stared at it. She remembered then that she had taken a picture.

She opened her photos on her phone and groaned when she saw the picture was nothing but a black screen. It must've been too dark to capture the handprint. She played around with the settings, increasing the light, and even applied filters in the hope of revealing something. She stared at the darkness and zoomed in. In the corner of the screen, it looked like there might have been a face.

Her phone started buzzing in her hand. Thankfully no one was around to hear her yelp.

"What did I tell you about calling during work hours?"

"Not to call you during work hours, but this is an emergency," Kayla said.

Lu shook her head. "What do you need?"

"You don't have to say it that way."

"Kayla. I'm at work right now. Is this an actual emergency, or is it a favor you're calling an emergency?" Silence stretched on. "That's what I thought. Now tell me what you need."

"I was just asked to go away for a long weekend with a few friends, and one of them wants to set me up with someone who will also be there."

"Okay…"

"Ken can't watch Lilly."

"I see." Having Lilly would be a welcome distraction. "I can take her if you can drop her off, but I won't have time to come get her on a Friday."

"That's fine," Kayla said eagerly. "We'll make it work."

"What weekend?"

"In three weeks."

"Okay. Done. Now the next time you have an *emergency* during work hours, you need to text me." Lu waited for a sarcastic comeback, but Kayla stayed quiet. "Anything else?"

"What? No. I was just texting Jess, telling her I can make it."

"Bye, Kayla." Lu hung up and shook her head.

For the first time that morning, Lu allowed herself to check the apothecary. The *Open* sign was shining bright as usual, but something seemed off, and it wasn't just the new plants outside the door. As much as she wanted to investigate, Lu sat back. She was set in her decision to keep out of Isla's way and not get involved. Lu couldn't—*wouldn't*—willingly subject herself to another day of Isla's unpredictable behavior. She couldn't be swayed by the worry she felt. No way. Even if her gut was telling her to get very, very involved.

❖

Isla paced frantically. "It's big and dark, and it is most *definitely* magic."

"Why are we open?"

Isla looked at Daria. "I don't want whoever or whatever this is to know I know."

"What happened last night?" Christopher said.

"I tried to see it or feel it. I needed to know what we are dealing with. None of this could've been a coincidence. So I put together a little ritual. I started to see a figure, but I passed out before I could see his face."

Christopher's eyes went wide. "You passed out?"

"Yeah, I found her sleeping on the floor this morning," Daria said with a small laugh.

"And how are you feeling?"

"The headache is still dull, but better."

"For now," Isla said ominously. "Keep drinking your tea. The last thing we can do is let our guard down and assume whatever this is has passed us by. I think they're after us specifically. Christopher, carry your tourmaline and fluorite at all times."

"I always do."

"Why do you think they're after us?" Daria said.

Isla thought of her vision. "I saw a person or a being walking toward me in my vision. That usually indicates whoever or whatever is coming at you. If I saw them walking away, then I'd know it was passing. These visions are usually very literal."

Daria's frown was deep. "And no face?"

"I tried to see it, I focused really hard, but I blacked out before I saw a face."

"What does that mean?" Christopher said.

Isla looked at Daria before answering. "It means whatever we're dealing with is very powerful to be able to control what I see and affect me that much in a vision."

They all turned when the door chimed, and Lu walked in. They must've looked like a bunch of deer in headlights because Lu looked at them oddly.

Christopher was the first to acknowledge her. "Lu. Hi."

"Hi," Lu said, looking in their general direction. She finally met Isla's eyes. "I wanted to see how you were feeling."

"I'm okay," Daria said. "It was just a headache—"

Isla elbowed Daria. "She's asking about me."

"Why?" Isla shot Daria what was hopefully a subtle look telling her to shut up. "I'm feeling better, thank you. I slept really hard last night and woke up better. I'm better."

Lu nodded. "It's probably the heat."

"Probably." Isla couldn't take it. Lu was so nice, and she didn't deserve any of it after how she had been acting. "Thank you for checking in on me. I'm sorry for how I acted. I'm dreadful when I'm dealing with even the slightest discomfort."

Lu's smile seemed forced. "I get it. I had my tonsils taken out when I was twelve, and I was the worst patient."

"I can't imagine you being anything other than a good patient," Isla said. She barely refrained from smacking her own face.

Lu looked at her strangely. "I assure you, I was terrible. But I'm here for a reason other than telling you about my tonsil temper tantrum. Can I talk to you about something?"

Alarms began wailing in Isla's mind. "I can't right now. We're having a staff meeting."

Lu's face fell. "Oh."

"Some other time?"

"Yeah. Sure. Anyway, I'm glad you're feeling better, both of you." With that, Lu left.

Isla covered her face with her hands and groaned. "Why is she still being nice to me?"

"I really don't know," Daria said bluntly.

"Wow. You really are feeling better."

"Guys," Christopher interjected, "I enjoy making fun of the odd relationship Isla has with the hot security guard, but we need to focus on the much bigger problems at hand. Like the mystery vision attacking both of your brains. We need your brains. I'm not the brains of any operation. I'm the beauty, obviously." They ran their finger behind their ear, as if they were tucking away long locks of hair they didn't have.

Isla blinked a few times before forming a response. "Christopher is mostly right. We need to focus on what's threatening us, and on Summerfest. Not on Lu or her kindness."

"Or that ass."

"Thank you, Christopher." Isla clapped her hands together. "We are protected, both divinely and by our own preventative actions."

Daria hummed. "Do you have any idea when we may get hit by this force?"

Isla's bravado slipped. "No. I don't, and I hate it because I feel like I can't keep us safe."

"Good thing we have each other for that," Christopher said.

"And our personal security detail outside with a dangerously chiseled face." Daria had a talent for being nonchalant with her teasing. "I'm sure Lu has a Taser or something they gave her in security school."

"She was actually in the military," Isla said, her need to defend Lu unrelenting. "I'm sure she has more to offer than just a Taser." She saw the amusement on their faces. "Shut up. Both of you."

Daria stifled her laughter. "We should probably monitor our customers more closely. Watch for new faces, people who don't belong." She cleared her throat, and all humor fell away. "We basically know everyone in town who's nonhuman or more than human, right? Especially you, Isla."

"Yeah. I know a lot from the years I spent helping my grandmother, and the list doubled since opening Hoffman's."

"Great. Now we just need to get the surveillance camera out back to work. I bet Lu could help with that."

"You did really good for two minutes," Isla said. "I was almost proud of you."

Daria laughed. "I'm sorry. For real, though, if we don't know someone who can help, we should just ask her. She's security for the strip mall, so I don't think it'd be weird."

Isla shook her head. "I want to keep her as far from this whole thing as we can. I don't even want her to catch a whiff of worry from us. Got it?" She waited for them to agree. "I'll call the company tomorrow morning. For now, I'd like to talk Summerfest. What are some of our items and services that would go over well?"

"Aura-reading photos," Christopher said.

"Yes."

Daria was next to pitch. "Crystals, and we can even curate bundles for special occasions. Like, these five crystals would be beneficial for a new job or new home or whatever."

"Yes, I love these ideas." Isla rushed to grab a pen and paper. "What about tea?"

"If we can come up with good iced recipes," Daria said. "No one will want a hot tea."

Christopher held up their finger. "But we could make tea packages to bring home or buy as a gift."

"I love all of this," she said as she scribbled. "We'll do the usual bath and smudge kits, but what about the more unique items like balms, salves, and ointments?"

Daria scratched her chin. "Maybe just advertise those?"

"Or we can keep some free samples on hand. The basic ones for, like, eczema or eye bags."

Isla pointed her pen at Christopher. "I'll print out some literature on products we won't have available at the festival, and we can hand it out whenever someone is interested in samples."

"Can I speak morbidly for a moment?" Daria said.

"That wouldn't be too out of the norm for you," Christopher said with a smirk.

Isla grinned at their banter. "I like it way better when you two tease each other."

Daria continued unfazed. "Do you think we're tempting fate by planning ahead for a future that's seemingly being threatened by someone or something we know nothing about?"

Isla squared her shoulders. "No. To stop living before the coward even shows their face would be the real tragedy."

Christopher looked at Daria and raised their eyebrows. "Very bold of her to assume they have a face to show." Daria erupted in laughter, Isla walked off toward her office, and they set about their tasks for the day.

CHAPTER ELEVEN

L u paced back and forth, waiting to catch her breath before starting her next set of leg raises. She woke up early three mornings a week to go to the gym, something she regretted every single time. She used to stop in on her way home from work, but she was less likely to make that happen after working long hours, day after day. She stretched her lower back and climbed back up on the Roman chair. She started her next set and focused on breathing in and out in time, counting each rep. After another fifty, she straightened out and dropped to the floor. The things she'd do for food. Lu lifted the collar of her tee and wiped the sweat from her brow. She did one more set before moving on to weights.

She liked doing upper body one day and legs the next, just to keep herself from feeling the ache all over. She settled in to start a set of butterfly presses when she felt like she was being watched. She caught her reflection in the wall wide mirror and saw an older man watching her with a smile from a bench not too far away. She'd put him at about fifty years old with a big, solid build and graying hair. This wouldn't be the first time someone at the gym mistook her for a man, and she wouldn't be surprised if it ended with her having to decline a date offer. She needed to push her chest out more or something.

Lu started the exercise and tried not to pay attention to her new admirer. She strained to keep her arms in the proper position as she pushed through the first set. After the count of fifteen, her chest burned, and she took a break. She sipped her water and cast a quick glance behind her. Lu was relieved to find him gone. She continued her usual routine, moving from chest to biceps, triceps to trapezius, then to her lower back, ending with thirty minutes of cardio. She was sweating profusely on a bike, nearing her third mile, when the strange man reappeared on the bike beside her. He pedaled lazily and stared up at the TV. Lu knew he had no interest in the news. She didn't like wearing headphones because she needed to hear her surroundings, but she'd kill for a pair right about now.

"I should've known you work out," he said without turning to look at her.

Here we go. "Excuse me?" she said, trying for an unfriendly tone.

He turned his head slowly. "I'm not surprised to see you here because you look like you work out."

"Sure."

"Not just your body, but the way you carry yourself."

"Do I know you?"

He laughed, but it sounded almost scripted. "No, I don't think you do. I've seen you working security. You like the pizza there, and so do I."

Although every alarm was going off in Lu's mind, it wouldn't be altogether impossible for someone to recognize her from patrolling the parking lot. She let her defenses down just enough to offer him a smile.

"Guilty," she said. "It's dangerous having good pizza so close. I don't think I've seen you there, though."

"I go during busy hours." He had a faint accent Lu couldn't quite place. "Just another face in the crowd."

"Yeah, that's probably it. Have you tried their buffalo chicken pizza? It's the best."

"My favorite. Anyway, I have to go. It was nice running into you like this."

"You, too." She turned back to her bike but watched him out of the corner of her eye, waiting for him to leave. When he did, she got up and walked to the front window to see what car he was driving. She opened the notes app on her phone, ready to take down his license plate, but he continued walking right out of the parking lot.

"Dammit." She walked up to the front desk and got the attention of the first person who looked at her. "Hi. I work security in the area, and the gentleman that just left looks like a suspect we're after. Can you tell me anything about him?"

The young woman was frazzled by the unexpected question. "Um, we're not allowed to give out names of our members."

"Can I speak to your manager?"

"They're not in yet, but I can give you their card." She handed Lu a small stack of cards after fumbling to separate one. "Call after nine."

"Do you know who I'm talking about? The guy who just left—about six foot six, graying hair, very broad build?" Lu asked desperately. Another worker looked at Lou. "Yeah, I know the guy. I asked him if he was ever a swimmer when he came in. His shoulders are unreal."

"Do you know his name?"

"Sorry, we can't give out member's names, but I can tell you he just joined this morning."

"And you've never seen him before that?" Lu watched as they both shook their heads in unison. "I appreciate your help."

Lu drove around the side streets close to the gym in search of her mystery man. She had no clue what she would do if she found him, but unfortunately, she never did. He must've been picked up or lived close enough to be off the road by now. She cursed all the way home and readied herself for work with short, frustrated movements. Lu was so annoyed by her own thoughts, she sped to the strip mall without a coffee or breakfast stop and parked in the first space in front of Hoffman's. She didn't care if Isla was in the middle of eighteen staff meetings this morning—Lu was getting some answers.

The door chimed as she entered the store, and she didn't see anybody on the floor. She didn't know exactly what was toward the back, but she started in that direction regardless.

"Lu?"

Lu recognized Christopher's voice but kept marching. She saw a closed door ahead with a cute floral *Office* sign.

"Lu you can't go in there. Isla has a—"

Lu grabbed the doorknob and swung the door open. She stumbled a bit in surprise when she saw Isla behind a large desk and a very attractive older woman buttoning up her shirt.

"Uh, sorry," Lu mumbled before slamming the door shut. She turned away, unblinking.

"Client. Isla has a client in there." Christopher cringed and wiped their brow. "Maybe you should—"

"I'll wait for her out front. Can you tell her it's urgent?" Lu didn't even wait for Christopher's response. She made a beeline for the door.

Outside, Lu took a deep breath even though the air was already humid and far from refreshing. Her stiff uniform felt too tight, and embarrassment caused her stomach to tense uncomfortably. Why was this morning so fucking awful?

"Hi."

Lu spun around too quickly and felt dizzy. "Hey. Hi. I'm sorry about barging in like that—I just have something important to talk to you about."

Isla looked over her shoulder through the window. "It's fine."

"I just, um…" *Don't say it.* "I tried talking to you yesterday." *Don't.* "I hope I didn't interrupt anything." Dammit.

"You didn't. The appointment was wrapping up anyway."

"Good." Lu nodded and tried to keep her expression neutral. Because it definitely looked like something was wrapping up, but she wasn't jealous. Not even a drop.

"What was it you wanted to talk to me about?"

"Stuff. Things happening." She cleared her throat. *Get it together.* "Have you noticed anything strange lately?" She would've sworn Isla's face lost color.

"Strange how?" Isla crossed her arms and held them, the way you would when you were cold, but a chill was unlikely with a temperature over seventy.

"Anything out of the ordinary." She read Isla's body language and watched as she dodged eye contact. "Any new faces that seem out of place or people behaving differently?"

"Does Christopher count?" Isla laughed.

Lu might not have known Isla well at all, but she knew she was dodging. And her laughter was definitely fake. She decided to share more than she probably should. "What about anything electrical? Lights flickering or TV signals going in and out? Anything out of place or vandalized?" Lu grew hopeful when Isla waited a beat before answering.

"No. Nothing like that. The strangest thing to happen around here was Daria and me feeling unwell on the same day."

Lu stepped closer, just into Isla's personal space. She lowered her head and spoke quietly. "You know you can tell me anything, right?" She looked at Isla through her lashes, Isla's eyes wide and trained on her. "Nothing will ever sound too big or too small, and I'll never think you're crazy."

"Wait here." Isla reached behind her and opened the door. She stepped into the shop.

Lu let out a long breath and shoved her hands in her pockets. She had no idea what she was doing, and she couldn't explain the way Isla made her feel. She slipped into a trance and got drawn in whenever they were close. She felt a *need* to be close to and protect Isla. She let her head fall back and closed her eyes. Had it really been so long since she'd been with someone that a pretty woman with an unpredictable attitude did this to her? Was she really that pathetic? She snapped to attention when the door chimed.

"I want you to have this." Isla offered her a small linen package.

She eyed the offering. "What is it?" she said, taking it and untying the purple string that held it together. She unrolled the linen slowly and revealed a bluish prismatic rock.

"There's also some herbs inside. It's New Age protection. That," she said, pointing to the rock, "is fluorite. You should carry it with you since you have a high-risk job."

She quirked the corner of her mouth. "Strip mall security?"

"You're obviously worried about something. Even if we hadn't had this conversation today, I can feel it."

"You can feel it?" she said, not even trying to mask her disbelief.

"Yes, I do. You said you'll never think I'm crazy."

Lu watched as Isla reached out and touched her hand. "I don't think you're crazy." She kept her breathing even, but her head was spinning.

"Then hold on to this." Isla covered the fluorite with her hand. She pulled away and stepped back. "I'll let you know if I see anything out of the ordinary."

"Thank you." Lu held up the small bundle. "And for this, too."

Isla bent her head and smiled before heading back into the shop. Lu watched her go, staring at the shop's purple door even after it was shut. She took the linen between her fingers and felt along until she touched the string holding it together.

"You must really like purple." She laughed at her own joke. Looking down, Lu noticed a faint white line in front of the door. She checked in the windows to see if anyone was watching her before bending and examining it. Without hesitation, Lu took a small sample to her tongue. "Salt?" She had seen enough movies to know what salt meant.

Lu scratched her head the whole way back to her patrol car. Once she was settled, she pulled out her phone and launched Google. She typed in *fluorite* and didn't have to look any farther than the first few results to grow even more curious. She read aloud, "*Cloaks your energy signature to avoid the effects of sorcery, psychic attacks, or curses.*"

Lu looked back up to the apothecary. "What do you know that you're not telling me?"

CHAPTER TWELVE

Isla hated grocery shopping. Too many people flooded the aisles, and she almost always bought way more than what was on her small list. She was convinced grocery store layouts were a scam. Every aisle had unnecessary hanging or standing displays of snacks and candy. Her cart wouldn't have limited edition Lady Gaga Oreos or two packs of Reese's Big Cups if they weren't next to the napkins and pasta. She turned the corner to head toward the checkout lines and nearly ran into someone. She looked up to apologize and smiled.

"Maribel, hi." Isla waited for recognition, but Maribel's attention seemed more than scattered.

Maribel looked at Isla with a dazed expression. "I didn't see you there. Did I run into you? I'm sorry." She grabbed Isla's cart with a white-knuckled grip.

Isla noticed her disheveled appearance. "Are you okay?"

"Me? Yeah. Of course." Maribel's eyes were red and swollen. "Henry had a craving for lamb, so here I am."

Isla moved slowly toward her and gently placed her hand atop Maribel's. She couldn't ignore the feelings simmering beneath Maribel's skin. "You're hurting."

Maribel's eyes went wide. "I'm fine."

"You can always talk to me. No appointment necessary," Isla said, adding a small laugh in an attempt to ease the other woman. "We're friends."

Maribel shook her head. "It's Henry. He just seems…" Maribel's eyes began to well up. "He's not himself lately."

"I thought you two were doing good." Isla lowered her voice. "Especially in the bedroom."

"We were, but all of that suddenly stopped." Maribel wiped away an errant tear. "Look at me, being a fool in front of the frozen food section."

Isla touched Maribel's shoulder and offered her a gentle smile. "Would you like to get a cup of coffee?"

Maribel looked at her oddly. "I thought you only drank tea."

"I get that a lot, but I like to indulge from time to time. After all, I'm only human," she said with a wink.

Maribel laughed. "Okay. There's a salad place across the street. They make the best espresso drinks. I know it sounds strange, but you have to trust me on this."

"Say no more. Let me pay for these quick," Isla said, pointing to her cart, "and I'll meet you there."

Maribel seemed lighter when she answered. "Okay."

Isla went through the self-checkout, only struggling once with an unexpected item in the bagging area. She stopped by her car and unloaded her bags. After a bit of searching, she spotted the salad place. The plain storefront was less than three hundred feet away. She opted to leave her car in the parking lot and walk across the street to meet Maribel. She opened the door to the small eatery, immediately enticed by the scent of coffee. Maribel wasn't hard to find in the open space, and Isla joined her at a small table.

"Can you keep a secret?" Isla said the moment she sat down.

"Of course."

"I drink tea regularly for the health benefits and to limit caffeine intake, but nothing compares to a good cup of coffee." Isla inhaled deeply. "It's one of my favorite things in the world."

"Mine, too," Maribel said. "I'll order for us. What can I get you?"

"Whatever you're having but with oat milk." Isla took in the simple decor and the short menu full of fresh foods. Sounded very much up her alley. She'd had no idea such a gem of a business sat close to home for months, and she wanted to blame being distracted by Lu. Again. She smiled up at Maribel, who approached with two mugs.

"And they even use real dishes," Maribel said as she set down their drinks.

"Thank you." Isla took the mug and sniffed the top of her frothy drink. "Cinnamon?"

Maribel leaned in. "It's a snickerdoodle cappuccino from their secret menu. They add a little vanilla and cinnamon."

"Cappuccino is my favorite." Her eyes lit up as she took her first sip and tasted the classic pairing of cinnamon and sugar. She swallowed and grinned. "It really tastes like a snickerdoodle. I love it." She set down the cappuccino and focused her attention on Maribel, silently encouraging her to open up.

"Over the last week or so, Henry has started to act differently, and it wasn't a slow or subtle change."

"What's he doing?"

"He's quiet, distant. He goes to work early and comes home late, and when I ask him where he's been, he gets mad and defensive." Maribel picked at her cuticle. "I suspect he's having an affair."

"No way."

"If it walks like a duck and quacks like a duck…"

"I refuse to believe it. Maribel, Henry is crazy about you. How long have you been together now?"

"Eighty-four years."

"That's a long time to just wake up one morning and throw it all away."

"Did you know most—" Maribel stopped herself from saying more. She checked her surroundings. "Most couples like *us* aren't monogamous. Imagining such a long lifetime with just one partner seems impossible, but not for me and Henry."

Isla spun her mug between her palms mindlessly as Maribel spoke. She wondered if she'd prefer a partner to experience hundreds of years with. Then again, she wouldn't even allow herself a partner in her own much more limited lifetime.

"Isla?"

She snapped back to the moment. "I'm sorry. I got lost in thought."

"What were you thinking about?"

"Whether or not I could remain monogamous for that long."

"And?"

Isla released a breathy laugh. "I don't even bother with relationships now."

"Yet," Maribel said confidently. "Someone always comes along and changes everything."

Isla shook her head, and when an image of Lu popped in her head, she started shaking it harder.

"Look, Isla, I don't mean to put you on the spot here, but I was wondering if you would do a reading for me."

"Daria does all our readings now."

"I want you to do it. Nobody else even knows about what I'm going through with Henry. I trust you."

Isla felt for Maribel, but she had rules to follow. "I'm sorry. I don't do readings anymore."

Maribel looked into the foam of her cappuccino, but her disappointed frown was still visible. "You were always so good. Why did you stop?"

She hesitated to explain, but Maribel had known her since she started studying under her grandmother, and trust went both ways. "It became too much for me. The stronger my powers grew, the more I opened myself up to everything around me." Isla recalled the first reading that literally knocked her down. "I couldn't control what I felt or absorbed from the other person. I made myself sick, physically and mentally, and I nearly died."

"Oh my."

"I had to make a choice to protect myself, but it wasn't an easy one."

"I had no idea," Maribel said. "I'll book an appointment with Daria."

"Just stop in. She'll have time for you—I'm sure of it."

They finished their cappuccinos while talking about the more inconsequential parts of life, and Isla felt tempted more than once to mention Lu. Ultimately, she decided to keep that confusing portion of her life private for now. Isla thanked Maribel for the delicious drink, and they parted ways.

She spent the short drive home replaying her conversation with Maribel. Isla knew Henry wasn't cheating, but proving it without evidence was impossible. Isla's train of thought continued to wander and wonder. What would cause anyone, but specifically a werewolf, to act erratically?

Isla pulled into the long driveway that ran along the strip mall and led to a small residents' parking lot behind the building. Daria's headaches, Maribel's marital problems with her werewolf—were the two connected somehow? After all, there was no such thing as coincidence. She suddenly got it. Her people. She put away the cold items, left the rest of the groceries on the kitchen counter, and ran back down to the apothecary.

"I just realized something," she said to Daria and Christopher, breathing heavily.

"That you need air to survive?" Daria watched Isla in concern. "When was the last time you ran?"

She shot Daria a look. "No. The *people*. We have to watch our people, too."

"Please hydrate. You're making me nervous," Christopher said, handing Isla a water. "We're watching out for our people."

"No, we need to *watch* them."

Daria looked appalled. "Spy on our own? Really?"

She looked at Daria quizzically. "I didn't say anything about spying. Think about it. You and I had some funky stuff happen to us, right?" She received a weak nod as an answer. "What if we're not the only ones being affected by whatever's going on?" She turned her palms up and looked at Daria and Christopher expectantly.

Christopher crossed their arms. "Go on."

"I ran into Maribel at the store, and she said Henry recently started acting strange. I know it's just one incident, but it got me thinking. She's going to come in for a reading with you," she said, pointing at Daria. "I want you to really focus and get her to talk. Get as much information from her as you can."

Daria looked hesitant. "Don't you think that's playing with her trust?"

"No. We're not using the information for anything bad. We're using it to save her."

Christopher stepped forward. "What can I do?"

"Ask everyone you help about their well-being lately. Even if you seem too attentive. We need to know if anyone else is feeling or acting differently. No symptom is too small. If Tom comes in tomorrow and says he's bored with gardening, we'll know it's out of the ordinary and make a note of it."

"Tom would never be bored with gardening."

Daria leaned into Christopher and softly said, "That's the point."

Christopher made a small O with their mouth.

"Are we all on the same page now?"

They both assured Isla they were.

"Good. I'm going to my office for a bit."

Isla closed the door behind her the moment she entered her office and looked at the painting above her desk to get a moment of clarity. She sat at her large wooden desk and opened the bottom drawer where she kept her miscellaneous papers. At the very bottom was a leather-bound notebook she'd used to keep notes during the apothecary's development. Isla pulled it out and opened it to a dog-eared page. Between two pages of handwritten notes was a Polaroid picture. She fingered the worn corner of the photo before flipping it over. The picture was of a young Isla and her grandmother. Isla took a deep breath and acknowledged the ache of grief in her chest. December would mark eleven years without her, but it never got easier. Her life had felt scattered ever since. Isla never believed in herself or her ability to be the witch and the woman her grandmother believed she could be.

"Oh, Grandmother, I don't know what to do." She ran the pad of her thumb over the photo. "Even with everything you taught me, I don't feel like I'm capable of protecting these beings, not from something this powerful."

My little Isla can do anything.

Isla's memory brought her back to high school, on that fateful night when her parents left, and her grandmother stepped in to pick up the pieces. Isla had cried harder than she ever had that day.

"I'm so sorry." She sobbed and fought to breathe through the onslaught of tears and hysterics. "I'm so, so sorry. I don't want them to go."

Her grandmother took Isla in her arms. "It's okay, my dear. They're the ones losing a bright light in their lives. You, on the other hand, are just moving on to the next chapter of your story."

Isla wiped her nose. "What do you mean?"

"This was meant to be part of your journey. Now, you'll grow up and learn. You will become the most powerful witch this town has ever seen."

"I don't want to be a witch," she said, crying harder.

"You don't mean that."

"Yes, I do."

"Being who you are is what makes you so very special."

"Being a witch caused all of this. I loved Kim and she loved me, and now she thinks I'm a freak and Mom and Dad…" Isla's eyes closed as her grandmother ran her fingers through her hair. The ultimate comfort.

"Kim doesn't understand, and that's okay. One day you'll meet someone, and they'll not only understand you, but they'll want to understand you. And that's true love."

"I'm never falling in love again."

"We'll see about that," her grandmother said with a chuckle. "We'll see."

In her daze, Isla dropped the photo. When she bent to pick it up, she knocked a mug full of pens from the corner of her desk, scattering them on the floor. With a huff, she stood and put her book on the desk. She picked up the pens, placed them back in the mug, and picked up the photo again. When she sat back down, her notebook was open, but she could have sworn she'd closed it. The page it was opened to was one of the first sketches she ever did while planning Hoffman's. Something about the plan looked familiar beyond it being her store. Isla turned the notebook upside down. Clear as day, the number four looked back at her.

"My lucky number," she said. Isla always gravitated to the number four, and the number gravitated back. She always picked it during the sports she joined, and every night for years she'd wake up at 4:44. Even now, subconsciously, she'd arranged her store in the shape of the number. Isla nodded, reading the sign loud and clear.

"I'm still not sure if I can do this, but I'm certainly going to try."

CHAPTER THIRTEEN

W"ell, Christopher, we're not next to a flag vendor," Daria said, squinting against the smoke passing through their tent.

"I didn't think they'd put us near a food truck."

"A smoked meat truck," Isla said. "I guess that's what we get for signing up late."

Daria squared her shoulders and mustered up some confidence. "It's okay. The wind direction will change, and it won't be so bad." She looked sympathetically at Isla, who seemed to be turning green. "You gonna make it?"

"Yeah," Isla said, covering her nose with her hand. "I hope we get some leads today. It's been awfully quiet lately."

"Quiet is good. Maybe it means the threat has passed."

"My feet still hurt."

"You never rest," Daria said.

"Maybe Maribel will stop by. I still can't believe she hasn't seen you for a reading yet. It's been weeks."

Daria grabbed her coffee and started sipping, pointedly ignoring Isla. Another pillow of smoke swept through, and Isla lifted the collar of her Hoffman's Apothecary T-shirt to cover her nose.

Daria grabbed a stack of postcard advertisements they had printed, forcing them into Isla's hands. "Go for a walk. Hand these out. See if anyone is acting suspicious."

Isla frowned. "But I'm Hoffman. I should be here."

"We won't have many customers or leads if you throw up all over the place."

Isla looked like she was about to argue, but another breeze full of meaty aromas wafted by. "Okay. I'll be back soon."

Daria gave her the okay sign. "And we'll be just fine."

"Do you think she'll get lost?" Christopher said when Isla walked away.

"I certainly hope so." Daria rubbed her forehead.

"Why? What's going on? Is your headache back?" Christopher looked back and forth from where Isla disappeared to Daria standing quiet. "Is this one of those catfights I always hear about?" They gasped. "Are we fighting for someone's affection? I knew you had a thing for Lu."

"I don't..." Daria eyed them up and down. "Have you been watching soap operas again?"

"No, late nineties rom-coms."

"Oh God. Please watch a horror movie or something to cleanse your brain. Okay, so, you know how Isla has been waiting for Maribel to see me?"

"Uh, yeah. She has talked about it every day."

"Well you see, I've talked to Maribel. Twice."

Christopher held up their hand. "Excuse me?"

"I haven't told Isla because I"—Daria licked her lips and looked around. Trying to explain herself was proving more difficult than expected, and she was only talking to Christopher—"I see things when I talk to her. I don't know what they are, and I'm the only one who sees them."

"Isla can help."

"Isla can't know. Not yet."

"Why not?"

"Because I don't understand what I see."

"What does it look like?"

"Sometimes it looks like Isla."

"Hey guys."

Daria and Christopher spun around to see Isla standing behind them.

"I'm happy to announce there are two stands that have funnel cake." Isla held up two funnel cakes and wore a proud smile. "On the store card, as promised."

❖

"All right, kiddo. You're the boss today, so where to first?" Lu set Lilly down the moment she stepped onto the festival grounds. "Do you want to see what kinds of games they have?"

"I'm hungry."

"We just had lunch." She laughed.

Lilly shrugged and pushed her long dark hair from her shoulders. "I didn't get dessert."

Lu looked down at the four-year-old and tried to come up with a fair argument, but Lilly was right. "You did not have dessert. What would you like?"

"Ice cream." Lilly took her hand and began leading her deeper into the crowded festival.

Lu followed along, only slightly regretting her decision to name Lilly her boss. But after they'd passed two stands advertising ice cream, she was beginning to wonder if Lilly had confused ice cream for another type of treat.

"Lulu, what's that?" Lilly said, pointing up to a large banner.

"Those are butterfly chips."

Lilly looked horrified, like she was about to cry. "Why would they eat *butterflies*?"

"No, no, no. It's just what they call fancy potato chips."

"Oh." Lilly tapped her lips with her finger.

"Do you want to try them?" Lu watched as a myriad of emotions played out over Lilly's face only to end with a fast head shake. "Then let's keep looking." They made it no more than fifteen feet before Lilly pointed again.

"What's that?"

Lu looked up at the hard apple cider stand. "Drinks for adults."

"Why are there apples?"

"For decoration."

"Can I have one?"

She took a deep breath. "Of course you'd want an apple."

"I want an apple." Lilly's voice was one step away from a full whine.

She walked up to the stand and grabbed the attention of an employee. "Excuse me, may I buy one of the apples?"

The young guy looked perplexed. "Um. No? I don't think so."

"Come on. I'll give you a dollar for an apple."

"They didn't say I could sell them."

"My niece wants an apple. In a sea of fried and sugary treats, she's asking me for an apple. Just let the kid have an apple." Lu reached into her pocket and pulled out a dollar bill. "Apples aren't even a dollar at the store. You're making a profit."

An older woman stepped directly in front of Lu. "Is there something I can help you with?" She wore a bright smile, but her tone clued Lu in to her authority.

She put on her best charming smile, hoping it didn't fail her this time. "My—"

"Hello, Judy," a familiar voice said from behind Lu.

She turned around to see Isla, wearing a very well-fitted T-shirt and cutoff jean shorts. Lu couldn't even try to fight the smile that grew on her face. Before she could say hello, the woman from the cider stand spoke.

"Isla! I'm so happy to see Hoffman's finally put up a stand at the festival. It really feels like the whole town is involved now."

"I can't believe I waited this long. Say, is there a reason why my friend is having such a hard time buying an apple for her niece?"

Lu raised her eyebrows and looked down at Lilly, who was now much more interested in cotton candy, but she couldn't back out. Lilly was getting a damn apple.

"It's no problem—we're just not used to having anyone ask about the actual apples."

"We'd like one," Isla said.

Lu held up her dollar bill. "Yes, please."

The woman handed Lu an apple but looked at Isla the whole time. "Keep your money. I'm just happy there's a kid here who wants fresh fruit."

"I'm afraid those intentions are waning." Lu nodded her head to Lilly, prompting the other two women to look as she pressed her face up against Plexiglas and watched as someone spun cotton candy. "I'm still taking the apple, and I'll get her to eat it. Even if it's the last thing I do."

"Tell her it's a magic apple."

Lu was surprised by the serious expression on Isla's face. "Does that work?"

"Nine times out of ten." Isla suddenly gave her a confident and very attractive smile.

Lu tried to coolly toss the apple up and catch it, but she fumbled and nearly dropped it. Her embarrassment faded the moment Isla laughed.

"Lilly, come here." Lu put her hand out and waited for Lilly to take it. "This is my friend, Isla." Lilly looked up at Isla and smiled shyly before burying her face into Lu's legs. "Say hi?" Lu heard Lilly's tiny muffled voice and could feel her mouth moving, but no discernible words could be made out. She knelt down to Lilly's level. "What?"

"You say *excuse me*, not *what*," Lilly said quietly yet firmly.

"Oh." She looked up at a very amused Isla. "Excuse me."

"She's pretty." Lilly hid her face again.

Lu's cheeks heated even though she wasn't the one confessing. "Maybe you should tell her that yourself." She felt Lilly nod and knew she had no choice but to pass the message along. Pity. "You're pretty."

Isla looked away and started fussing with her hair.

Lu wished she could say more under the guise of a four-year-old. Isla wasn't just pretty, she was the most beautiful woman Lu had ever seen. She tore her attention away when Lilly tapped her thigh.

"I have to go potty."

"Of course you do." She shrugged at Isla. "When you gotta go—"

"You gotta go. I'll see you later. Bye, Lilly. It was very nice meeting you."

Lilly turned shy again, and Lu ushered her toward the bathroom.

Isla fanned her face the moment she was free of Lu's intense blue-eyed gaze. She replayed Lu's words over and over, reveling in knowing Lu thought she was pretty. Sure, Lilly might have been the one who started it, but anyone with eyes and ears could tell Lu meant it when she said it. She walked slowly back to the Hoffman's stand in a daze, trying to avoid the inevitable scent of meat. She returned to the delightful sight of a busy tent.

Daria waved her down. "Welcome back. Raquel here is interested in our beginners smudge packages."

She nearly jumped with excitement. "Great. Is this a new place or somewhere you've been living for a while?"

Raquel adjusted her large, thick-rimmed glasses and looked around. "Um, I've lived in my apartment for a year and a half now."

Isla sensed her hesitancy. "Tell me more. Anything you share will only help serve you in the end. Why does smudging interest you?"

"A friend of mine does it every full moon to cleanse her space."

"That's recommended."

"But she also does it whenever she feels like bad energy has entered."

She noticed the difference in tone and knew this was closer to Raquel's truth. "Your friend is smart. Anytime you feel like someone bad or someone carrying ill intent enters your world, it's very important you do what you can to rid yourself and your home of the energy they brought in."

"I think that's what I need."

"May I ask who brought the harmful energy into your home?"

"My ex-boyfriend."

She could hear the pain in Raquel's voice. "Did he live there with you?"

Raquel nodded.

"What do you want for your apartment now?"

Raquel twisted the strap of the bag. "I want it to feel less like him. Maybe lighter? Freer. I want it to feel like I'm ready to move on."

Isla lacked recent experience, but she could commiserate with Raquel's wishes and broken heart. "We start with white sage," she said, picking up a small bundle. "Hold it at a forty-five-degree angle and light the end. Let it burn for about fifteen to twenty seconds before you blow it out. Take your time cleansing your space with the smoke, and concentrate on areas your ex preferred or lingered. His closet space, his side of the bed, the couch, and anything else."

Raquel appeared to be taking in the instructions. "Okay."

"While you're doing that, repeat to yourself your intentions, and even come up with a mantra."

"A mantra?"

"A short saying you can repeat to build yourself up. You can say things like you're strong and independent, or you're deserving of love."

Isla grabbed an abalone shell and three candles. "Use the shell to rest the sage or catch its ashes. When you're all done, light this pink candle by your door to welcome love, this white candle in a common area to promote peace and serenity, and this blue candle in the bedroom." She put all the items in a linen bag with the apothecary's name on it. "Light the blue candle and sit quietly for at least five minutes. Close your eyes and think about the person you are and the person you're working to become."

"What does the blue candle do?"

"It helps heal emotional wounds."

Raquel bit her lower lip to fight back the tears already welling in her eyes.

Isla placed her hand on Raquel's shoulder and felt the sadness start to take over. "You'll be okay. Better than." She pulled back and sent Raquel to Christopher for payment. She watched the young woman walk away with her head hung low. Isla reminded herself she did what she did to help people like Raquel.

After two hours of nonstop business, a lull between customers gave them a moment to breathe.

"I need a sausage sandwich," Christopher declared.

"No one's stopping you," Daria said as they stormed off.

Isla laughed. She started restocking what she could from the boxes stacked behind their makeshift checkout counter. She was pleased to see their inventory was dwindling. With only a few hours left, they were nearly halfway sold out.

"We should've brought more teacups."

"How were we supposed to know this many people would be interested in learning to read tea leaves?"

Isla nodded. "We'll have to remember this for next year."

Daria grinned. "Does that mean Hoffman's will be back?"

She hated Daria's I-told-you-so tone. "We should have done this sooner."

"On that note," Daria said while patting her stomach, "Christopher isn't the only one who's hungry. Did you happen to notice where Annabeth's pierogi stand is? I've been thinking of those delicious little potato pockets all day."

Isla thought hard. She had walked the entire festival grounds and stopped to say hello to everyone she knew. She never saw Annabeth. "I don't think she's here."

"What? That can't be. She has a stand every year."

"I didn't see it. I walked up and down every aisle."

"That's weird."

Isla felt the ache begin in her feet. "Too weird."

CHAPTER FOURTEEN

L u dragged her feet up the long walkway. Watching after Lilly was exhausting. She walked right into her sister's house without ringing the bell or knocking, figuring having a key and the kid was good reason enough.

"Kay?" she shouted. She took Lilly's overnight bag and placed it on the couch. "Hello? Anybody home?"

"Hello?" Lilly said, matching Lu's tone and inflection.

"Well, well, well, look what the cat dragged in." Kayla came from around the corner and scooped Lilly up. She planted kiss after kiss on Lilly's chubby cheeks. "Was she good?" Kayla barely paused before adding, "Good enough? Was she better than terrible?"

Lu chuckled. "She was a perfect angel." She didn't bother to mention the three temper tantrums and minor accident involving markers and hot cocoa on her couch. "We had the best time together."

"Is that right?" Kayla said to Lilly. "What did you do?"

Lilly started playing with Kayla's necklace. "We watched movies and ate pizza and stayed up really late."

Kayla glared at Lu.

She felt betrayed. "Not *that* late."

"We went to a fest'val—"

"Festival?"

"Fest'val and played games and ate ice cream."

"Wow. That sounds like so much fun." Kayla bounced Lilly and got a belly laugh.

"And, and Lulu's friend got me an apple."

Kayla looked at Lu with raised eyebrows. "What friend was this? I haven't heard about many of Lulu's friends."

"Uh, well, she's just a shop owner I know from work. I work

the patrol—patrolling the area around the shop." She swallowed and stuffed her hands in her pockets to keep from smacking her own face. "Her shop."

"Wow. Sounds like a real BFF," Kayla said, clearly fighting back laughter. "Lilly, sweetie, what was Lulu's friend like?"

"I know what you're doing. Stop using your child as a—"

"She's pretty!"

Lu sighed. "We made such a nice family, but I'm afraid I'm never going to speak to you again after tonight."

"You should never threaten your sister like that."

"I'm talking to the kid."

Kayla guffawed. "Lilly, sweetheart, was the friend nice?" She nodded along with Lilly, all while shooting an amused look at Lu.

"Fine. Her name is Isla. She owns an apothecary in the strip mall where I work security."

"I'm still not over you working as a security guard."

Lu pursed her lips. She wanted to tell Kayla her job was much more than it appeared, but now was not the time. She shrugged instead.

"But your job doesn't matter. Isla matters."

"There's no way you're going to drop this, is there?"

"I'd drop it if you didn't react this way, but you're very obvious."

She hated her inability to hide most things from Kayla. "We're friends. That's it. She's very kind and brings me tea almost every morning."

"She brings you tea? That is the cutest thing I have ever heard." Kayla put Lilly down and patted her butt. "Go wash your hands and then come back to have a snack." Lilly scampered off.

"It's not cute—it's nothing. She owns a shop that makes herbal tea. It's no big deal." Lu knew she was trying too hard to sell her point. "Whatever."

"Are we talking tea bag and hot water, or does she actually craft a cup of tea for you?"

She pictured the many jars containing ingredients lining the counters at Hoffman's. "Shut up."

"Mm-hmm. Tell me more about Isla."

"There's not much to tell."

"How old is she?"

"I don't know," she said, racking her brain for a memory where they might have discussed age. "Younger than me, I think."

Kayla paused with a bag of Goldfish crackers halfway open. "Not gross younger, right? You're not having a midlife crisis?"

"Oh my God. Can anything be normal with you? Why do you always jump to extremes?"

Kayla held up her hands like she was innocent and went back to the elephant dish before her. It was divided into sections, and she was filling them with various goodies for Lilly to choose from. Kayla started cutting grapes in half before she spoke again.

"I'm happy she's age appropriate for you," Kayla said.

"She's not anything *for* me. We're just friends."

"Is she single?"

She looked at Kayla in disbelief. "Will you please drop it?"

"Answer me, and I'll drop it."

Lu let out a frustrated breath. She didn't believe Kayla would drop it, but desperation left her no choice. "Yes, she's single, and no, she's not interested in a relationship. Especially not with me."

"Is she straight?"

"Uh…" She recalled their conversation about her sexuality. "No, she's not, but it's more like she's in a relationship with her business. Business-sexual."

Kayla finished pouring two glasses of apple juice and set one in front of Lu, who threw it back in one gulp. "Her tea business?" Kayla said, pouring more juice for Lu.

"An apothecary." She pictured Hoffman's, the memory vivid enough to smell the herbs. "She makes all kinds of natural remedies and sells New Age things like crystals and stuff. She really helps people with whatever they've got going on, and they really trust her." She finished her second glass of juice, feeling Kayla's eyes on her. "You'd like her candle section."

"You should ask her out."

"That ship sailed," she said without thinking.

"Ha! I knew there was more going on than you were telling me."

She rolled her eyes. "You're ridiculous, and I'm leaving." Lu stood and started for the door. Lilly came running, fully dressed in princess attire. "I'm out of here, kiddo. Give me a hug." She held Lilly tightly and hesitated to let go. The days with her tiny niece were fleeting, and she wished she could slow it all down. "I'll see you soon."

"Bye, Lulu."

Kayla was hot on her heels. "Going so soon?"

"It takes me two hours to get home, and I have work in the morning."

"Oh. I thought maybe it was something I said."

She stared at Kayla. "You're a jerk." She pulled Kayla in for a quick hug.

"I just care about you. I haven't seen you get serious about anyone since the divorce."

"I couldn't—"

"I know. First it was the military and then getting discharged and then moving. You are a master at excuses."

Lu laughed. Only her sister could manage to see things like Don't Ask, Don't Tell and moving across the country as excuses. "I'll be just fine."

Kayla crossed her arms. "Text me when you get home."

"I will." Lu didn't look back as she walked to her truck. She appreciated the way Kayla cared, but that didn't make it any less annoying.

The drive home was long and tiring, the highway being straight and monotonous. Late summer traffic slowed her down a few times along the way, but Lu still managed to make it home just as the sun dipped below the horizon. Samson was happy to see her, his shuffled walk picking up speed as he greeted her at the door.

"Hey, buddy. What do you say to a quiet night on the couch with *The Golden Girls*?" If she hurried, she could be on the couch in less than a half hour, ready for the comforts of television and her dog. She looked into Samson's soft brown eyes and smiled. "Don't take this the wrong way, but maybe I do need to put myself out there."

Once Lu had changed and settled down on the couch with a dinner of Cocoa Puffs in a large bowl, she fired up Hulu and hit *Keep Watching*. She tapped her spoon in time to the theme song and tried to encourage her brain to shut off. Any problems, any thoughts of her lonely existence could wait. Halfway through the episode, when no more than a small puddle of vaguely chocolate milk sat in the bottom of her bowl, Lu's mind wandered, and she turned her attention to her phone. She started aimlessly scrolling, liking pictures and posts along the way, but even this activity felt stale after a short time. She threw caution to the wind and searched *Isla Hoffman* but wasn't entirely surprised to find zero results. Isla was either very private or not on social media. Disappointing.

Boredom not yet satisfied, Lu did the unthinkable next. She pulled up the App Store and typed in *dating apps*. In under a minute, she had started her Tinder profile. She used a recent selfie that left much of her identity a mystery, but her smile looked good. She filled in the question prompts quickly and just wanted to get on with it. She felt desperate, yet exhilarated. She was ready to say good-bye to her crush on Isla and see what kind of women were out there. The best part was she didn't have to drag herself to a bar on a Friday night after a long week at work. Modern technology wasn't all that bad if you were into instant gratification.

Lu started swiping the moment her profile was finished, and every single swipe was left. A few too many were women already in committed relationships just looking for fun, not something Lu was into. She felt hypnotized by her rhythmic swiping after a while, nearly missing a very promising-looking profile.

Shay had long blond hair and bright blue eyes and was only a couple years younger than Lu. Her profile also boasted a love for all animals, not exclusively her two pit bulls, and an affinity for all things summer. Lu found herself smiling more and more with each word she read, but her fear grew, too. Swiping left was easy because nothing could come of it. Swiping right was putting herself out there. Lu took a deep breath and swiped right. She jumped when the phone buzzed in her hand.

A message from Kayla. *Did you make it home okay or should I continue to assume you're wrecked on the side of the road somewhere?*

Lu snorted and replied, assuring Kayla she was alive and well. She locked her phone and set it down, resolving to pay attention to her dog and her show, and not get into any more trouble.

Chapter Fifteen

Isla needed to learn to say no. For the sixth time in recent history, she found herself working alone at night after approving both Daria's and Christopher's requests for time off. This Monday evening was particularly slow, so she had very little to complain about except her boredom. She had no one to talk to or to laugh with, and her evening dragged on without someone poking fun at her from time to time. She checked the clock and had less than twenty minutes until close. The store was immaculate, fully stocked, and prepped for the next workday. She knew she could take advantage of being the business owner and close early, but what if someone needed her? What if there was a last-minute crisis only she could solve?

"Yeah, right," she mumbled, starting for the door. She was going to lock up and go home, but before she even made it halfway, the lights suddenly went out. The store was pitch black, odd since a hint of light had still clung to the night sky just moments before. Isla strained to see out the large front windows, but everything appeared ominously dark. She took a deep breath to remain calm, and she walked carefully back to the counter. She searched for her phone but couldn't find it. Next, she checked the drawer beneath the cash register for matches. She knew for a fact several books of matches were there for customers who bought anything that'd burn.

She froze when the door chimed, and a beam of light hit her directly in the face. "Who's there?"

"It's Lu. Is there anyone in here with you?"

"No. Just me, myself, and I." She heard the door lock and Lu's footsteps as she approached, causing Isla's heart to speed up. "Shouldn't you check on the rest of the stores?"

"Most of the stores are already closed, and Pat keeps a gun under his counter."

"Really?"

"No," Lu said, a smile evident in her voice. "But he does have a baseball bat and an attitude." Lu pulled a stool over to the exit and climbed up to check the emergency lights. Not even a flicker.

"I was wondering why it seemed darker than usual," Isla said.

"It's eerily dark. Every light is out, and it looks like it's the whole block. At least." Lu got down and double-checked the lock on the door. "I'll stay with you while you get your stuff and close up for the night."

Isla was flattered by the special attention, but it went against her nature to accept help on this level. She was more than capable of taking care of herself during a blackout. "I'm fine. I live right upstairs. The worst that'll happen is I'll stub my toe along the way."

"Not on my watch, you won't."

"Lu, seriously, I'll be okay. You should head home. Who knows what the roads are like right now."

"This is my job," Lu said firmly, standing much closer to Isla than before. "I'm here to keep the stores and the people in them safe." Isla heard a rustling sound, and she sucked in a breath when Lu grabbed her hand.

"Sorry. Did I scare you?" Lu asked.

She cleared her throat. "Yes. No. No, not really." She opened her hand at Lu's urging and waited. Something cold and metallic was pressed into her palm. "I'm not afraid of the dark." *Just being with you in the dark.*

"Here's a flashlight. Do what you need to do, and then grab your stuff. No need to rush. I'll keep watch by the door."

She felt around the flashlight and found the on button. The store grew even brighter, but the far corners remained pitch dark, and the hairs on the back of Isla's neck stood on end. She wasn't one to spook easily, but something about this blackout left her unsettled.

"I can't believe how dark it is," she said, stating the obvious, desperate to hear anything to keep her mind off her unease.

"Last time I saw darkness like this was in the desert."

She looked at the outline of Lu standing watch at the door. "The desert?"

"Iraq," Lu said matter-of-factly, without elaborating.

"How long were you there for?"

"A while."

"Army?"

"Air Force."

"Oh."

Lu chuckled. "Let me guess, not a fan of the military?"

What she wouldn't give to avoid this conversation. "Not particularly, but I respect our servicemen and women. It takes a lot of courage to willingly sign up for the job."

"Or stupidity."

She could hear a new bitterness in Lu's tone. "Why do you say that?"

"Are you almost done?"

Isla hadn't even moved. "I'm sorry." She started gathering any loose papers and stowed them away for the morning when the power would hopefully be restored. "I'll just be another minute."

Silence stretched on as she moved about carefully, thinking of any possible mishap that could be caused by a power surge. Her apothecary was assembled with catastrophe avoidance in mind, which meant Isla didn't have much prep work to do.

"I expected more respect from the military."

Isla stilled. She was afraid to respond or make a sound. Lu very clearly didn't like talking about this part of the past, but why would she mention it if not for Isla to engage?

"What do you mean?" She felt Lu's eyes on her. When she turned to look back, the indirect glow of the flashlight highlighted Lu's strong face. She was ghostly and beautiful.

"They wanted me to be everything they needed, and what they needed wasn't the real me. I was there to serve my country and the freedoms we all have, but I wasn't allowed to live freely as myself."

After struggling for a second, Isla understood. "I thought they ended Don't Ask, Don't Tell forever ago."

"Yeah, 2011, but I joined in 2002, right out of high school." Lu walked toward her. "At first it didn't bother me. Then I met someone when I was twenty-four, and we got married. Being married and in the military was hard enough, but being a married gay woman in the military was a challenge I never planned for."

"Why get married?"

"We were young and stupid. A lot of servicemembers get married early in life. I'm not sure if it's the danger of the job or absence making the heart grow fonder."

"Is the hiding why it didn't work out?"

"Sort of. I suspected she was cheating on me, and then I cheated on her. We had an unhealthy dynamic from day one, but that didn't make any of my actions right. I still regret everything I did."

Emboldened by the darkness, Isla reached out and placed her hand on Lu's upper arm. The heat of Lu's skin was evident through the cheap fabric. "We all make mistakes, especially when we're young and hurting."

"Have you ever cheated on a partner?"

She recalled the one person she ever loved and felt pathetic for the devotion she showed, even as a teenager. "I only ever had one partner. We were sixteen, and I loved her madly. I would sooner stab my own heart before betraying her like that."

"Then what happened?"

"She betrayed me." Isla pulled her hand back and fixed her hair. "Ready to go when you are."

Lu held the flashlight up and illuminated her face from the chin up. "Lead the way."

Isla walked out of the store and locked up behind them. The short distance to the connected stairwell felt like miles with Lu's footfalls echoing behind her. She battled internally with whether she should invite Lu in for a nightcap. She gave a silent thanks to the darkness surrounding them and the full moon hidden behind dense clouds. Neither one of them would've opened up the way they did if not shrouded in the blackout.

"I appreciate you walking up with me."

"It's what I'm here for."

She turned suddenly and shut off her flashlight. "Is it, though?" She took Lu's flashlight and shut it off, too. Crickets sounded louder, and the air felt hotter in the dark.

"No," Lu said, her voice straining.

"Then why are you here?"

"Because I needed to make sure you were safe."

She closed her eyes and allowed herself to feel, to open up and absorb Lu's energy. Their bodies were no more than a few inches apart, and that small space was electrified. She could smell Lu's skin.

"Lu…"

"I think about you all day. Every day."

Isla knew she was playing with fire, but the darkness encouraged her to fan the flames. "What do you think about?"

"If you're busy or if you're watching for me from the window. I think about the way you look when you laugh." Lu's next words were no louder than the summer bugs around them. "Every day I've wondered what it'd be like to kiss you."

Isla's stomach clenched, and her breathing turned shallow. She whimpered when Lu touched her cheek. She couldn't see much, but a small sparkle came to life in Lu's eyes. Isla wanted to weep at the gentleness of Lu's touch.

"We shouldn't," Isla said weakly.

"Tell me to go, and I will," Lu said, pausing long enough for a response that never came. "There's something about you, Isla. I can't explain it. I feel like we're inevitable, even after you push me away or I tell myself it makes no sense. But as soon as I see you again, I'm drawn in by the way you look at me."

"The way I look at you?"

"Like you've known me forever."

She swallowed hard, the gulp sounding loud between them. "Maybe I have."

Lu ran the pad of her thumb over Isla's full bottom lip before taking Isla's face in her hands. "Can I kiss you?"

Isla opened her mouth, and a small squeak came out. Not trusting herself to speak, she nodded instead. She should say no, but in the dark, in this moment, Isla felt free enough to allow her heart and desires to lead the way.

Lu's lips touched hers, and in an instant, she felt the kiss everywhere. Her cheeks warmed, her heart raced, and her hands went right for the front of Lu's uniform. Isla balled the material in her fists and pulled Lu closer and closer still, until their bodies were touching at every possible point. Lu continued to kiss her, alternating between soft reverence and deep explorations. When she opened up to Lu and felt the velvety softness of her tongue against her own, Isla's knees buckled.

"Whoa there," Lu said, tightening her arms around Isla's waist. "Are you okay?"

"Yeah," she said, happy Lu couldn't see her embarrassment in the darkness. She took a steadying breath. "I'm good. Really good." She shook her head to try to gain some control over her body. Her ears weren't the only part on fire.

"Good." Lu gave Isla's hips a squeeze, equal parts playful and strong.

"I should probably get insi—"

Lu cut her off with another kiss, this time pressing Isla against her door. The kiss turned more heated. Isla ran her hands up the back of Lu's neck, and the short bristly hair on the back of her head. Lu dipped her head to kiss Isla's neck, smiling against her skin when Isla moaned in response.

A loud crash tore them apart.

"What was that?" Lu panted.

"I don't know, but it sounds like it came from the store."

"Go inside, and I'll go check it out." Lu started for the stairs.

Isla grabbed Lu's wrist. "No way. It's my store, and I'm not about to sit here while God knows what is going on in there." She moved around Lu and tried to get in front of her, but Lu pulled her back by her hips. Lu's strength was a major turn-on.

"At least stay behind me."

They walked awkwardly close and quietly down the stairs together. Isla's heart was lurching with every step. Another loud, indistinct sound caused her to jump, but she never stopped moving forward. Once on the ground, they turned the corner, and Isla let out a loud gasp. She covered her mouth in horror.

The large front window of Hoffman's was smashed, and the word *TRAITOR* was painted across the door in red.

CHAPTER SIXTEEN

S tay here," Lu said, holding Isla's forearm tightly. She could feel the heat of danger creeping up the sides of her face. "I'm going to run to my car for something. Do not move from this spot." She stepped away from Isla slowly, walking sideways so she could watch both the path to the car and the apothecary. Once she made it to her vehicle, she opened the passenger door and reached for the glove box, pulling out her agency-issued Glock 19M. She had no need to check the ammo thanks to her weekly routine of cleaning and tuning her handgun, but she mentally prepared herself to use the weapon as she approached the vandalized door.

Lu held the gun slightly behind her back and held up her free palm to Isla, who looked ready to spring into action. "I'm going to check the inside. I don't want you anywhere near the door. Actually, you should go back upstairs and lock your door."

Isla looked disgusted by the idea. "No way. You're not going in there alone."

"How did I know you were going to say that?" she said, wiping the sweat from her brow. "I'm trained for this. You're not."

"I'm sure your security training was great, but this is probably some punk kid pulling off a dare from one of their friends."

"Why would a random kid call you a traitor?" She looked at Isla expectantly, but no answer came. "And from my experience, most punk kids write profanity or draw dicks on public property."

"I'm coming with you."

Lu moved her firearm just enough for Isla to see it. "Please, let me do my job and keep you safe."

Isla's eyes were wide. She nodded and didn't argue.

Lu took a deep breath and let her military training take over. She allowed the dark to tell its story: tiny pieces of glass continued to fall from the window frame, crickets chirped, and she heard shuffling inside the store. She crouched and moved past the window to the door, gripping the handle. It was still locked, so if anyone was inside, they had to have come in through the broken window. Lu examined the window and carefully leaned into the opening. She shone her flashlight on the debris but didn't see any sign of forced entry. The glass appeared to be broken cleanly, the shards all falling straight down instead of at a trajectory associated with an object being thrown into the window. No one entered the apothecary this way, which gave Lu hope no intruders were lurking inside.

"Toss me your keys," she whispered to Isla, who reacted immediately. She opened the door and held the flashlight against the grip of her pistol. She proceeded with caution, putting one foot in front of the other and sweeping her sight and the light from side to side. Hearing the sound of crunching at her back, she pivoted quickly. She growled in frustration when Isla held up her hands and stood no more than five feet behind her.

"I'm sorry, but I couldn't just stand there."

"I could've shot you."

"I knew you wouldn't."

"You're infuriating sometimes."

"Yeah, well, you're no walk in the park either."

Lu clenched her jaw and went back to investigating instead of arguing. Nothing in the apothecary appeared to be out of place. The cash register was untouched, merchandise sat perfectly on the shelves, and the office door remained shut. Another beam of light came on and waved around. She looked back at Isla.

"Notice anything out of place?"

"I don't think so," Isla said, stepping around Lu and venturing deeper into the store toward the office.

"Be careful." She winced when she heard a thud.

"Just my elbow. Ow." Isla let out a gasp.

"Did you really hurt yourself?"

"My picture is gone."

Lu looked where Isla shone her light but couldn't remember what once hung in the blank space. "What picture?"

"An old painting of an island."

She couldn't recall the image, which struck her as strange. Lu was very observant and had a near-photographic memory. "Was it worth anything? Did it look like a painting that could earn a few bucks?"

"No. It was just a family heirloom."

Lu's heart ached for Isla and the broken tone of her voice. "It was valuable to you."

"Priceless."

"I'm sorry. Hopefully, we'll be able to get it back once we file a police report."

"I'm not filing a police report."

"Isla, come on. You have to."

"I don't *have* to do anything. As far as I can see, only the picture is missing. I'll get the window replaced and repaint my front door in the morning. It is what it is—why complicate it?"

"You're not complicating things by calling the police. They can help you get your painting back and keep this from happening again."

"Please. The police don't care about me or my little shop. I'll take care of it myself like I always do."

She didn't miss Isla's bitterness. "This has happened before?"

Isla didn't turn to look at Lu as she answered. "I've been robbed a few times, and I called the police like I was supposed to. The first time, I got an older officer that talked to me like I didn't know how to run a business. The second time, I was all but told too bad, and the third time I was asked if any of my voodoo could make their jobs easier by telling them who did it."

Lu couldn't believe what Isla was telling her. She had met many of the officers working in Bender, and they all seemed like stand-up people. "I guess it's a good thing you have a great security guard now."

Isla snorted. "Yeah. Lucky me."

She stared at Isla's back for a moment, unsure of what to do next. She wanted to console Isla and make her feel safe. They had kissed no more than thirty minutes earlier, but the dynamic had since shifted, and Lu no longer felt like she was welcome to Isla's physical touch.

"Are you okay?" she asked.

Isla turned around and screamed before dropping her flashlight. "Lu, look out!"

A sharp pain radiated across Lu's skull, and everything went black.

❖

"Lu," Isla said, running to where Lu lay on the floor. She didn't care if the dark figure she'd seen was anywhere around. Her sole focus was Lu's well-being.

"You need to be more careful about the company you keep," a deep voice growled.

"Who are you?" Isla looked around the shadows surrounding her. The lights came back on, seemingly brighter than they'd ever been. She squinted and waited as a hairy figure came into focus. "Henry?"

"Don't tell Maribel."

She was outraged. "Don't tell Maribel you assaulted my—" She looked down at Lu. "My security guard?"

A new voice came from behind her. "Relax, Isla, I taught him how to knock someone out with minimal headaches the next day. She'll be fine."

Goose bumps spread across her flesh. She recognized the unmistakable timbre of the voice. A man stepped out of the corner, his eyes dark and his stance broad. He stood close to seven feet tall and wore a black suit, looking exactly the same as he had decades ago.

"Uncle Ronan. I thought you were—"

"Cast out because of you? Yeah, I heard my brother's very creative story."

Isla felt confusion and nausea and anger all at once. "I don't understand what's going on."

"It's quite simple. You opened a very dangerous can of worms when you outed your family to your little girlfriend back then. I thought living our authentic lives in public was a good thing, but Marcus and Mother disagreed. They couldn't handle the threats and the attempts on their lives. They chose to be cowards and run, as usual, leaving you behind with Celeste."

"And you?"

"I chose to leave, too, but my intentions were much different. I traveled the world and studied the way our kind is accepted or rejected in different societies," he said, running his hands over his slicked-back salt-and-pepper hair. "Do you want to know what I learned?"

"What?"

"The United States will deny anything they're not ready to believe, even if the evidence is spelled out right in front of them. They'll listen to the news, but only the news that fits their own beliefs. Henry here could knock on their front door, and they'd tell him to his face that werewolves don't exist because CNN released a private study."

Her mind was reeling. "But why would he tell me you were gone because of me?"

Ronan chuckled. "Marcus wanted to scare you, guilt you into believing your actions had fatal consequences."

"Scare me? What was the point if I was already hurting?"

"To keep you in line even after he abandoned you."

Her heart sank. "They were so afraid I'd tell someone our secret again."

"Not just anyone, humans. And I guess his worry was justified," Ronan said, nudging Lu's still body with his large foot.

She tightened her grip on Lu. "She doesn't know anything I don't want her to know."

"Oh, I don't care who you tell."

"Then why are you here?"

"For you."

"Me?"

"And to stop you from betraying your kind any further."

Her attention was torn between Lu and Ronan's senseless words. "Excuse me? I have devoted my life to my people."

"To helping them hide, yes. You have devoted your life to the message we should all deny who we are."

"I've done no such thing."

"Henry?" Ronan smirked cockily.

"Everything you did for me was to keep the wolf at bay."

"Because it's what you asked for." Isla's head was spinning. She did not take kindly to anyone questioning her devotion or morals. "I never pushed you to be anything other than what you wanted. You and Maribel wanted a simple life, a boring life, to raise a family."

"Because you teach us it's the only way to survive. Ronan helped me see the truth."

Lu groaned, and Isla held her tighter.

"What is the truth?" she said through clenched teeth.

"Hiding ourselves from inferior humans is the same as surrendering in a war we know we can win. We are turning our backs on the sacrifices our ancestors made to get us here. It's disgusting," Henry said, sounding like he was reading the lines straight from a propaganda pamphlet.

"And?" Ronan said.

"And we're done hiding. We are stronger and smarter. We should be in charge, not humans."

She leveled a stare at her uncle. "What are you going to do? Start a revolution?"

Ronan laughed. "My sweet dear, I already have. Henry is one of the many I've recruited, and there's plenty more coming."

"You're corrupting them."

"No, I'm waking them up."

"You sound crazy."

"I want you to join us."

She laughed. "I would never. Endangering my loved ones and the innocent people around me isn't exactly my style."

"You are very powerful, Isla. Perhaps more powerful than you even know."

"I am well aware of my power, thank you, and I use it for good."

Ronan approached her slowly and crouched to be as close to eye level as possible. "Imagine a world with no more hiding. You could use your powers for good on a much larger scale."

She knew manipulation when she heard it, but she still struggled to ignore the possibilities. "I'm proud of what I do here."

Ronan stood abruptly. "Think about it. With your powers and Celeste's book, you could be my most powerful asset."

She struggled to keep her face neutral. "How do you know I have the book?"

He tilted his head. "I see everything." Ronan snapped his fingers, and in an instant, everything was back to normal. He and Henry were gone, the apothecary was like it had never been touched, and her picture was back in its spot above her desk.

Lu moaned as she came to.

"Shhh." Isla ran her fingertips through Lu's short hair. "Try not to move too much."

"What happened?" Lu blinked one eye open. She slowly sat up and rubbed the back of her neck. "The window?"

"Long story," she said, wondering how much of the truth she'd have to tell in order to keep Lu safe.

CHAPTER SEVENTEEN

L u couldn't get past the smell but knew she had no choice but to push through. "What's in this again?"

"Turmeric."

"Is that spicy? Spicy sometimes upsets my stomach."

"There's ginger in it also. That'll settle your stomach."

"Oh. Good." She brought the teacup to her lips again and tried her best to not inhale. "You have a nice place," she said, trying to buy time and distract Isla from watching her. "Bigger than it looks from the outside. Were you able to get this at the same time as the store, or did you have to wait?"

"Same time. Now drink your tea."

She raised the mug to her mouth and, this time, forced herself to drink. Would Isla be offended if she pinched her nose? The first sip was jarring to say the least, hot and spicy and too aromatic for a cup of tea. She started coughing immediately after swallowing.

Isla patted Lu's back. "Are you okay?"

"Yeah," she said, raspy from both the concoction and coughing. "This is some strong stuff you're handing out."

Isla laughed. "It's good for you. It'll help with any inflammation and headache."

"I'm fine." She sat up straighter on Isla's insanely comfortable couch. "That's not the first time I've been knocked out. Probably won't be the last, either."

"That's not exactly comforting to know."

She liked knowing Isla cared. She took another drink of her tea, not because she wanted more, but because it's what her body knew to do when holding a mug. Her jaw tensed. "Very lemony."

"What do you remember?" Isla bit her nails and wouldn't look at Lu.

She carefully considered what to say next, not wanting to lie or withhold, but Lu was worried about whatever was making Isla so nervous. "I remember everything up until the world went black."

"I'm going to get the ice pack again." Isla stood up, but Lu reached out to grab her hand and stop her. Isla looked down at their hands. "Ice is good—"

"I don't doubt everything you're offering is good for me, but right now what I need is an explanation." Lu put her tea down and angled her body to face Isla fully. She took Isla's hands in her own and gently caressed the soft skin on the inside of Isla's wrist. She loved being able to touch her. "What happened while I was out? How did the window fix itself?"

"It didn't exactly fix itself."

"I know you didn't fix it in a matter of minutes."

Isla pulled her hands back and started pacing. Lu wanted to go to her, to hold her until her nerves faded away, but she knew she wouldn't be welcomed. Instead, she drank her tea as a sign of trust and waited.

"My family's history is complicated." Isla paused long enough to make Lu believe that was her explanation.

"Okay?"

"And I'm the reason it's complicated."

"Do you have a history of shattering windows?" Her joke fell flat.

"If I tell you about my family and my history, I will be breaking every rule I've put in place for myself since I was sixteen years old."

"I'm not taking that lightly, if that's what you're worried about."

Isla pressed her hands to her head and paced faster. "Of course, I already broke a rule by kissing you."

Lu couldn't stop her small smile. "I'm pretty sure I kissed you."

Isla stopped pacing and tilted her head as if to say *really?* "I've lived my life a certain way, and it's worked really well for me. I'd be taking a huge risk by telling you."

"I understand living according to a plan or rules you set for yourself, I really do, but we also grow up and change, and the plan or rules have to change with us." Lu grabbed her tea and took another sip. "I'm actually starting to like this."

"I'm a witch."

"And?" Maybe she should've acted more surprised, because Isla looked mad.

"I'm serious."

"So am I," Lu said with a shrug, Isla glaring even harder at her.

"I don't appreciate being mocked."

"I'm not mocking you." Lu stood and rested her hand on Isla's shoulder. Her skin was chilled. "Your store isn't exactly *not* witchy. You make stuff to heal people, you burn stuff to cleanse spaces, and you have Daria, who wears black all the time." She held her breath, hoping to hear a laugh, and blew it out slowly when Isla chuckled. "So does Christopher, actually."

"That's fair, but I'm afraid what you're accepting is not what I mean when I say I'm a witch."

She struggled to come up with the right words to tell Isla she knew, without being straightforward and saying she knew. "I think *witch* says it all."

"Here," Isla said, pressing her fingertip to Lu's teacup.

"I want to take my time, but I'll drink it." Isla kept her eyes on Lu's, and in less than ten seconds the cup and tea were heated to almost boiling. "Ow, wow, okay." Lu placed the cup down and started waving her hand. She looked at Isla skeptically. "You just did that?"

Isla nodded and looked scared. "When I was sixteen, I was in love, and I told my girlfriend about me and my family and our abilities."

"Your whole family can do this?" she said, pointing to the mug.

"I come from a long line of witches and warlocks, all very powerful."

"Witches and warlocks." She had heard the stories a hundred times, but Lu still felt underprepared for hearing the truth. She wished Isla hadn't told her. "What happened?"

"She lost it, told me I was a freak, and then told anyone who'd listen. My family was tormented and forced to move."

"That's horrible."

"The horrible part was my mom and dad not wanting me to go with them. They left me here with my grandmother and told me to deal with my mess." Isla shrugged. "They said my uncle disappeared, and it was my fault."

Now Lu wanted to beat up the ex-girlfriend and Isla's parents. "That's the opposite of what parents are supposed to do. How are you still so nice after all of that?"

"My grandmother taught me we all have a choice. You're dealt your cards, and whether they're good or bad, it's up to you to decide how you interpret them. The bad could be a life lesson that helps you grow into a better person or a path that'll lead you into the darkness. I never wanted the darkness."

"Your grandmother sounds like a smart woman."

"The smartest." Isla's eyes started to water. "I can't believe you're still here." She let out a hollow laugh.

"I'm here for the tea."

Isla's laugh turned genuine. "You should really finish this. If you do, I'll read your tea leaves for you."

"Read my tea leaves?"

"It's an ancient practice. When you brew loose-leaf tea, it leaves bits and pieces in the bottom of the mug. They can reveal a lot about the drinker."

"I don't know if I believe in that."

Isla sat down and presented Lu's tea to her once more. "You don't really know until you try it, right?"

"Sounds like something I told my first girlfriend." She saw amusement in Isla's eyes, but she knew she wasn't off the tea-leaf hook yet. She should not agree to do this, but Isla looked at her expectantly, and she was powerless. She took the cup and sat back down. "That's why you won't get into relationships?"

"Bingo. I didn't want to risk that happening again. I couldn't trust like that and put more people in danger."

"You didn't want anyone else to leave or disappear like your uncle."

"Yeah, but the joke's on me because he's the one responsible for tonight."

She almost spit out her tea. "No way. Like a ghost?"

"No, not quite. My uncle Ronan is alive and well. He was never harmed or banished or any of the other horrific things I imagined. All this time I thought I caused the breakup of my family, but it turns out they all left me because they wanted to."

She hated Isla's broken tone and posture. "Can I be honest?"

"Of course."

"I don't like your parents very much."

Isla guffawed. "That makes two of us—three, actually, because Ronan isn't a big fan either."

"Score one for the asshole who knocked me out."

"That wasn't actually Ronan—that was Henry."

"Who's Henry? Another uncle? Cousin?" Lu finished all but a mouthful of her tea and placed the mug down with more force than necessary. She was starting to get very agitated on Isla's behalf.

"No. You'd probably recognize him from coming into the shop."

"He's a customer? And tangled up with Ronan? I don't understand."

Isla started rubbing circles on her temple. "I barely understand it myself. Ronan is recruiting other nonhumans to start a revolution."

No, no, no. "That's not good," she said without thinking.

"Maybe it will be, I don't know. It just goes against my upbringing."

"Nonhumans?"

"Inhumans, nonhumans, whatever you want to call us." Isla sank into the couch, leaning back on her elbow, exuding a level of relaxation Lu only dreamed of. "Henry is a werewolf," Isla said nonchalantly.

"Of course he is." Lu's mind reeled, and she tried to figure out what this all meant for her. "Who else?"

Isla pursed her lips and blew out a breath. "There's roughly one hundred and seventy nonhumans living in Bender."

"Jesus."

"Jesus is not one of them."

Lu stared at Isla with an open mouth. "You know them all?"

"Pretty much. I started my business to help them. Up until tonight, I believed we all wanted to live our lives with no conflict between us and humans. To me that meant keeping quiet and living under the radar. A lot of humans think they know we exist, but we only see what we want to see. Believing and knowing facts are very different." Isla leaned forward and picked up the mug. "Are you ready?"

No. "Ready as I'll ever be."

Isla placed the mug back on the table. "I want you to spin the cup three times, and I'll be right back."

Lu followed the instructions. When Isla returned, she placed the mug upside down on a saucer.

"Now," Isla said, placing her hand over the inverted mug, "I want you to close your eyes and focus on your life and your future. Make a wish."

"A wish?"

"Focus on something you hope for your future, a wish." Isla closed her eyes.

She watched Isla's face for a moment before following suit. Lu thought of the life she was living now and what she hoped for herself one, two, and even five years down the line. She opened her eyes and found Isla looking back at her with a serious expression.

"Ready?"

"Ready."

Isla turned the cup over and examined the contents. "The rim represents your present, the sides are your not-so-distant future, and the bottom is your distant future." Isla turned the cup slightly. "I see many good things for you, but I'm concerned about your present."

She leaned forward and tried to peek at what Isla was seeing. "Why?"

"You have conflicting symbols of good and bad luck. Clouds, which mean serious troubles, but also birds and a butterfly, which symbolize good luck, success, and pleasure." Isla looked at her for a second and smirked. "In your near future, I see challenges being overcome, happiness and success, and even travel."

"Let me see." She grabbed the mug, covering Isla's hand with her own. She held Isla's gaze as the touch warmed her chest. "I don't see what you see."

"Look," Isla said, pointing to a clump of dull green leaves, "birds and a butterfly."

Lu frowned, struggling to see it. "I see squiggles, and maybe that looks like an hourglass, not so much a butterfly."

Isla pulled away and looked at Lu with large eyes. "Not an hourglass."

"Yes, an hourglass."

Isla shook her head. "That means imminent danger."

"I was just clobbered on the head by a werewolf." She couldn't believe those words left her mouth effortlessly. "What does my distant future say?"

"I see a ring."

"A ring?"

"Marriage."

"Oh."

"Or a failed marriage since it's on the bottom."

"This isn't a very exact practice, is it?" She chuckled.

"I'm a little rusty." Isla stood and marched off toward the kitchen.

Lu watched her retreating form and tried to unpack everything she was just told, pre- and post-tea reading. "I think I should go."

"Are you sure it's safe?" Isla shouted over running water.

"I'll be fine. I have to get home to Samson."

Isla reentered the room, drying her hands. "Samson?"

"My dog. He expects his dinner no later than nine."

"It's almost ten."

"And he'll nag me about it." Lu smiled and walked up to Isla. "I'll see you tomorrow. We'll figure out what to do about your uncle, and everything will be okay. I promise."

"You can't promise that."

"Yes, I can," she said, wrapping her arms around Isla's waist. "You have your tea leaves and witchcraft, but I have my gut. It's never wrong." She leaned in and kissed Isla gently, slowly, and pulled back as soon as she felt her self-control falter. "Good night, Isla." She walked to the door.

"Good night, Lu."

Lu walked out into the humid night and scanned the parking lot before getting into her car. She let out a heavy sigh, one laden with the warring feeling she had struggled with since opening her eyes. She had a job, a duty, and she couldn't just ignore it. She picked up her phone and dialed.

"Cadman. We haven't heard from you in days."

"Put the boss on," she said, in no mood for chitchat.

"You better have something to report."

"I do," she said, swallowing hard. "There's rumors of a werewolf."

"Rumors of a werewolf? You're calling me about a rumor? Dammit, Cadman, I'm pulling you from that spot, effective immediately."

"No, sir, you can't do that."

"The hell I can't. You are there to do one specific job, and you've yet to call me and prove you're capable of it." A long pause stretched on, and the silence grew uneasy. "You are there to investigate and report any suspected Inhuman activity to me, not to bring me news from the rumor mill."

"I know that, sir." Lu looked at the apothecary and remembered the mess it had been, only hours ago. Why did things have to be so complicated? "The shop owner is the one who told me about the werewolf."

"And what about her?"

"Who?"

"The shop owner. What can you tell me about her?"

"Nothing. Furthest thing from a threat." She shook her head at herself. "I'm going to follow up more tomorrow, but I didn't want to risk blowing my cover."

"You have twenty-four hours to give me more than a rumor. You got it?"

"Got it." The line went dead. Lu pondered her next step and fully understood what it was like to be stuck between a rock and a hard place. Or in this case, a witch and a hard-ass.

Chapter Eighteen

I need to get out of this. I need to dismantle everything I just set in motion, and I don't know how. None of this was supposed to happen, and now I have a resurrected uncle, a maybe girlfriend, and a possible supernatural revolution on my hands." Isla took a long deep breath.

Daria began fixing herself a cup of tea. "How much caffeine have you had this morning? It's barely eight thirty."

"Why aren't you worried? You should be worried."

"Should I?" Daria fixed her bangs and waited for the water to come up to temperature. "Maybe I'm just too tired to worry, but I really feel like we'll be fine. You're powerful, I'm powerful, and we have Lu with her big bad gun."

Isla looked at the drawer she had stored Lu's gun in after their run-in with Ronan. "Yeah, but—"

"But nothing. We come up with a plan, and we handle it."

"I'd really prefer you and Christopher stay out of this."

"That doesn't work for me. Christopher? Sure, keep them on the sidelines and away from danger. But you and me? We're a team and have been for years now. Do you remember the first time we met?"

"When you hit on me at the bar by introducing yourself with your full name? That time, Daria Kane?"

Daria closed her eyes and shook her head. "No, um, the second time we met?"

Isla laughed. "Yes. You knocked on the door while I was trying to get this place opened and asked me for a job. You didn't remember our first meeting then, either." She quirked her eyebrow.

"Because I was shit-faced in the bar that first night."

"But you still had great taste," she said, tossing her curls over her shoulder.

"*Anyway*, you interviewed me right then and there. You told me what you were looking for in an employee, and I told you what I was looking for in an employer. We shook hands and got right to work." Isla switched on the *Open* sign. "I don't see what that has to do with everything I told you."

"Since that day we've tackled everything together. You welcomed me into your world, and we formed our very own coven. How could one witch go into battle without her coven?"

She crossed her arms. "Do you always have to be right?"

"No, it just comes naturally." Daria stirred a spoonful of raw honey into her cup. "Before we start planning, I need to know more about your maybe girlfriend. Did you tell Lu the truth?"

"I did."

"Holy shit." Daria almost dropped her tea.

"I know. I didn't really have a choice. With Ronan and Henry showing up in a dramatic display—"

"Wait. Henry was with him?"

"Yeah. They're working together. Or maybe Henry is one of his minions. I don't know."

"That explains it," Daria whispered.

"Explains what?"

For the first time in a while, Daria's stoic exterior faltered and deep worry broke through. "I'm going to tell you something, but you can't get mad."

"What?" Isla dropped her voice. "Daria. Tell me."

Daria blew out a long breath. "I met with Maribel."

"When?"

"Before the festival. Twice."

She was taken aback. "Why didn't you tell me? I asked you if you had spoken to her, and you lied to me. You kept telling me no and giving me all these excuses."

"I didn't know what to say because I didn't understand what was going on."

"Explain it now." She fought against her rising anger, trying to understand Daria's actions.

"Okay, so, when I spoke to Maribel and offered to read her, she was really happy. She opened right up for me, and I saw everything. I felt her anxiety and her worry, and I saw choppy moments between her and Henry. But the more I tried to focus on them, the more slippery my control got." Daria began pacing. "When I pushed to be a part of their conversations, I hit a wall. A thick, dark wall, and in the next minute all I saw was you."

"Me?"

"You, with your back against a wall and very clearly in danger. Both visions were the same, except you were shadowed in the second one."

"What else?"

"That's it. I kept it to myself because I couldn't make sense of it."

She shook her head. "You should've told me."

"I know that now, but you were stressed about your feet aching, and I didn't want to add to that unless absolutely necessary." Daria pressed her hands together. "I really thought I was doing the right thing. I'm sorry."

"I believe you, but please don't keep things like that from me."

"I promise," Daria said with her right hand raised. "Now what did you tell Lu? *How* did you tell her?"

"I just came right out and told her because I can't lie, and there isn't a cover story on earth that would work anyway. One second the shop was in ruins, and the next it was immaculate, and she definitely noticed it."

"And how did Lu handle it? Did she freak out like you expected?"

"No, she actually—" The door chimed, and she turned to greet the customer. "She's walking in right now."

Lu's smile was broad, bright, and directed only at Isla. "Good morning."

She felt her cheeks warm. "Good morning."

"Good morning," Daria said loudly.

Lu looked at Daria only briefly before walking to Isla. "I'm sorry it's so early."

"Don't be," Isla said, fidgeting with the strap of her linen romper. "We just opened."

"I know. I was waiting."

Her heart sped up. "Oh?"

"I wanted to see you again, and I realized I couldn't text you to tell you how much I wanted to see you again because I don't have your number. I maybe also want another tea like the one you made me last night."

Isla went soft knowing Lu was growing to like and accept some of her ways. "Really?"

"Really." Lu looked in her eyes and said no more.

Isla was taken by the kaleidoscope of blue and grays dancing around Lu's pupils. She had never seen such bright eyes or genuine kindness directed toward her. Lu was an honest soul.

"Not to interrupt y'all, but I think this is when you're supposed to exchange numbers." Daria walked behind Isla and gave her a small nudge.

"Give me your phone," Isla said, extending her hand. Lu handed it over right away. She went about adding her name and number as a contact. Feeling cheeky, she added a moon and sparkle emoji next to her name. "Text me whenever you want, but I do have to confess—I'm not much for talking on the phone."

"I can understand that."

Daria poked her head around the corner. "She will decline literally every call from you and text you instead."

"Thank you, Daria."

"I'll text you," Lu said, looking from Daria to Isla. "Before I go, do you have my...you know?"

Isla was too distracted by Lu's lips to pick up what Lu was putting down. "Hmm?"

"You know? The thing I left behind last night?"

Daria sighed. "I wish I didn't know about your gun because this would've sounded much more interesting."

"You know?"

She cringed. "Daria knows," she said, lowering her voice as if the store was full of spies. "She and Christopher are my partners. We're a coven, and we trust each other and tackle whatever comes our way. Together." An unreadable look flashed across Lu's face. Maybe Isla had pushed her acceptance too far.

"Here," Daria said, handing Lu her gun. "I expected it to be heavier."

"Thanks. I'll text you soon." Lu looked over the weapon and turned for the door. "Don't tell anyone I carry this, please."

"Your secret is safe with us. Right, Daria?"

"Right."

Lu smiled stiffly and left.

Isla dropped her head back and groaned. "Well, that went great."

"Eh, it'll be fine."

"I hope you're right."

❖

"Shit. Shit, shit, shit." Lu placed her gun in its lockbox and slammed the trunk shut. "*Shit.*" She got in the car, started the engine, and turned on the radio. Maybe music could distract her from the shitstorm of a situation she found herself in. Her job was on the line if she didn't give her boss what he was after, and Isla just kept hand-feeding her exactly that.

On one hand, that was great. It meant her time in Bender wasn't for naught. She was producing results and getting the job done. When she'd initially been transferred to the CIA's Supernatural Division, she'd felt delighted. The gossip mill had been hot with talk about a new department, but no one knew specifics, and no one could just apply. The CIA decided whether or not you were worthy, and when Lu received her transfer email, she thought she'd hit the lotto. Until the day she arrived in a new state with new orders and found out she was about to investigate the boogeyman. Her training felt like a joke, and the first three months on the job seemed like some elaborate prank reality TV setup. But now? She was gathering evidence at warp speed and literally had her hands on a real witch.

However, Isla was caring, strong, generous, and understanding. Isla wanted to help people and make the community a better place, all noble and positive traits. Lu knew in her gut Isla wasn't looking to hurt anyone, human or not, but proving Isla's innocence wasn't her mission as an agent. Her job—her *duty*—was to report back any being or incident that was otherworldly. Simple, but why did doing her job feel so wrong?

"What am I going to do?" She looked at the time. "Twelve hours." She had Isla to consider, Ronan to worry about, and a job to keep. "Ronan."

Lu pulled out her phone and composed a message. She smiled at the little emoji next to Isla's name, and the familiarity of the simple first name warmed her heart. She typed out the message and tried her best to keep her tone light. The last thing she wanted to do was alert Isla to anything else going on. She'd tell Isla the truth about her job and what brought her to this parking lot on her own terms.

How do you think we can get Ronan to visit again? She hit send and tapped her phone against her palm.

I'm not so sure I want that.

He's not going to stop unless someone stops him. I think it's up to us.

I don't want anyone getting hurt. Especially not you.

Lu could really get used to Isla caring about her. *I'll wear a helmet. Ha. Ha.*

At least think about it. We'll get lunch and discuss a plan. You pick the place, so we don't end up at Chili's again.

Okay.

Great. I'll come get you at twelve.

See you then.

Lu felt a few butterflies in her stomach when a winky face appeared on her phone screen. She closed her eyes and rested her head back. For just one second, she'd allow herself to be someone other than a CIA agent. She was Lu, a simple security guard with a hint of jittery nerves when she thought about a lunch date with Isla. To calm herself, she took a short trip down memory lane to last night when their lips met, and Lu found out Isla's mouth was dangerously addicting.

"No surprise there," she said before turning up the radio. Classic rock could help her through any life turbulence. She sang along to Queen's "Somebody to Love," letting all the high notes drag the stress out of her like therapy. With every word she sang, another piece of a possible plan fell into place.

If they could lure Ronan into another meeting and get him to explain his plan while being recorded, Lu would have evidence. She could call her boss before the meeting and get a backup team to capture Ronan and bring him and his accomplices in for questioning. It could work. Lu knew her boss couldn't resist hard proof and multiple suspects. Maybe, just maybe, she could keep any and all suspicion away from Isla.

All Lu had to do was get Isla on board.

CHAPTER NINETEEN

Isla wiggled her feet to make room between the stack of empty coffee cups and the water bottles on the floor of Lu's car. She tried to do it as quietly as possible, worried she'd embarrass Lu, but she couldn't help crushing one or two. "Sorry," Isla said sheepishly.

Lu grimaced. "I'm the sorry one. I should've taken the time to clean my car before I picked you up."

"I'd say you used your time wisely, changing clothes." She looked Lu over, very enticed by the mossy-green V-neck T-shirt she was wearing with dark wash-distressed jeans. "Very wisely."

"I couldn't keep wearing my uniform every time I saw you. I brought an outfit and changed in Pat's bathroom."

"Are you and Pat friends?" She was genuinely amused by the idea. Not because she didn't like Pat or consider him friendly, but because he was easily twenty years Lu's senior, and Isla wondered what they had in common. "Was it your mutual love of pizza that brought the two of you together?"

"You are very funny. I'm actually surprised by how funny you are."

She gasped dramatically and placed her hand over her heart. "I think I'm offended."

Lu rolled her eyes. "Where are we off to?"

"Seed to Sprout. Take a left onto Main Street, and it's right before you cross over Route 66."

"Seed to Sprout? Sounds healthy."

"They have all kinds of food and a great bakery." Isla knew she wasn't really convincing Lu. "I know you prefer your bestie's pizza, but I promise you won't hate it."

Lu drove in silence for a couple minutes before saying, "I knew you wouldn't be humorless, but you have a very natural and easy sense of humor. You also aren't afraid to poke fun at me, which is refreshing."

"Really?"

"I think a lot of people see my butch exterior and assume a lot about me that isn't true. Like I'm a hard-ass or something."

"I don't think it's the butch thing—I think it's the military thing. Your serious face is *very* serious."

"Maybe." Lu slowed to stop at a red light.

"To me, your eyes are too soft, which makes it impossible for any other part of you to seem hard." Lu's eyebrows rose, and she shot Isla a sideways glance. "Don't miss the turn." Would Lu always frazzle her this easily?

Lu pulled into the lot and parked in the first available spot. She unbuckled her seat belt and went immediately for a kiss.

Isla kissed Lu back without hesitation, allowing herself to relax into Lu's loose embrace. She brought her hands up to Lu's jaw as she pulled back. "Hi."

"Hello. Sorry, but I've wanted to do that since you got in my car."

"Why didn't you?"

"I wanted to be professional."

"You are too cute to be a hard-ass."

"As long as you think so, that's all that matters."

Isla kissed Lu again, this time slowly and deeply, turning up the heat just enough before she pulled back abruptly and spoke against Lu's parted lips. "Let's eat."

Lu's cheeks were red. "Let's."

The inside of Seed to Sprout was small and earthy. Indoor trees and plant stands stood in the large front window, and dozens of smaller plants lined the dining room. Colorful dining tables stood on the boho-chic area rugs, while a large old-school peg-letter menu hung above the counter where patrons ordered.

"I love it here. They have the best barbecue seitan."

"Satan?"

"See," she said, moving in closer to Lu. She was craving the intimacy of simply *being* with someone. "They sound the same, but I still know you're talking about the devil."

Lu smirked.

"Seitan is a meat substitute made from gluten."

"Yum." Lu's lips were tight.

She held Lu's elbow as they stepped into the line. "Everything here is vegetarian or vegan." The wider Lu's eyes got, the harder Isla laughed. "This is my revenge for Chili's."

"I didn't know you were a vegetarian then, though."

"Trust me, you will find something to order, and you will love it." She looked into Lu's eyes, so happy they stood eye level with one another. "I promise."

"Order for me."

"That's a lot of pressure."

"You promised." Lu shrugged.

She squared her shoulders. "Fine." She stepped up to the counter and smiled at the woman behind the register. "Hey, Jen."

"Isla, I haven't seen you in a while."

"The shop's been busy, but I'm here now with a newbie. I want to knock her socks off."

"Say less," Jen said with a bright grin.

"We'll get the Shanghai spring rolls, the rib platter, an arugula salad, and do you have any specials?"

"Buffalo chik'n mac and cheese that'll have your new friend questioning everything she knows about food."

"I'll take it." Isla turned back to Lu. "Water or soda?"

"Is the soda vegetarian?"

"Two Mexican Cokes, please." Isla paid Jen and led Lu to her favorite table in the corner closest to the window. She could watch people pass by, but the trees offered privacy.

"You didn't have to pay."

"I insist." She looked across the small table at Lu, and an inexplicable flutter moved across her chest. "I'm really happy to be here with you."

"Isla, I—"

"I think we need to talk about us and what this is and how we plan on moving forward," Isla said almost too quickly to be coherent, but she must've been clear enough because Lu looked terrified. "I'm kind of born-again when it comes to relationships, and I need to know we're on the same page. Giving this a try is huge for me."

"I know," Lu said, shifting in her seat, "and I don't take that lightly. And for what it's worth, it's been a while for me, too. Not twenty years or anything like that, but a hot minute." Lu's smile was easy but still looked somewhat guarded. "I think we both want the same thing."

"I'd like to date you and see where things go."

"Ditto."

Isla giggled. "Who are you? Patrick Swayze from *Ghost*?"

Lu leaned over the table and kissed Isla, causing her to go scatterbrained for a moment. Lu sat back with a satisfied grin. "I'm going to kiss you every time you tease me."

"Are you trying to make me stop? Because I assure you it will not work."

"No way. I'm making it more fun for me."

Jen appeared tableside with a large, overflowing tray. "We have a whole bunch of goodies here." Jen placed all the plates down and handed Isla and Lu silverware and napkins. "And two Cokes." The glass bottles were the last additions, fitted between plates. "Enjoy."

"Thanks, Jen." Isla placed a napkin on her lap and nearly salivated over the feast in front of her. "I want you to try everything and tell me what you think. Be honest."

Lu surveyed the food in front of her. "I have to admit, it smells very good."

"Let's dig in."

They didn't speak as they ate, but Lu made plenty of satisfied sounds. Isla recognized a newcomer's amazement immediately, and she felt accomplished to know she had convinced a meat eater. Score one for the vegetarians.

"What's the plan you want to discuss?" Isla sat back and tried to hide her heavy breathing. Overeating was probably one of her most toxic traits.

"Dinner or a movie soon, preferably."

She knew she was falling for Lu. "Yes, but I was talking about my uncle this time."

"Oh. Right," Lu said, wiping her mouth and placing her napkin down. "Business. I think you should lure Ronan back to your shop and try to get more information from him. Who knows? Maybe his endgame isn't as devious as it seems."

"A revolution? Not devious?"

"Okay, fair point. I guess what I mean is the more details we know, the better prepared we can be for whatever's to come. Perhaps we can change his mind, or the two of you can come to some sort of compromise."

She tried to see the situation from Lu's point of view but struggled, considering Lu's levelheaded plan didn't sound like a human's perspective at all. "Are you not freaked out by having a lunch date with a witch and discussing what her powerful warlock uncle has planned? With a werewolf as an accomplice? Is none of this shocking you?"

Lu turned serious and cleared her throat. "Look, I've seen and heard a lot of things in my life. I've been all over and heard stories of the supernatural from vastly different cultures, and I believe there's some truth to all of it. Then I had an experience of my own when I was stationed in Iraq. One night I was standing guard and I heard a loud noise in the distance. It wasn't a cry or a scream, but it was definitely a sound of anguish."

"What was it?"

"I'm not sure. I went to go check it out, but the moment I stepped away from my post, I felt frozen. I couldn't move, I couldn't speak, and I swear to you I felt something right next to me, examining me. Inches from my face." Lu rolled the Coke bottle between her hands. "A second later, I was moving and everything else stopped. No more presence. No more noise."

Isla rubbed the goose bumps on her arms. "Wow."

"The next day, my buddy and I searched the area in the daylight. I figured we'd find some kind of animal tracks or a bone."

"What did you find?"

"Footprints, unlike any I've ever seen. We never spoke of that night again."

Isla shivered.

"I'd be crazy to deny the existence of any of this stuff."

Isla was speechless. Out of all the outcomes she'd imagined as she avoided dating over the years, this was never one of them. Across from her sat a beautiful butch woman who was strong and kind, but also open to a world she knew very little about, a world that would scare the average person away.

"Okay," she said resolutely. "I'll see if I can get a message through to Ronan and tell him I want to meet. We'll try things your way and see what we can find out."

"Thank you."

"But," she said, holding up a finger, "you have to trust me if I say your way won't work, and then you'll follow my lead."

"Deal." Lu extended her hand, and Isla eagerly took it. "What'll you do in that case? Like, what's your plan."

"To stop him."

"By doing what?"

"Whatever it takes."

CHAPTER TWENTY

Lu tapped her fingertips to the steering wheel as the phone rang. An unfamiliar male voice picked up, and her drumming stopped.

"Director Langdon's office."

"Who is this?"

"McCafferty. Who's this?"

"Cadman," she said, looking at the phone to make sure she dialed the right number. "Since when do you answer phones?"

"Since I was here, and it rang. What do you want, Cadman?"

She stared ahead in disbelief. "To speak to Director Langdon, obviously." She pinched the bridge of her nose and waited to be transferred. How was she supposed to take her department seriously with agents like McCafferty working cases?

"You better have something for me, Cadman."

"Actually, sir, I'm requesting an extension."

"No way."

"Sir, I understand why you're reluctant, and I *will* have something for you. I'm working on something big, but it involves a meeting, and I don't know if I'll be able to make that happen before nine o'clock tonight." She held her breath.

Langdon chewed gum loudly on the other end. "How much more time?"

"Just until the end of the week, maybe less."

"Fine."

"When I have a day and time, I'm going to need backup."

"Don't push your luck."

"We're dealing with a werewolf and a very powerful warlock, sir."

"You'll get two guys."

Lu opened her mouth but didn't speak fast enough.

"McCafferty will be one of them. He's familiar with the area."
She ground her teeth together. "I'll take what I can get."
"Report back to me as soon as you have a time."
"I will."
"Get to it, Cadman." He hung up.

She relaxed and congratulated herself. She was one step closer to closing this whole crazy case and pushing the CIA as far away from Isla as possible. Hopefully. She looked over at the apothecary and was happy to see the store busy. Lu had a lot of pent-up energy to get out, so she decided to go for a walk around the perimeter of the strip mall. She often walked along the storefronts, but she didn't patrol the sides and back of the building nearly enough. If they were going to have a meeting with Ronan, she'd feel much more confident if she knew there'd be no surprises. She paused halfway across the parking lot. She was dealing with witches, warlocks, and a werewolf. Predicting anyone's behavior would be impossible.

She started for the end of the building and waved to Pat, who was cleaning his windows. Lu appreciated what a hard worker he was. She rounded the corner and checked along the foundation up to the roof. The strip mall had a flat roof, which worried her. It'd be much too easy for someone to sit and wait to ambush. Around the back were dumpsters, one for recycling and three for trash. There was no overflow, which told Lu everything she needed to know about sanitation's schedule. Once she approached the back door to Hoffman's, she took pictures of the surrounding area and the door. She probably wouldn't need them, but having them for reference later could be good. She'd be able to notice any changes or any evidence of trespassing. She touched the plants beside Hoffman's back door. Between the lavender plants grew another bush, one she recognized but couldn't name. She broke off a sprig of the piney plant and brought it to her nose. It made her think of potatoes. She took a picture and sent it to Isla.

What kind of plant is this? She took a bit between her teeth to taste it.

Rosemary. It's an herb, not a plant.

Sorry. She added a smiley emoji with its tongue out. *Why do you have it by your doors?*

Rosemary and lavender are very powerful. Both reduce stress, and lavender also protects from evil spirits.

Now she knew why the planters had appeared recently. *Rosemary makes me want potatoes.*

SMH.

And Lu could easily picture Isla shaking her head.

She walked back around to the front of the building and looked in the window of the now vacant dance studio. Finding nothing unusual, she moved on to the apothecary, and even though she knew she shouldn't risk her professionalism by popping in, she opened the door with zero hesitation.

"There she is," Daria said with a broad grin. "I was worried I wouldn't see you today."

She narrowed her eyes. "You were?"

"Don't encourage her," Isla said as she stepped out of her office with a middle-aged woman. "Remember, Amanda, two drops of the oil under your tongue at bedtime. Nightly. Don't miss a dose. Otherwise, your transitions can become unpredictable and uncontrollable." Amanda looked at Lu and back to Isla with wide eyes. "It's okay. She's safe."

What she said warmed Lu's heart but hurt it soon after. She hated keeping the whole truth from Isla and vowed to tell her as soon as the dust settled. She couldn't go on hurting her, but she didn't want to risk the trust she had started to earn with the community. She swallowed a surprising lump in her throat.

Isla walked up to her after leading Amanda to the register. "I wasn't expecting to see you again so soon."

She lost herself to the way Isla's eyes softened while looking at her. "I was checking the perimeter and couldn't walk past without saying hi."

"Hi."

"Hi."

Amanda giggled as Daria handed her the receipt and said, "You two are gross and sweet. All at the same time."

"You know, it doesn't cost anything to mind your own business," Isla said without looking away from Lu. "Would you like to go to my office where there's less sarcasm and fewer big ears?"

Daria covered her ears with her hands. "I do *not* have big ears."

"You sure hear everything."

Lu started to laugh. "Lead the way."

Isla did lead the way, holding Lu's hand. She shut the door behind them, and her expression went serious. "What's up? Is something wrong?"

"Nothing—hey, the picture's back."

"All part of Ronan's illusion. Asshole." They looked at one another.

Lu gave in to temptation and kissed Isla firmly. She held Isla's face in her hands and memorized the soft, smooth skin of her cheeks. She pulled back and said, "I think I need to visit you less." She ran her thumb over the small mole beside Isla's left eye.

Isla's mouth dropped open. "What? What do you mean?"

"I can't stop myself from kissing you, and that's very unprofessional."

Isla wrapped her arms around Lu's neck. "I'm the boss around here, and my rules say it's perfectly okay for you to stop in for some kissing."

A shiver went down her spine. "Well then, in that case…" She kissed Isla again, this time with renewed fervor. She dug her fingertips into Isla's hips, swallowing Isla's moan. Isla tasted of spearmint and lemon. She bit at Isla's lower lip and slid her hands around to her lower back, teasing and hinting at moving lower still. Lu followed Isla as she stepped backward, never breaking their kiss.

Once against her desk, Isla sat back and wrapped her legs around Lu. She caressed Lu's shoulders and neck down to her chest before her hands came to rest against Lu's abdomen. She unbuttoned three buttons and snaked her hand into Lu's uniform shirt before she stopped in surprise.

Lu couldn't stop herself from laughing. "I'm sorry."

"It's ninety degrees outside and you're wearing layers?"

"These uniform shirts are very itchy. I hate the feel of them scratching against my skin." She looked down into Isla's hazel eyes and picked up a very mischievous twinkle.

Slowly, Isla untucked Lu's shirt and reached up to touch the skin of her bare abdomen. "That's better."

Lu's breathing grew shallow, and she fought to keep her brain present. Lu kissed Isla hard and pressed her hips forward, smiling against Isla's parted lips as she groaned.

Someone knocked on the door. "I can hear you two out here with my big ears," Daria said.

"Then try not listening." Isla breathed heavily and dropped her head back, much to Lu's delight.

"We should probably stop," Lu whispered, but she made no move to follow her own suggestion.

"We probably should."

"Daria will walk in on us on purpose."

"She might." Isla scratched Lu's waistline.

Lu sucked in a breath. "You're killing me."

"Mm. We're just getting started."

"Ahem." Daria cleared her throat loudly from the other side of the door. "I'm really sorry, but we have a line out here."

"Dammit," Isla said, nearly growling at the interruption. "I'll be out in a minute."

Lu stepped away and adjusted herself, nearly whimpering when the seam of her pants pressed against her throbbing center. She tucked in her shirt and smiled at Isla. "We'll continue this soon, I hope. Maybe after dinner?"

"I'd love that." Isla checked her hair in the antique mirror she had hanging on the wall. "Oh, and before I forget, I got in touch with Henry and told him to pass along a message to Ronan. We should be hearing from him again soon."

"That's great. What was your message?"

"That I wanted to see him. But if he breaks another window, I'll break his face."

Lu didn't hide her shock. "That certainly gets the message across."

"I thought so. Now, about that dinner…" Isla adjusted Lu's stiff collar. "My place or yours?"

"Mine. You can meet Samson."

Isla lit up. "I'd love to meet your dog."

"You should be nervous. There's my dog and my sister to meet, and Samson is by far the more important of the two."

"Well, now I feel the pressure." Isla tucked her hair behind her ear. "I always hoped I'd have a dog as my familiar, but that's yet to pan out."

"Familiar?"

"They're our little spiritual companions disguised as small household pets. We bond with them pretty deeply."

"And you've never had a dog?"

"No. Just a chipmunk."

"A chipmunk?"

"Yes," Isla said with a warm smile. "Chippy. I'd leave peanuts on my windowsill every morning, and he'd come sit with me. We'd have very peaceful mornings together, and he'd listen to me vent about my problems."

Lu tried to imagine any relationship between a person and a

chipmunk, and all she could conjure up was an image of two cartoon critters going on adventures. "What happened to Chippy?"

Isla's expression went flat. "I put peanuts out one day, and he never came. I suspect his time on this earth was up, but I know his spirit will find me again someday."

Lu didn't personally understand a lot of what Isla was sharing about her life as a witch, but she recognized the same emotions she had felt throughout her life as a boring human. They weren't all that different. "I bet he will." They looked at one another for a silent beat. "I'm gonna get back to work," she said, pointing her thumb behind her.

"You should text me if you're bored," Isla said coyly.

"Okay, but you have to tell me if I get annoying."

Isla stepped up to her slowly and embraced her. "I don't see that happening."

Lu felt her knees start to shake. No one had ever shown her this kind of softness—no past relationship had given her this kind of comfort. And her relationship with Isla was just starting to bloom. "Be careful what you say. I can be very talkative." Just then, her phone buzzed. Lu moved enough to get her phone from her pocket but refused to disconnect fully from Isla. She tried to stuff the phone away as soon as she saw the preview on the screen, but Isla saw it anyway.

Isla stepped back and away. "Was that Tinder?"

"Yes. No." She dropped her head. "Ugh, yes. I downloaded it before—"

"It's fine," Isla said with her hands up between them. She might as well have built a brick wall. "You don't owe me anything, especially not an explanation." Isla stepped around Lu and opened her office door.

She felt appropriately excused. "Isla…"

"I'll let you know if I hear from Ronan." Isla would not meet her eyes.

She left Isla's office, and the only thing she hated more than the wounded look in Isla's eyes was the implication of Daria's smirk.

Chapter Twenty-one

Isla decided to close the apothecary early, a rare occurrence, so she could be with herself and think. A walk along the bay would serve her well.

If only Daria hadn't insisted on coming.

"You didn't even hear her out?" Daria said loudly as she snacked on a fruit cup she picked up from a 7-Eleven they just *had* to stop at on the way. "You should've heard her out."

"Why?" Isla said, looking toward the sunset. "We just started doing whatever it is we're doing. Who am I to assume or expect her to see me exclusively?"

"You were banging a succubus while you were crushing on her."

She took a deep, calming breath. "Exactly. We're both single adults, and she's a very attractive person. I have no reason to believe *she* wasn't banging someone." She failed to keep the mocking tone to herself. "But we didn't actually bang the last time."

"Oh? But I thought Rumi was *irresistible*," Daria said with disgust.

"Seriously, what is your problem with Rumi?"

Daria wouldn't meet her eyes. "She slept with..." She mumbled the last few words.

"She slept with *who*?"

"My boyfriend at the time. After I introduced them at McColligan's. Like, literally the same night."

She pulled a face. "Oof. I'm sorry."

"Whatever. Let's get back to you. If you're really okay with all this, why are you brooding?"

"I am not brooding."

"Long walks along the bay to think and clear your head? Not your norm. Sorry." Daria popped a grape in her mouth.

"Maybe I'm here because of what's going on with Ronan."

Daria bobbed her head from side to side. "No. You do that kind of thinking with your grandmother's book in hand."

She wished her grandmother had given her a handbook on this subject. Isla laughed lightly, no more than a passing of air through her lips. "My grandmother was romantic through and through. Even after everything that happened," Isla said, crossing her arms and welcoming a cool breeze across her skin, "she kept reminding me that true, loyal love was out there for me."

"And you called her crazy."

"Yup."

"What do you think now?"

The bay air filled her lungs. "I still think she was crazy."

Daria rolled her eyes. "Have you heard anything from Lu?"

"Yes, she sent me a few texts throughout the day. Mostly to check if I had any news, and one explaining she only went on Tinder once."

"That's good. What did you say back?"

"I didn't," Isla said under her breath.

"Excuse me?"

"I didn't say anything, okay? I ignored her texts because I didn't know how to handle my feelings." She shocked even herself with the confession. "I have been so steadfast on not getting involved with someone. I haven't wanted to trust anyone, and just days into my first time trying, reality smacks me across the face."

"What reality is that exactly?"

"Dating is hard, and I've never really done it," she said. "I don't know the first thing about having an adult relationship. How long before we're exclusive? How do I handle irrational jealousy? How do I know if my jealousy is even irrational?" She walked right up to the dock's edge and looked into the dark water. Each ripple of the surface distorted her reflection. "What does love really feel like?"

"Oh, sweetie," Daria said, putting her arm around Isla's shoulders. "No one really knows, even when they think they do."

She held Daria's arm. "What am I supposed to do with that advice?"

"I really don't know." They shared a laugh. "But what I do know is you have to talk to Lu. If you leave all of these unanswered questions swimming around in your head, they'll build up, and nothing good will come of that."

"I know you're right," she said, patting Daria's arm. "Can you tell me why I'm even taking dating advice from you? You haven't had a relationship in years."

"Months," Daria said, correcting Isla with a raised finger. "I've been dating in secret because I'm convinced I doom every relationship I have the moment I talk about it."

She looked at Daria skeptically. "Do you really believe that?"

"I did, but then my last two attempts went down in flames. Now I'm starting to think it's just me."

"I don't think so."

"Yeah, me neither." Daria laughed. "As if."

Isla looked out over the water, the sky becoming a deep navy blue. She studied the stars as they started to show themselves. She didn't often wish she could go back and have a redo, fully believing every step of someone's journey was necessary. But every once in a while, something small would happen that Isla wanted to erase. If she could rewind to the beginning of this day, she would gladly take the opportunity to change the way she'd behaved. And steal another kiss.

They went their separate ways, and after careful consideration, Isla decided to send Lu an apology text. She'd want Lu to talk to her if the tables were turned. She must've typed and retyped the message a dozen times before settling on a flat greeting.

Hi. What are you up to?

Isla started biting her thumbnail and waited anxiously. Too many what-if scenarios ran through her head one right after another. The final one, a chance of Lu going out with a Tinder match as revenge for Isla's cold behavior, was what pushed her to her limit. She did the unthinkable and called Lu.

"Hello?" Lu's voice was deeper than usual and heavy with confusion.

"I'm sorry I'm calling so late."

"I'm shocked you're calling at all."

"I know, I just…" She just what? Isla's thoughts were scattered. This was why she preferred texting. "Did I wake you up?"

"No. I got home a little bit ago, and I'm just out of the shower."

A nice visual distracted Isla from her misery. "I wanted to apologize for earlier, and I got worried when you didn't text back." She stood in front of her living room window and hugged herself with one arm. "That probably sounds a little silly. I only messaged you twenty minutes ago."

"It doesn't sound silly."

"I know I didn't behave the best today—"

"Your reaction to a Tinder notification was pretty appropriate."
Lu's laughter sounded husky, even sexier over the phone than in person.
"It was more about how you tried to hide it."

"I panicked and handled it poorly. I would've liked to talk about
it, though."

"We can talk about it now." Even though talking it through was
all Isla could think about, she wanted Lu to be in control of how this
conversation played out. "I'll understand if you don't want to."

"I downloaded Tinder once I convinced myself we would never
happen," Lu said quickly. No hesitation. "I felt a little sorry for myself
because I kept hoping, even after you told me you weren't interested
in a relationship. All it took was some teasing from my sister, and I felt
sad enough to put myself out into the digital dating ring."

"Your sister teased you?"

"Oh yes. After Lilly decided to expose my friendship with a
certain very pretty lady she met at the festival, my sister wouldn't let it
go. Kayla is many things, and at the very top of the list is a major pain
in my ass."

Isla's smile broadened as she thought of Lu having a sibling
rivalry. "Is Kayla younger or older?"

"Younger."

"I feel like the younger ones are always spiciest."

"That is one word I would use to describe Kayla. For sure."

Silence carried on, and Isla decided to say exactly what was on her
mind. "Have you had any luck with Tinder?"

"No. Today was the first time I ever got a notification. Go figure,
but I already deleted it."

"So you're not seeing other people or sleeping with anyone in
the meantime?" She tried to act casual by wiping at a smudge on the
window, as if Lu could see her.

"No," Lu said, laughing like Isla had delivered the funniest
punchline of all time. "I'm sorry for laughing—it's just, um, I haven't
really dated since the divorce. I don't count the two blind dates Kayla
set me up on."

"Really? I find that hard to believe. You could have any woman."

"I mean it. Isla," Lu said in an oddly serious tone, "I won't lie to
you. I promise."

She wasn't ready to accept the tenderness or the serious turn their conversation had taken. "And you've been divorced a year?" she said dramatically.

"A little over a year, and we were separated for a long time before that. Technically we were married for almost fourteen years."

"That's a lot of years."

"Yeah, but like I said, we were separated for a long time. Until the divorce was finalized, I didn't feel emotionally ready to date, and I won't sleep with a woman unless I'm emotionally invested. I guess I'm old-fashioned like that." A crinkling sound came through the phone. "And I'm not about dating multiple women. Again, old-fashioned. When I like someone, I like some *one*." The crinkling continued.

"What are you doing?" Isla said.

"Eating."

"Eating what?"

"A Snickers," Lu said, obviously through a mouthful of candy bar.

"You really do have the worst eating habits." She shook her head. "And somehow you still have an incredible body."

"Incredible?"

Oh boy. "Don't act surprised. You know you have a nice physique." She thought about the way Lu's clothes hugged her thick thighs, strong biceps, and the slight slope of her breasts. "You might forget from time to time because you're constantly wearing that terrible uniform."

"I thought women loved uniforms."

"Most of us do, but your security guard getup could be much, much sexier."

"I'm sorry it's such a turnoff."

Isla smacked her forehead. "That's not what I'm saying—"

"I'm kidding. It sounds like we need excuses to get me out of that uniform"—Isla's heart sped up—"and into street clothes."

Or just out of clothes completely. "Yeah. That's exactly what I was thinking." She swallowed hard. "I'm sad we missed our dinner date this evening."

"Me, too, but I can think of a few ways to make up for it. I found a place just outside of Peabody that boasts great ambiance and a menu with anything you could want. It's only a fifteen-minute drive."

"What's the name?"

"My place. No uniforms allowed."

"Sounds wonderful," she said. Isla turned and looked around her empty apartment. She could hear Daria's and Christopher's voices in her head, egging her on to go after what she really wanted. "Or I could come over now. The night's still early."

"Oh. I, um—"

"Never mind." She wanted to curl up from embarrassment. Her ears were on fire. "It's after ten. It's late. That'd be crazy."

"I love the idea of you coming over, but I'm not very good company this late because I get up really early. I'd probably try to convince you to go to sleep with me."

Desperate to save face, Isla kept her tone light. "That doesn't sound like a bad idea."

"Do you like to cuddle, Isla?"

She couldn't mistake Lu's husky tone. "I do."

"Good."

Now Isla was lost in a daydream of burrowing deeply into Lu's arms and getting the best night's sleep of her life. Just as she was about to ask for more details, her phone vibrated. She didn't recognize the number.

I got your message.

She didn't need a witch's intuition to know exactly who it was, but she didn't have to give herself away too quickly either. *Who is this?*

You know who this is. I will meet you tomorrow night. Same time and place.

With fewer theatrics this time.

Lu's distant voice could be heard in the ominous silence. "Isla? Hello? Did I scare you away? Are you still there?"

"Looks like we won't be having dinner tomorrow night either."

"Why not?"

"We have a date with Ronan."

Chapter Twenty-two

L et's go over the plan once more," Lu said, checking to make sure her gun was loaded. For the fourth time.

Daria rolled her head to the side and sighed. "We've gone over the plan a billion times already."

"Okay. If we've gone over it a *billion* times, you can walk me through it yourself." She looked at Daria expectantly.

"You really are military," Daria said with a huff. "Fine. Christopher and I will be working even though it'll be obvious we're not *actually* working. We'll have our eyes on you two and Ronan. Basically, we're security's security guards."

"That's not how I put it—"

"But it's the truth. Don't worry, you'll be safe with me."

Christopher raised their hand. "And me. I'm very protective."

Lu looked at Isla, exasperated. "You work with these two every day?"

"Sometimes I get lucky, and one of them needs a day off." Isla's little smile was absolutely adorable.

Lu shook away the warm and fuzzy thoughts. She needed to get into the right mindset. Tonight wasn't just about figuring out Ronan's next steps—it was about clearing Isla's name and getting the CIA's attention as far from Isla as possible. All while keeping the CIA part a secret. For now. Telling Isla she was a CIA agent tasked with watching Bender would derail any hope of her plan going off without a hitch right now. The less everyone knew at this point, the better.

"Are you okay?" Isla said with her hand on Lu's forearm.

She licked her lips. "It's been a while since I've done anything like this. I want to make sure everyone is safe." She leaned in. "Especially you."

Isla kissed her cheek. "I think you know by now I can handle myself."

"That'll never stop me from protecting you." She sucked in a breath as Isla touched her cheek.

"Hi," Christopher said, toying with their long, gauzy scarf nervously, "I'm sorry to interrupt, but what do we do if he shows up with a posse again?"

"He only had one person with him last time—"

"And Henry won't hurt us," Isla said confidently.

Lu, on the other hand, had no reason to have faith in anyone but the three people she shared the room with. "We don't know that."

"I do."

"At the very least, we need to be prepared for the possibility Ronan shows up with someone willing to hurt us. We can't risk being underprepared."

"I agree," Daria said.

Isla looked at Daria before meeting Lu's eyes again. "Agreed."

"The whole purpose of this meeting is to get Ronan to talk. That's it. No confrontations and no being a hero."

"Mm-hmm," Christopher hummed. "What if we have the chance to stop him right here and now?"

"Then we take it," Lu said, purposely lying for the first time since the start of this. "But the only way we can really do that is if we know exactly what he's doing and who else is involved. If we go ahead and jump on him today, he might have dozens of worker bees out there who will carry out his plans regardless."

Christopher lowered their head. "I didn't think of that."

"But you're ready and eager to put an end to this," Lu said in a gentle, reassuring tone. "We need that kind of energy right now."

Isla stepped into the center of the main sales floor and looked around at everyone. "I need you all for this. Without you guys, I would be much weaker, both in power and spirit. Daria and Christopher, I appreciate how supportive you both are. And Lu..." Isla looked at her with such an open and vulnerable expression. "Technically we barely know each other, but you've been willing to step up with me and for me. I am grateful for you."

Lu felt the tightness of emotion creep up her neck. She managed a wink in return and shifted her attention to the time. She couldn't risk being distracted. "He'll be here any minute. I'm going to check the back one more time." She wanted to make sure the locks were secure and Isla's lone security camera was pointed at the exit. Just in case. Lu stopped moving the moment she heard the door chime.

Instead of rushing up to the front, she opted to hide behind a display and scope out Ronan and his minions. She spotted a dark-haired man but couldn't make much out about him because Daria was in the way. He was surrounded by two men and a very petite woman. If Lu had to guess, she'd say the newcomer was a fairy. She'd have to ask Isla later.

"Three may be a crowd, but seven is a party," a man said, his voice sounding vaguely familiar.

Lu wrestled with the decision of whether or not to expose herself now. She could lie low and let the supernatural squad work their magic, but the risk of missing important information was too great. She took her phone out of her pocket and set the camera to record. She placed it in an inconspicuous place to try to capture everything that transpired. Now she just had to get Daria to move.

"Eight," she said loudly enough to cut through the chatter. All heads turned to her. "Eight is definitely a party." Lu's years of training took over her brain, and the world felt like it switched into slow motion. She stepped up to Isla, eyes on hers with every step, and nodded subtly. After a deep breath, she turned to survey the faces in front of her. "Son of a bitch."

"Hello again," Ronan said.

Isla did a double take. "Again? Hello *again*?"

Lu clenched her fists at her sides. "I should've known. I should've put two and two together."

Ronan raised his palms and said, "Perhaps your investigatory skills are rusty since wasting away in this parking lot."

"Will someone tell me what the hell is going on?" Isla shouted.

"Ronan has been stalking me." Her ire rose when Ronan laughed at her.

"I'd hardly call it stalking."

"Playing the role of gym creep kinda proves otherwise." Instinctually, she stepped in front of Isla. "What are you after, Ronan? You follow me to the gym and fake small talk, then show up here and trick us into thinking you've destroyed the place. And no, I haven't forgotten the part where you knocked me out."

"That was me," a surprisingly scrawny man Lu could only assume was Henry said as he stepped forward.

Isla nudged Lu to the side. "Why were you following her?"

"I wanted to get to know this person who might get in the way of family."

"I really wouldn't consider me your family. We may be related by blood, but I haven't heard from you in twenty years." Isla turned to her. "Why didn't you tell me about him?"

"Gym creeps aren't all that new, and I had no concrete reason to believe he was in any way connected to you." She grew mildly embarrassed. "And then I forgot."

"Guys," Daria said, clapping her hands for attention, "I think we have more important things to take care of at the moment."

Lu hated to admit it, but Daria was right. "What exactly are you after, Ronan?"

"I thought I made myself pretty clear the other night. Oh, that's right, you weren't awake for that part of the discussion." Isla held her back. "I'd be more comfortable discussing my business without a pesky human here." Ronan looked at Lu in disgust.

"Witches and humans aren't all that different," Christopher said meekly from behind Lu. "Sure, we have powers, but we popped out of our moms all the same."

Daria snickered, and Lu held her breath. The last thing they needed was to provoke Ronan to violence. She was desperate to shift the focus.

"Who are you?" Lu said to the other woman with as much harshness as she could conjure.

"I'm Annabeth."

"Annabeth works at the post office," Isla said.

"And him?" Lu pointed to the quiet guy by the door. He was of average height, and nothing really stood out about him. "What's his deal?"

"That's Raj. He's a bouncer for McColligan's Pub downtown."

"And he's…"

"A vampire."

"Of course." Lu didn't have a regulation stake on her, so she hoped everything went smoothly.

Ronan let out a breath of annoyance. "Now that we're all acquainted, I'd like to discuss an offer I have for Isla." Everyone remained quiet. "I'd like your apothecary to be the center of our operation. A lot of our kind come in and out of here every day and consider this a safe space."

"You want to use my apothecary, the business I busted my ass to build over the years, as a recruitment center for your army?"

"Isla, I think you miss my point completely."

"What point is that?"

"I'm not waging a war. I'm advocating for freedom." Ronan stepped closer to Isla and softened his voice. "Don't you have any sympathy for the ones you help?" Lu stood her ground and would not let Ronan get any closer to Isla. "Don't you think it's unfair for them to have to stifle their gifts to remain safe?"

"I…"

Lu stopped looking at Ronan to watch Isla's face. Ronan was getting to her. "He's messing with you, Isla."

"Think about your grandmother," Daria said.

"Poor Celeste. She lost too many eggs from her basket before her time was up."

Isla tried to lunge forward, but Lu stopped her. "Do *not* speak of her that way," Isla hissed.

Ronan shrugged. "I'm only speaking the truth. Decades ago, Celeste was the first of us to step up and encourage everyone to be proud and use our powers regardless of human feelings."

Isla stiffened in Lu's grip. "I don't believe you."

"And then she had your mother, and she became soft."

"No way." Isla started to shake.

"You don't have to believe me, but it's the truth."

Lu shook her head. "Why would having a kid suddenly change her mind?"

"Because the child was not purebred."

"Purebred?" She looked at Isla, who started laughing.

"He's saying my mother wasn't a full witch, that her father was a human with no powers. This is how I know he's making all this shit up. My grandfather was almost as powerful as my grandmother."

"Randolph," Ronan said, checking the time on his large gold watch, "was not her father."

She had to physically restrain Isla again. She held her tightly around the waist. "You can't go after him."

"The hell I can't, and do you really think you holding me will stop it from happening?"

"Please, Isla, trust me." Lu placed her lips to Isla's ear. "Please."

Isla relaxed and nodded, but Lu could still feel she was ready to pounce at any moment. "How would you even know this?" Isla asked.

"Your father told me," Ronan said like it was the most obvious thing on the planet. "They found out after the loss of their first child."

Lu was lost. "First child?" she whispered to Isla.

"I would've had a brother, but he drowned before I was born."

"The trauma of the loss caused side effects a witch would never experience. Your mother was devastated by the discovery, and it took years for her to confide in Celeste again. Eventually they made up and everyone really leaned in to the peaceful cohabitation garbage Celeste had been spewing. Your mother had become the poster child for hybrid relationships." He looked back and forth between Isla and Lu, who was still holding her. "I see the apple didn't fall far."

Lu had had enough. "We get it, jackoff. Now tell us exactly what you're planning to do."

"I don't answer to humans."

"You will answer to me," Isla said, pushing out of Lu's grip and stepping right up to Ronan. "Not only because I am a witch more powerful than you, but because you need me."

"I don't need you," Ronan scoffed.

"You think I haven't been reading you this whole time?" Isla sounded smug. "I may be younger than you, and I may have human in my bloodline, but one of my greatest gifts is my ability to read others. I've been in your mind, Ronan, in your bones, and I feel you shaking."

Lu looked at Daria. "She can do that?"

"Yeah, but she's tried to turn it off for a long time because too many feelings were making her sick."

Without thinking, Lu stepped away from Isla. If Isla dove into her brain and could see *anything*, Lu's entire plan could go up in smoke, and their relationship would likely stop before it really had the chance to start.

"You need me. Otherwise, none of your grand plan will come to fruition."

"You're wrong. I will gain the trust of many Inhumans, and we will fight for our freedom."

"Humans will stop you," Lu said.

Ronan made a sound in the back of his throat. "Nonsense. Humans are weak. We will make them see us for who we really are and change the order of things."

"You, Henry the werewolf, Raj the vampire, and Annabeth the…" She looked at Annabeth for confirmation.

"Fairy."

"Knew it," Lu said under her breath. "You think your supernatural *Breakfast Club* is going to waltz in and take over the world? Just like that?"

The corner of Ronan's mouth twitched. "You're catching on." He looked at Isla and said, "Think about the offer." He snapped his fingers and was gone in an instant. The other three disappeared, too.

Lu looked around in a panic. "What the hell just happened?"

"Some witches and warlocks have the ability to teleport, but he can't go far," Daria said. "He must be close all the time. He went to your gym and watched you, can teleport here, and is hanging with some of our well-known community members."

"I'm shocked he got to Annabeth," Christopher said, finally stepping out of the corner they'd hidden in.

Lu looked back at her phone. "We almost had him."

CHAPTER TWENTY-THREE

L u sulked the whole way back to her car. Her good night with Isla was a cold embrace and a stiff kiss on the cheek, she had gotten reamed by her boss on the phone for producing no results and wasting everyone's time, and the worst part of it all was dealing with McCafferty. She could still see his greasy fingerprints all over her phone from when he insisted on checking in with Director Langdon himself.

"Why I have to explain myself to a guy dumber than a loaf of bread is beyond me," she muttered as she climbed in her car. She needed a hot shower and some quiet time with Samson. Maybe this was what happened when you had personal ulterior motives. She always focused on her mission, never strayed, and spent every day proving her loyalty to the institute she was working for. Now she felt split in two, and she was wrong fifty percent of the time.

"I don't like what you're doing to my niece." She jumped and looked at her back seat. Ronan sat there like he didn't have a care in the world. "She has so much power. She could do so much for her kind, and she's wasting away in this place being courted by a human."

"A human that could kick your ass."

Ronan hummed. "I do appreciate how protective you are of my Isla—"

"She is not *your* Isla, and the sooner you understand she's not joining your crusade—"

"It's no surprise your boss is interested in her."

Lu froze. Her mind went a million miles a second, trying to come up with denials and lies and even a few threats to throw Ronan off the scent, but it was no use. He knew. "Where do you get your information?"

"This is your problem, Agent Cadman. You only see what you

want to see, and you accept even less. With everything you witnessed tonight and all we told you, do you really believe I need an informant?"

Lu looked ahead and let out a long, shaky breath. Backed into a corner, she didn't have many options. "I guess this is where you blackmail me."

"Why must you use such a dirty word? I would like something, and you would like to keep something a secret. It's more like striking a deal."

"What do you want?" she said, staring at the apothecary. She felt the future she imagined with Isla slipping farther and farther away. The conflicting symbols in her tea leaves were beginning to make sense.

"Not much. I won't ask you to encourage Isla to join me, but stop discouraging her, and your secret will be safe with me."

"Fine."

"Unless you become a threat to any of us. Then I'll have to stop you."

She didn't even care at this point. "Whatever."

"Your defeat surprises me. I expected more of a fight from you."

"Look," she said, turning around again, "I'm not in a winning position here. Do I want to keep hiding from Isla? No. Do I want to hand her over to you? Absolutely not. But no matter what I do, the end result will always be the same: I hurt Isla. That's the last thing I ever wanted to do." She wiped at her face roughly. "I don't even know why I'm telling you this. You're the dickhead causing all these problems."

"It's like a death row confession."

"Get out of my car," she growled. "Do that snap thing again and make sure no one sees you." In a second, Ronan was gone.

She pulled out her phone and assessed the video from earlier in the night. She had no way of editing the video to keep Isla innocent. She had names and roles, even places of employment where the other players could be found, but none of it was enough to bring to her boss. Lu felt more confused than ever. She didn't want to implicate Henry, Raj, and Annabeth, but if it's what she had to do to protect Isla…

You really did it this time. She perked up when the apothecary lights went out. She watched and waited for Isla to leave. She didn't have to wait long. Isla stepped out of the front door and locked it behind her. She leaned forward and hoped Isla would look for her, but she didn't. Lu deflated and sat back. Her chest ached, and she felt the familiar warm prickle of tears come to life. Life felt unfair.

❖

Isla cried unabashedly. The whole night had been an emotional triathlon, running between unsavory truths about her family and wrestling with the possibility her grandmother wasn't the peacekeeper Isla had always believed her to be. She put her hand out toward the podium that held her grandmother's book and pushed all her emotions to her fingertips. The podium flew onto its side, and the book went tumbling.

If at one time Celeste really believed Inhumans were superior, would that make Isla's entire mission obsolete? Or did Celeste's change of heart conquer anything she might have done or believed previously? She had always believed people could change, even fundamentally, as they grew, educated themselves, and evolved. But how would she ever know? She had no answers and nowhere to turn because the only person who could help her was gone. She wiped her tears and stood up. Crying solved nothing.

Isla picked up the book and flipped through the pages. She had read every word dozens of times, and not once did she imagine her grandmother was antihuman. There were spells for all ailments and occasions, anecdotes to help guide and comfort, and even small notations of ways to help the neediest. Her mind reeled. How was she ever supposed to hold up her world as it crumbled?

A knock sounded at the door.

Isla pulled herself up and out of her pity party and adjusted her bathrobe. She had tried to shower several times but kept getting distracted by anger and annoyance. She'd put on a brave face by the time she got to the door, not wanting Christopher or Daria to see her such a wreck. She opened the door and gasped. There stood Lu with her shoulders slumped, looking the worse for wear. Lu wore dark gray joggers, a plain white T-shirt, and moccasin-like slippers.

"I couldn't sleep," Lu said quietly.

"Come in." Isla stepped aside and locked the door behind Lu. "I'm sorry for the mess. I—"

"You're pissed. I get it." Lu looked at her, concern on her fatigued face. "Have you been crying?" Lu said, walking up to her and taking her face in her hands. "I'm sorry."

Isla fought back a fresh wave of tears. Lu's gentleness was overwhelming. "You have nothing to be sorry for."

"Tonight was my fault. It was my idea to call Ronan here and get him to talk. I wanted him to confess to everything or at least tell us exactly what he had planned. I never expected him to do what he did."

"Dismantle my life? Yeah, me neither." She pulled away from Lu, not because she needed to get away from her, but because she needed to move. "I keep replaying it over and over in my head."

"Which part?"

"All of it, starting with my whole childhood." She ran her fingers through her hair and scratched at her scalp. The pleasurable pain was a welcome distraction. "My grandmother was revered in this community. Do you know how many lined up to give their lives when she was dying?"

"We all wish we could do that when someone we care about is passing."

"Literally. If another Inhuman is dying, we can give them our life force. You don't hear of it happening often because you're giving up your life for another, but dozens stepped up for Celeste. They couldn't bear the thought of a world without her."

"But now they have you."

"Ugh," Isla groaned. "I feel like I'm losing it."

"Listen to me," Lu said, gripping Isla's shoulders. Lu's crystal blue eyes bored into her. "Your childhood and the relationship you had with your grandmother were all real. Your memories are real."

"How do you know?" she said desperately. "You're talking *to* a witch *about* a witch. She could've cast a spell to fabricate everything I remember about our time together." She felt sick at the possibility. "She could've planted false memories, and I'd never know any better."

"Come here." Lu led Isla to the couch and sat her down. Sitting next to her, Lu said, "The truth of the matter is you have no way to prove whether those memories are real or not."

"Thank you. I feel so much better." Lu looked at her. "Sorry."

"You said it yourself—you're intuitive. You're smart and you *feel*. You know the truth in your heart, but the outside noise is keeping you from seeing it." Lu took her hands and started tracing the lines of her palm.

Isla tried to control her breathing. "I can teach you how to read palms."

Lu smiled. "No, thank you. I'll leave the magic to you."

She watched Lu and the content expression she wore. This woman was too pure to be of such a nasty world. "How are you this good?"

Lu shook her head, and Isla saw the muscles of her jaw jump. "I tried…" Lu said roughly. She cleared her throat. "I've always tried to do the right thing."

Isla felt her heart slipping deeper into her feelings for Lu. "You do. I know you do."

"Really?" Lu looked at her with red, shimmering eyes. "I need to know you believe that."

"I do," she said, touching Lu's cheek and then her jaw. "I knew it the moment we met." She touched the faint darkness beneath each of Lu's eyes and then her lips. "Remember when you said I look at you like I've known you forever?"

Lu nodded.

"I think I have."

Lu closed her eyes. "I'm sorry I failed tonight."

"You didn't. We tried, and we'll try again." She encouraged Lu to lay her head on her shoulder. She pulled Lu down to lie with her on the couch. Over and over, she ran her fingers over the buzzed hair on the side of Lu's head. Their breathing matched until it evened out, and they fell into a contented slumber.

CHAPTER TWENTY-FOUR

Isla stirred and tried to spread her legs out but couldn't. She came to consciousness slowly, realizing she wasn't in bed and her hand was touching bare skin. She opened her eyes and saw the skin of Lu's neck. Her arm was wrapped around Lu's body, and her hand tucked into the waistband of Lu's sweatpants at her hip.

"What time is it?" Lu said, her sleepy voice gravelly and sexy.

"I have no idea." She fumbled around in the dark in search of her phone. She couldn't remember where she put it.

"My phone is in my pocket." Lu reached down between them, her hand grazing Isla's inner thigh. Lu pulled out her phone, and the lit screen was blinding. "It's a little after four. I should get going."

Isla tightened her grip without thinking. She couldn't bear the thought of losing this closeness, of losing Lu. "Don't go," she whispered. "Come to bed with me. No expectations. I just…"

"You just what?"

The darkness offered a veil of safety that bolstered Isla's bravery to confess what she wanted all along. "Want you." She stood as gracefully as she could, waiting for Lu to join her. She smiled the moment Lu took her hand. She walked slowly to her bedroom, offering Lu the time to change her mind. Once in her bedroom, Isla turned on a small Himalayan salt lamp to its dimmest setting.

Isla never made her bed, calling it a personality quirk. She always had clean sheets and blankets, but the bed was never tidy. She didn't see the point when she was going to crawl into it again as soon as possible. She watched Lu as she took in the space. A moon phase tapestry hung on the wall behind her, candles and crystals sat on nearly every flat surface, and original art depicting women and celestial bodies hung around them.

"This room is very you," Lu said. "I don't mean it in a jerky way. It's nice. My place is very plain, boring really. This is nice."

Isla didn't know what to say to that. Why was she nervous? She moved instead of speaking, removing her robe to reveal a burgundy lace bralette top and mismatched indigo panties. She climbed under the covers, patting the mattress in invitation for Lu to lie down.

Lu lay flat the moment her body hit the edge of the bed, and didn't move. Her hands were folded on her stomach, and she was as rigid as a board.

"Are you okay?"

"Yeah," Lu said, staring up at the ceiling.

"Am I making you uncomfortable?"

Lu turned her head to look at Isla. "I'm actually worried about making *you* uncomfortable."

"Don't," she said, reaching out. "I want you to hold me." She inched closer then paused. "Can you maybe come to me so we're not hanging off the bed?" They laughed.

Lu shifted closer and lifted her arm, an invitation Isla took immediately. "You smell good," Lu said.

Isla burrowed her face into Lu's neck. "So do you." She propped herself up on one hand. "Thank you for staying."

Lu's eyes were dark in the dim light. "Of course," Lu said, tucking a runaway strand of Isla's hair behind her ear. "I'll do anything to make sure you're okay."

Isla felt Lu's sincerity in her chest, but she could also feel the heaviness of the day's loss. "You're burdened," she said, more to herself than Lu. Lu raised herself up to eye level, and Isla placed her palm against Lu's cheek. Lu closed her eyes to the touch. Isla felt uncertainty and fear but also immense attraction. She placed a soft kiss on Lu's forehead. Feeling Lu lean in to her, she kissed her eyebrow next.

"I don't deserve this," Lu said, opening her eyes. "I don't deserve you."

"I'm afraid you think I'm someone much greater than I am."

"And I'm terrified you see me as someone much better than I am." Lu touched Isla's lower lip and traced a line down to her clavicle. She followed the prominent bone to the bend of her shoulder.

Isla closed her eyes. If she didn't know better, she'd have thought Lu's fingertips were fire. She shivered. "Please keep touching me."

Lu obliged, paying attention to her chest and along the thin straps of her bralette. Slowly, Lu worked her way back up to her collarbone, throat, then jaw.

Isla went from a hint of arousal to wet and ready in seconds. She leaned in and waited for Lu to meet her halfway, moaning once their lips finally met. She kissed Lu hard, pouring every emotion into the firm press of her lips. She had so much to tell Lu but no words to do so. She pushed Lu on her back and straddled her supine body, smiling as Lu looked up at her with a mixture of wonder and nerves. She grabbed Lu's hands and placed them on her hips.

"Are you okay? We can stop and go to sleep. I wasn't lying when I said zero expectations." When Lu didn't answer, Isla pulled back just enough to look at her face. A war waged behind Lu's eyes, and Isla wondered what could cause such a sexy, confident woman such struggle and uncertainty. "I mean it."

"It's not you."

"I know."

"There's so much going on, and it's dangerous and—"

"And we'll get through it together. I really believe that, and I need you to, too," Isla said firmly. "I need to believe we'll be standing together on the other side of this, as close as we are now. Do you?"

Lu hesitated briefly before pecking her lips. "If you believe it, I believe it."

"So you're with me?"

Lu's small smile finally reached her eyes. "Always."

"Always." She loved the sound of that.

"Promise me one thing?"

Isla would agree to anything if Lu kept looking at her this way, wide-eyed and adoring. "Okay?"

"No matter what, no matter how this all plays out, you'll be willing to pick up the pieces and believe I did the best I could."

Her heart broke, then melted into a new one that beat exclusively for Lu. She couldn't believe Lu was so worried about failing. "Let's focus on what we have right now, what we feel right now." She guided Lu's hands to the bare skin of her stomach.

"Are you sure?"

She brought Lu's hands to her breasts. "Yes."

Lu seemed to shake off whatever hesitation was holding her back and snapped into action by sitting up and pulling Isla's body flush against hers. Isla's center pressed against Lu's lower stomach.

Isla whimpered at the unexpected pressure. The pounding arousal and intensity of feelings rushed through her. She hadn't felt this way in a long, long time. Sex with Rumi was always the same—powerful, but a means to an end. Their lack of emotion kept it simple and businesslike. But this? She never had so much passion and need and fire dancing in her chest.

Isla grabbed the sides of Lu's head and pulled her back, kissing her roughly. She tasted Lu's tongue and swallowed Lu's panting breaths. She could not get close enough. It was as if her soul was trying to imprint itself on Lu's. Lu put Isla on her back, Isla staring up in wonder at Lu's strength.

"You're so fucking sexy," Isla said.

Lu kissed her throat and down her sternum. "As long as you think so," Lu said. Lu skipped over the bralette and kissed her stomach down to her navel. "You have the softest skin I've ever touched."

"My God..." Isla was confident in her skin and always enjoyed being stripped down by her sexual partners, but being with Lu felt different. She felt more exposed and vulnerable than ever, admired inside and out. "What are you doing to me?"

Lu looked up at her with devious eyes. "Anything you ask for."

Isla spread her legs, showing Lu what she wanted next without saying a word. The feel of Lu's weight settling against her sent a tremble through her body. She pulled Lu in with her legs and kissed her again. Lu started to move her hips and began kissing Isla's throat.

"How did you know my neck is a sweet spot?"

"Just a good guess," Lu said, biting her neck.

Isla hoped for a permanent mark, a constant reminder of the moment she and Lu became one. She whimpered at the next gentle nibble. Isla was going crazy, and Lu hadn't even fully touched her. "I'm wet," she whispered roughly. Lu sat back abruptly. She nearly screamed at Lu for leaving her writhing and wanting, but her reward was Lu removing her white T-shirt and sports bra. "Jesus."

Lu's upper body was magnificent and nothing at all what Isla had imagined. Lu's breasts were fuller than she expected, with small dark nipples so hard Isla wanted to take them between her lips. Lu's arms were thick with visible strength and her belly soft. She was the butch woman of Isla's dreams. With a smirk, Lu stood and removed her sweatpants, revealing a sleeve of colorful tattoos covering her left leg. She licked her lips. The sight of Lu in nothing but boxer briefs was a treat, but the cartoon sloths printed across her underwear made Isla's heart swell with happiness.

"You're perfect in every way." She reached out her hand to Lu, trying to not rush her but needing her back against her skin. "As cute as they are, they need to go." Isla tugged at Lu's adorable boxer briefs.

Lu pushed them down and kicked them away as she joined Isla again, all awkward moves. "Better?" Lu said as she lay between Isla's legs. Isla nodded, unable to speak thanks to her mind going blank.

"I'm feeling a little overdressed," Isla said.

She wasted no time leveling the playing field, and *finally* they were both naked and touching at any point their bodies would allow. "You fit," she mumbled quietly.

"What?"

"Nothing." Isla closed her eyes and pressed her fingertips into Lu's sternum. She felt an energy exchange unlike anything she'd experienced or heard of, and she knew her heart chakra was in charge. The buzz began in her hand and was carried throughout the rest of her body by her spine. *I'm falling in love with you.*

"Touch me." Isla gasped the moment Lu touched her pulsing flesh. She burrowed her head back into her pillow, her toes curling from the way Lu spread her wetness around her entrance. Her clit was crying out for attention, but Lu seemed to be on a mission to take her time.

Isla kissed Lu's lips and then her chin, unable to focus on any task but moving her hips in time to Lu's circling. Once Lu finally entered her and pressed into her clit with her palm, Isla was on the precipice of orgasm.

"No, no, no," she said between heaving breaths. She thought her ribs were about to split with how hard her heart was beating.

"Are you okay? Do you want me to stop?"

"Dear God, no!" Isla anchored herself by digging her nails into Lu's hips. "Fuck me."

Lu was very, very good at following directions. She started pumping slowly at first, giving Isla time to stretch and acclimate. If Isla hadn't already noticed Lu's long fingers, she knew them very well now.

The pressure began building too quickly for Isla, but she couldn't have stopped her orgasm even if she wanted to. Isla grunted and ground her teeth as she came. Bright white exploded behind her lids, and an electric shock set fire to her insides. Everything went black.

CHAPTER TWENTY-FIVE

When Isla came to, she saw Lu's smiling face above her. She tried her best to smile, but every muscle in her body felt like Jell-O.

"Hi," Lu whispered.

"Did I pass out?"

"I think so. Is that not normal for you?"

"No." She pushed a few strands of runaway hair from her damp forehead. Her pulse was still strong between her thighs, but the craving for Lu invigorated her. She regained her seat atop Lu's lap and licked her lips as she looked over Lu's body. "Where should I taste first?"

"Anywhere," Lu said quickly. "But do it soon, because I'm dying."

She smirked and bent over to kiss the center of Lu's throat. She stuck her tongue out and let the tip touch Lu's salty skin. With a firm touch, she licked straight down Lu's sternum and felt the vibration of Lu's moan beneath her lips. *She's very sensitive.* Isla wrapped her lips around one of Lu's delicious-looking nipples and sucked gently. The noises coming from Lu's full parted lips were a delight.

She couldn't wait any longer. She needed to taste Lu's essence and made quick work of kissing various spots of naked skin along the way. Lu's labia glistened, droplets of wetness clinging to her small patch of hair. Isla's mouth watered at the sight and the scent of her. She slowly introduced her tongue to Lu's slick flesh. She circled Lu's prominent clit first and then sucked it between her lips. Up and down, she bobbed her head to create friction and suction around Lu's most pleasurable spot.

"Yes, Isla..." Lu wove her fingers into Isla's long hair and gave it a tug, the slight pain sending a bolt of pleasure right to Isla's crotch. Lu leaned up on one elbow to look down at Isla. "I'm so close."

Isla dipped her tongue into Lu's entrance. She tasted sweet, like a summer morning and strawberries. She was greedy with her tongue, lapping and circling and pumping until Lu started moaning loudly. Isla was grateful she didn't have any neighbors.

"Keep your tongue on my clit," Lu said roughly. "I'm gonna come, I'm gonna—" Lu threw her head back and screamed. Isla's efforts were unrelenting until Lu pushed her away.

Not ready to disconnect from Lu fully, she kissed each inner thigh and Lu's lower belly. She crawled up Lu's body and kissed her deeply. Isla knew by the way Lu's eyes drooped it was time for bed.

"Good night, love," she said, kissing Lu's forehead and finding her own slumber next to Lu.

❖

Lu sat on the edge of Isla's bed and stared at her phone. Two missed calls from her boss, one from Kayla, and three unread texts. The sun wasn't yet up, birds had just started to wake, and Lu sat simmering in anxiety. She couldn't even look at Isla and find peace, because the contentment she'd once found was now tainted by guilt. Her thumb hovered over the message icon on her home screen for seconds before she finally touched it.

Call the office immediately.
We need to talk, Cadman.
Either you bring me Isla or you get new orders.

She read and reread the final message over and over, a sick feeling twisting inside at Isla's name in the stark print. How did he know Isla's name? Lu couldn't remember a time she mentioned it. *Bring me Isla.* Taking Isla into custody was never part of her orders. She was tasked with surveillance only, documenting and deeming whether or not an Inhuman was a threat. Why the sudden change in orders?

"What're you doing?" Isla said in a sleepy slur.

Lu's heart ached. She swallowed her pain and put on her best smile. "Hey. My internal clock is set to the same time every day." She turned away and hoped Isla would fall back asleep, but the shifting of the mattress at her back told her to keep wishing. "Go back to sleep." She quickly locked her phone and dropped it onto her pile of clothes.

Isla kissed the back of her shoulders and then the back of her neck. "Come with me."

She turned and kissed Isla. "I wish I could, but I have to head home to take care of Samson. I can't be late for work."

"You sure do take your job seriously."

"I want to avoid Samson getting hangry," she said as she stood. She cast a quick glance at Isla and caught her unabashedly admiring her naked body. The sheet was wrapped loosely around Isla's torso, right below her breasts. Lu tried her best to burn the image into her memory. She wanted this moment to be locked away forever. "I will see you later, right?"

Isla stretched, making her all the more enticing. "What would Hoffman's Apothecary be without the Hoffman?"

"Daria's Apothecary?"

Isla shuddered. "Don't even joke like that."

Once dressed, she crawled across the mattress to kiss and touch Isla one last time before leaving her and nearly got lost somewhere between kissing her neck and her ribs. She wanted to cherish this lightness, the closeness and intimacy. She knew her reality and was aware of the potential end of everything she had come to love over the past few months. She ran her fingers through Isla's hair, only catching one small tangle and laying a kiss on the spot where she caused pain. She never wanted Isla to feel pain.

"I'll wave from the parking lot," she said, standing and backing away from the bed. She needed to get out of Isla's gravity before the pull became too much. She wiggled her feet into her slippers.

Isla sat up and held the covers against her body. "I'll wave back."

"Can't wait." Lu winked and turned away.

"Let's have that dinner tonight."

She paused. "Definitely."

"Great."

She blew Isla a quick kiss and walked to the front door. She took the stairs quickly and all but ran for her car. Panic started to bubble up from her gut and made her queasy. She needed to gain some kind of control in the situation, but she had no idea how to do that. She drove and drove, hoping the orange sun peeking above the horizon would bring her some clarity. By the time she made it to the CIA's local office, the world had come fully to life. She took two consecutive deep breaths before exiting her car and walking up to the building.

Lu passed through security without meeting anyone's eyes. She knew how she must look, in house clothes with her hair mussed. That she possibly smelled like sex only occurred to her once she stepped on the elevator. She looked at her reflection in the shiny door and wondered if she had finally gone mad. Every second up until this moment was a blur. As the doors opened, Lu began second-guessing her decision.

"Cadman?" Director Langdon said. He wasn't supposed to be right there. He was supposed to be in his office, and Lu was going to march in dramatically and demand answers. But now he stared at her with a furrowed brow, and the elevator doors slid closed between them.

There was no turning back. She pushed the button to open the doors and stepped off the elevator immediately. "We need to talk," she said to Director Langdon without making eye contact. She kept walking back to his office and waited for him to shut the door before speaking again. "I understand I haven't been producing many results—"

"*Any* results. You've given me nothing except an elaborate story and requests for understanding and more time. Quite frankly, Cadman, I should've pulled you from Bender a long time ago, but you came to this department with recommendations from colleagues whom I trust." He threw the file he was holding down on his desk. "Now I'm questioning even that since you're standing in front of me wearing sweatpants and speaking well out of turn."

"Sir, this is a unique case that requires time and attention."

"You mean Isla Hoffman requires *your* attention." Director Langdon leaned forward with his fingertips on his desktop. "Is that what you mean?"

"No, that's not what I mean." She was not a liar. Honesty was the best policy, after all.

He narrowed his beady eyes. "You have accolades for days. You were top of your class, a top performer in boot camp and any other physical assessment the Air Force did. You worked your way through law enforcement and government agencies because they scouted you." Director Langdon recited Lu's résumé like he had studied it nightly. "But your loyalty is what landed you here."

"I'm here because I'm one of the best," she said, chin up and shoulders squared. "It's well known that I get the job done."

"Then what is the problem this time?"

She took a deep breath. "I don't think you're being upfront about the details of this case and my role in it."

"Are you questioning your superior officer?"

"Yes. I am." She grew irritated when Director Langdon remained quietly smug. Clearly her job was on the line. "I was sent to watch and report any findings. My time in Bender has been very quiet until recently, but when I tell you the uptick has nothing to do with Isla Hoffman, you tell me to bring her in. As far as I was told, this department wasn't in the business of apprehending innocent people."

"Apprehending *creatures*, and none of them are innocent."

"I disagree."

"You would." He took a seat and leaned back casually. "Since the beginning of time, these creatures have cared very little about human lives. Nothing has changed."

"Not all. The actions of *some* members of a group do not represent the whole. Humans are plagued with criminals and bad people, but our entire society shouldn't be struck down because of it. It's why we have police officers and a judicial system. It's why we have agencies like the CIA. We watch the bad guys and capture them," she said passionately. "We should be protecting the innocent, both human and non." Director Langdon nodded, and Lu thought she was getting through to him.

"Nice speech," he said, looking down at his hands. When he looked at her again, something sinister flashed in his eyes. "But your assignment, including the new details, remains the same."

She felt a sickening twist in her gut. "What's the point of all of this?"

"You know everything you need to know. Now make use of your closeness to Miss Hoffman, or I expect your resignation on my desk by tomorrow. Do I make myself clear?"

She clenched her jaw. "Crystal."

"Good. Now get out of my office. Oh, and Cadman?" Lu stopped and turned around. "Maybe you can plan another late-night rendezvous."

Everything inside bottomed out. She felt dizzy and sick. "How…?"

Director Langdon shot her a look more belittling than any words. "I know everything."

Once back in front of the elevators, Lu's mind started to scramble. She needed to figure out how he knew what he knew. Her boss was up to something, or maybe her entire department or the agency had kept her in the dark. She started at the phone buzzing in her pocket, and she checked it to see a news update. She stared at her reflection in the phone screen, and the look of realization stared back. They'd bugged her. "McCafferty, you sly son of a bitch." She covered her face with her hands. Of all nights for her boss to listen in.

The doors slid open, and she stepped onto the elevator, looking down at her clothes. She'd do no sleuthing in sweats. The elevator stopped at the next floor, and Lu forced a neutral expression when Maria Ramirez stepped on. She was a smart agent and the only coworker who ever asked Lu on a date. Turns out Maria didn't handle rejection very well.

"Hey, Maria."

"Hi," Maria said curtly, looking Lu up and down. "Did I miss an email about a department sleepover?"

She faked laughter. "Good one, but no. I forgot something, and I ran here early to avoid being late to my shift. Say," she said, clearing her throat, "can you remind me where they take the suspects once they're brought in? I'd ask the director, but he's a little mad at me right now for not getting any results on my last case." She didn't lie completely, and she knew giving Maria a juicy tidbit about her failure would throw her off the scent.

"That sucks. Good luck getting back on his good side." The elevator doors opened, and Maria stepped out. Lu's shoulders fell. "They're questioned and then moved to the basement for holding."

"Then where do they go?"

"How the hell am I supposed to know?" Maria walked off toward the cafeteria.

"Have a nice day," she said. Lu tilted her head. The button panel lacked a button for the basement. "What the hell is going on here?"

CHAPTER TWENTY-SIX

The sun was bright and hot even though it was September. Hard to believe the leaves would be changing in no time. Isla stared out the front window of the apothecary, trying desperately to look casual and not like some lovesick teenager distraught over the absence of their lover. She kept commenting on the weather even though Daria and Christopher weren't fooled by the deflection.

Daria threw a crumpled-up receipt at Isla to get her attention. "Sometimes people run late."

"And some people run late all the time," Christopher said, shooting Daria a look.

"Why you gotta do that?" Daria put her hand on her hip. "I was trying to comfort our friend here, and you have to come at me."

"You walked right into it." Christopher smirked.

Isla normally found their interactions amusing, but she felt raw this morning and didn't have patience for much. "I'm going to my office." She heard footsteps following and wanted more than anything to shoo them away, but she couldn't do it once she turned and saw the concern in Daria's eyes. "I'm fine," she said, trying to ward off the third degree.

"You're not. Do you want to talk about it?"

"Not really." She sat at her desk and rested her head back against her cushy chair.

"Is this about Celeste?"

"It's about the last twenty-four hours changing *everything* in my life. Everything I knew, everything I thought I knew, and everything I stood for. It's all changed."

"That's not true."

"No?" She knew her voice dripped with doubt. "Please, tell me how it's not."

"You are still Isla Hoffman, witch on a mission to help others. That's embedded in your heart, and no family secret is going to change that."

"And the fact that I've been doing this all for nothing?"

"Now you're just talking out your ass. There's no way you believe that."

"I do."

"What about Mike Carroll, the human that owns the steak house down the street?"

Isla remembered Mike, but she couldn't think of why he mattered right now. "What about him?"

Daria sat on the corner of Isla's desk and crossed her arms. "He came in here with chronic heartburn. He tried everything the doctors recommended and hated being dependent on a prescription with a long list of side effects. What did you do?"

"I made him a cup of tea and mixed together some oils for him to take." She started to see Daria's point but refused to admit it.

"He told you it's like he has a new stomach. He's back to eating and enjoying the foods he loves. You gave him back his passion and happiness. *You* did that." Daria looked at her with a mixed expression of disbelief and sadness. "Tell me that was for nothing."

She took a deep, slow breath and exhaled heavily. Her brain was a fuzzy mess, a jumble of thoughts and outcomes wrestling together, but not one came out on top. Not one stood out. All she had was a jumbled mess. Isla looked at Daria and shrugged weakly.

"I'm going for a walk," she said. "I need to clear my head."

She stepped out the door into the humid morning, welcoming the heat and discomfort on her skin. Feeling something in the here and now gave her focus, much like her evening with Lu. She scanned the empty parking lot again. How was she supposed to tell her friends that beyond the problems with Ronan and her family, she struggled with the possibility that Lu ran away after sleeping with her.

Isla walked and walked, only pausing to kick a pebble from one parking spot to another. She cut through a lightly wooded area and stepped out onto Ocean Avenue. The bustling downtown was her favorite part of Bender, and she still wished she could've found a vacancy on the busy street for her apothecary. She stopped and looked at a window display for an upscale boutique. Maybe someday.

She skipped over two cracks in the sidewalk and came up to her favorite little coffee shop. Blue Mountain Coffee offered a small menu of classic drinks like pour-over coffee, lattes, and cappuccinos, and not one tea bag to be spotted anywhere. They even brought in breakfast pastries from local bakeries. But Isla's favorite detail, besides the pop culture posters and brightly painted walls, was the small bulk candy section they had in the back. Nothing screamed *created by passion* like an odd combination of offerings.

Her mood instantly brightened as she joined the long line of caffeine-hungry patrons. The smells of sweets and coffee engulfed her. Coffee brought Isla a happiness she never felt right admitting to. Tea was a healing medicine, a treatment for all ailments. Coffee? Well, it tasted so dang good.

"Can I help you?" said the young female barista. She had big brown eyes and a floral tattoo on her neck.

She smiled and faked the need to look at the menu. "I'll have an oat milk cappuccino, the largest you can make." She scanned the large glass case of baked goods. "And a banana nut muffin. Actually," she said, holding up her hand, "make it two and a large Colombian coffee with a little vanilla, milk, and sugar. Please."

"Name for the order?"

"Isla."

The barista strained to hear her. "Mya?"

"Isla, like island but without the *N* and *D* at the end."

"Got it. Sweet name." She started scribbling on a cup.

"Thank you."

"I'll have this right out."

The noise in the coffee shop quieted Isla's mind enough to keep her thoughts on Lu. She closed her eyes and swore she could still feel Lu's hands on her. She remembered what Maribel said about Henry, how she could still feel him. Their love always amazed her. Henry was eternally devoted to Maribel, and Maribel gave back just as much love and adoration. The sound of the espresso machine coming to life brought Isla back to the moment. Through all of the unease she held, she dared to wonder if she and Lu were destined for something extraordinary.

"For Island."

She turned around to see her order ready on the counter. The barista winked and walked away. Isla grabbed the goods, and as much as she would've loved to continue her stroll downtown, her curiosity demanded she return to the strip mall to see if Lu had turned up. Sure, she could've shot Lu a text by now, but the last thing she wanted was to seem too clingy. Isla was too far out of the dating loop to take risks. She'd feign casualness instead. At least for the next ten minutes.

By the time Isla cut back through the woods, she felt lighter. She was strong enough to handle everything Ronan threw at her, and as long as Lu was still by her side, she had no reason to be scared. Much to her delight, Lu's car was parked in its usual morning spot, but as she approached, she noticed it was empty. Isla walked to the store and took a hopeful breath before opening the door.

Lu stood against the counter chatting casually with Christopher. She turned and grinned the moment she saw Isla.

Yes, she had no reason to be scared anymore.

"There you are," Isla said with an easy tone that didn't match her earlier discombobulation.

"Here I am." Lu took the paper cup Isla offered and looked at her.

"Coffee," Isla said, holding up a small paper bag, "and a banana nut muffin."

"Be still my heart." Lu peeked into the bag. "What's the occasion?"

"I was craving coffee today." She raised her own cup to her lips and smirked.

"This feels like some odd form of foreplay," Daria said. Isla nearly choked on her first sip of cappuccino, but she couldn't chastise her because Lu looked insanely attractive with a rosy blush along her cheeks.

"You were running awfully late this morning," Isla said as a way to change the subject, but then the thought of how her very own morning started popped into her head. Now she was the one blushing.

"I had to run to the main office before heading here." She took a long sip of her coffee, clearly pleased by it. She nodded and said, "Vanilla? Where did this come from?"

"A little place downtown. I'll take you sometime."

"Can't wait."

"So," Christopher said, drawing out the word, "sorry to interrupt, but are we going to talk about what happened last night?" They looked worried. "Are you going to give us some good news? Say something hopeful?"

She had nothing to offer, she had nothing to say, but she had to muster up something because as the leader of the coven, she needed to prove herself. "I'm sorry, Christopher—"

"There's nothing we can do right now," Lu said. She put her coffee down and gave Christopher her full attention. "Unfortunately, there's no next step that's safe or logical." Everyone, including Isla, looked at Lu like she had just killed their puppy. "I know that's not what you want to hear."

"That can't be true," Daria said. The thick black headband she wore accentuated the dark circles beneath her eyes. "We have to do something."

Isla looked at Lu and saw the somber look in her normally bright blue eyes. "I believe Lu," she said, taking her hand. "She has a lot of experience I don't have. I trust her to take the lead."

Christopher and Daria exchanged looks and nodded in tandem. Daria leveled a lethal glare at Lu. "I'm only trusting you because Isla does. Don't fuck this up."

Lu saluted Daria. "Aye, aye. Right now, we need to regroup and wait."

"For what? For Ronan's army to start marching down the street?" Christopher's voice strained with what sounded like impatience, but Isla knew they were actually scared.

Isla shook her head. "That won't happen."

"How do you know?" Daria said curtly. "This morning you weren't even sure of yourself, and now suddenly you're confident the bad guy won't win?"

She knew Daria was right. This whole morning was such a seesaw of emotions. "He said he wasn't looking to start a war. And I have to believe the good guys win."

"We will," Lu said. "But in order to win, we have to be patient and plot our next move carefully."

Christopher turned pale. "I'm not so sure we have time for that."

Isla felt imminent danger crawl up her spine and spread across her skin as goose bumps. The ache in her feet returned, and she heard a harsh whisper in her head telling her to turn around. She looked slowly over her shoulder.

Ronan stood in front of the apothecary. He smiled at Isla and held up his hand.

Lu leaned in and whispered, "What is he doing?"

She squinted to see him more clearly. He snapped his fingers. "I don't—*ah*!" Blazing pain radiated from the base of her skull, around and through her temples, and ended in her eyes. Isla dropped to her knees.

CHAPTER TWENTY-SEVEN

Lu froze in panic. She had never been faced with a choice between someone she cared for deeply and doing her job. She looked between Isla's crumpled form and Ronan's shit-eating grin.

"Daria," she said loudly and firmly. "Keep her safe—you got that?" Daria rushed right over to Isla and started caring for her. "Christopher, I need you to watch them and the doors. Okay?" Christopher stood wide-eyed and frozen. "Christopher!"

"Yes?" They shook their head.

"Can you watch them?" She pointed to herself and then Daria and Isla. "Don't watch me. Watch them." Christopher's nod was anything but reassuring, but Lu needed to accept it and move on.

She took a deep breath to steady herself and pulled the gun from the back of her waistband. Something told her to carry today, and she was grateful for the small voice. She held the firearm at her side, finger off the trigger, as she stepped outside. Ronan acted as if he was posing as she looked him up and down. She saw no weapons, just a man dressed in a suit despite the heat.

"Little hot for the three-piece, don't you think?"

"I like to dress professionally. That's cute," he said, pointing to her gun.

"I like to carry professionally." She started walking around him. "I thought we weren't going to have a problem."

"A little bird told me my time with Isla may be limited, so I decided to move things along."

"That bird was wrong." She surveyed the area for the best, safest position to be in. She didn't want to lure him out into the parking lot, but she also didn't want to put the storefront in danger. "Are you married,

Ronan? Got a wife and kids in a cave somewhere?" She continued to step back and off the curb.

Ronan's attention remained on the apothecary. "This world is no place for children."

"I think you're a lunatic, but I do agree with you on that. What about the wife? Maybe a husband or boyfriend?" She internally gave herself a high five when he turned to look at her with raised eyebrows. "Pool boy?"

"If your plan is to annoy me enough to make me go away, I must say your effort is remarkable."

"But is it working?"

Ronan cracked his knuckles.

"Is that a no?"

"Perhaps it's time I spoke with Isla." He looked her up and down.

Lu felt her anxiety rise. "Sorry, but Isla can't come out to play right now."

"Give that to me," he said with a come-hither motion.

She raised her gun and pointed to it. "This? This is mine. You'll have to get your own." In an instant the firearm was out of her hand and in Ronan's.

Lu looked at her hands. "Witchcraft."

He disassembled the gun with one hand and a few moves. He kicked the pieces aside and folded his hands together. The change in his breathing gave away his impatience, and now that Lu had no gun, she felt a bit unsure and unsafe. A chiming bell cut through the tension.

"That's enough," Isla said from the store's doorway.

"Go back inside," Lu said to her.

"I think maybe *you* should go inside," Ronan said, walking up to Lu. "Leave the adults to talk." He placed his hand on her shoulder, and she felt paralyzed.

"Let her go, Ronan." Isla's loud, broken voice sounded panicked. "You want me, and here I am."

"You are right, but this one really likes to get in the way." He tightened his grip on her shoulder.

"Okay, buddy," Lu said, "you might want to let up a bit. She's gonna be so pissed if you hurt me, and you really don't want to see her pissed." She tried to signal Isla to stop, but either she didn't notice or she was too stubborn to listen.

"This is between you and me," Isla said.

"Let's keep it that way." Ronan gave Lu's shoulder a tight squeeze, and pain exploded throughout her.

I'm about to die.

Lu's spine felt like a firecracker's fuse, and her face grew hot. She fought to keep her eyes open and on Isla's. *Isla.* She had so much left to say to Isla, so many truths and apologies, but the tension and electricity traveling throughout her body wouldn't allow her to speak. A tear ran from her eye, and she mustered up all her strength to mutter a simple, "I'm sorry."

Isla tried to step forward again, but the power Ronan was emitting wouldn't allow her to get close. "I'm sorry. I'm the one who should've been protecting you."

Lu turned her head from side to side best she could. Her vertebrae felt tight enough to snap. "I—"

"This is all very touching," Ronan said with a yawn. "But let's move on. Isla, my dear niece, you are unwilling to listen to a word I say, but you blindly follow this human. I can feel how fickle her body is. Imagine her mind?"

"Stop," Isla said.

"It would take nothing to end her right now."

Isla balled her fists at her sides. "I said stop."

Lu's breathing sped up as heat and pain surrounded her skull, but she wouldn't look away from Isla. If these were her last minutes, at least she was still connected to the shining good in her life.

Ronan eased up on his grip and laughed. "You don't even know her. Go on," he said, nudging Lu with his knee, "tell her." Lu hung her head. Ronan gripped the back of her neck and pressed down until she thought her head would fall off. "Tell her. Now."

No matter how many times she had imagined her own death, an odd habit she'd developed in Iraq, she never imagined this. Her nobility and honesty no longer mattered—she couldn't bring herself to say the words. Not like this. She shook her head and prepared for the worst.

"Fine," he said, releasing her long enough to push her onto her knees. "Your trusted security guard is actually a special agent with the CIA."

Lu couldn't bear to watch Isla's face, but she heard a whisper of shock.

Ronan walked his fingers along the top of Lu's skull. "What is the

CIA doing in your quiet parking lot, you ask? Great question. To watch *you*, my dear."

"What?" The pain and confusion were evident in Isla's voice. "I don't believe you."

"Stop being blinded by love and open your eyes. Why would this ignored strip mall require security? Half of the stores are vacant, and the others are run by people who've been here forever. They'll probably die in these stores, their bodies left undisturbed."

Isla's nostrils flared. "Any landlord would want their property to be safe."

"When was the last time you even saw or spoke to your landlord? They don't care."

Lu started to regain some composure and strength. She brought her right foot up to stand. "Isla..."

"*Stay*," Ronan said, pushing down on the crown of her head. She could taste blood. "I never expected you'd grow up to be this naive. What makes you believe her over me?"

"Lu wouldn't. She'd never lie to me, and I know she'd never keep something like this from me."

Ronan's chuckle was deep and menacing. "Go ahead," Ronan said. "Speak. Tell Isla the truth."

The fiery vise eased away from her spine, but the throbbing ache didn't go anywhere. Lu slowly raised her head and stood up. She looked Isla in the eyes, shattered by the pain and tears she saw there. She said she wouldn't lie to Isla, but how was she supposed to put any of this into words, here and now?

Ronan didn't even give her the chance to explain herself. "There's only one way for you to know the truth." He nudged Lu forward.

The panic in her chest started to rise as Isla stepped closer. "It was just a job," she said weakly, trying to prevent the inevitable, but Isla only hesitated a second before holding her head in her hands. Lu opened her mind and her heart, hoping how she felt for Isla would rise to the top and show Isla her truest intentions. But the horrified look on Isla's face told Lu all she needed to know. "I'm sorry," Lu said roughly through tears of pain and sadness. "I never meant—"

"No." Isla dropped her hands and stepped back, her chin starting to quiver. "You told me you'd never lie to me."

"I didn't—"

"And I believed you! Even though I knew better."

"I didn't lie to you." The force of her words made her chest hurt.

"Playing the role of security guard and keeping the truth from me is just as bad. What's it called?" Isla looked around. "Lying by omission. That's what you did to me."

"It wasn't like that."

"Do you see now, Isla? These are the humans you want to cohabitate with. These are the humans who run the world that should be ours." He put his hand on Lu's shoulder. "We'd be much better off without them."

Lu screamed as a current of what could only be described as needles and flames went through her whole body. Birds flew from the trees as the sound echoed around them. She fell to the ground, the pain unrelenting as the world grew dimmer around her. The last thing she saw before losing consciousness was Isla's glowing eyes.

CHAPTER TWENTY-EIGHT

Isla could hear her heart racing in her ears. Life moved in slow motion—Lu's body folding, Ronan's crooked teeth as he smiled in triumph, and the guttural scream from Daria.

"No!" Isla ran toward Ronan and pushed through the resistance of the field he'd built between them. She landed her fist on his chest and pressed it forcefully into his sternum. "*Corpsi plasum tarsdum falici usse toi.*" She looked into Ronan's dark eyes as realization washed over him.

He gripped his chest and stumbled backward. "What did you do to me?"

Isla looked down at her hand as her fingertips stopped glowing. She ignored Ronan and rushed over to Lu, flipping her onto her back. Daria came running out of the apothecary, and they flanked Lu's body.

"Lu? Come on," Isla said, patting Lu's cheek gently.

Daria laid her head on Lu's chest and looked at Isla in worry. "Her heartbeat is there, but it's weak."

She fanned her fingers and put her hands on Lu's chest. "*Reduk mun spiritist meim. Sannah vulneira tuan. Vitnam grafi et gervitii solutant.*" She focused all her energy on her hands, not her broken heart or the fear paralyzing her thoughts. Everything she had went into the connection between her hands and Lu's body.

"What are you doing?" Daria asked.

"I'm bringing her back."

"We can't bring people back, Isla," Daria said, reaching for Isla's hand, but she pushed her away.

"She's not dead," she said so loudly her voice broke. "Please. Come on, come on. Do you hear me? You're not done here." Her voice shook. "Please…" She lowered her head and closed her eyes. Tears trickled down to the tip of her nose. One let go and landed on Lu's forehead. Lu sat straight up and gasped. She coughed and coughed, until she sounded raw and began gagging. Isla sat back and watched in relief, but movement from the corner of her eye caught her attention. Ronan was trying to crawl away.

Isla walked up to him and wiped the tears from her face. She squared her shoulders and nudged his body with her bare foot, flip-flops lost during the altercation. "You're not going anywhere," she said.

He looked up at her from the ground. Fear was evident in his eyes, but he put on a smug face. "You're not going to kill me."

"I vowed to never use my powers or my knowledge to harm anyone, but if it's a choice between your life and the lives of many innocent beings, I know what side I'll be on."

"How do you still not see it?" His voice was distorted by a strange gurgle.

"Because I'm not like you," she said, looking over her shoulder to where Daria was tending to Lu. Christopher joined them with bottles of water. "I'm one of the good guys."

"You're a fool."

She turned back to Ronan and knelt next to him. "You're right, I am. Because I'm going to let you go." The cocky hopefulness in his eyes irritated her. "But before I get your heart back to beating normally, I want to remind you: I am more powerful than you. I carry my grandmother in my heart and my spirit, and that's something you'll never have."

"You can't stop what I put in motion."

"But you can," she said, pointing into his chest with her index finger. "I want you to leave here, get as far away from Bender as you can. Do you understand me?"

"I'll never stop."

"I can only hope you change your mind, but if I catch wind you're still up to this revolution nonsense, I'll be able to find you very quickly." She zapped a little more power into his chest and added, "And I'll stop you for good."

He slammed his fist against his chest and looked around in a panic. "Fix me," he said, gasping for air.

"You can live with a slow heart rate. It's fine." Isla stood up and started to walk away. She stopped and smiled when Ronan called out her name.

"Fine," he said shakily. "I won't hurt humans, but I'll never encourage our kind to continue living in the shadows. We don't deserve it."

She returned to her crouched position and tilted her head to look at Ronan. He was nothing more than a jaded man trying to make a place for himself in a fucked up world. She could relate. "Fine," she said, punching his chest with a little more force than necessary. "Go." She watched him scramble to his feet and disappear. She had to admit, she was mildly jealous he was able to teleport.

The celebration lasted only a second. Isla now had to deal with Lu, and that was far scarier than any altercation or family drama. She walked slowly, not exactly eager to join Christopher and Daria at Lu's side.

"She's breathing, and her pulse seems to be strong and stable," Daria said. Christopher echoed with a nod of their head. "We should move her inside."

"No," she said. "Leave us be." She looked at Daria and Christopher.

"Out here?" Christopher waved their hands around. "Where anyone can see?"

"If nobody saw what went down with Ronan, I'm not worried about this."

"Wait," Christopher said, taking off their long black cardigan. They rolled it up and put it under Lu's head. "Okay." They stood and took Daria's hand, walking inside together.

Isla looked down at Lu's face, eyes closed and peaceful even with scuffs along her skin and a thin sheen of dirty sweat. Lu's eyes began to flutter, and Isla prepared herself for another battle.

Lu cracked one eye open, sadness and worry playing across her face. "What happened?" Lu groaned and tried to sit up.

She wanted to tell Lu to take it slow, be careful, not hurt herself, but she also knew to keep her distance. Isla had to rebuild the walls around her life and her heart. "We won. Ronan won't be showing up again."

"Who's Ronan?" Lu's blue eyes were clear and red-rimmed.

Isla's stomach sank. "What?"

"Just kidding." Lu started choking, and it took her a minute to calm the fit. "I remember everything," Lu said, looking her straight in the eyes, "unfortunately. Isla, I—"

She held up her hand. "Please, don't. There's nothing you can say that'll change this, especially how you made me feel."

"Can I at least try to explain myself?"

"I do not owe you your moment."

"No, you don't, but I know you feel as strongly for me as I do you. Or at least I know you did." Isla wouldn't give Lu permission, but she remained silent. "I felt lost after my discharge from the Air Force. I was in a loveless, toxic marriage, and I felt like I didn't belong in the world I had prepared myself to be in. I floated around law enforcement for years, first as an officer with the NYPD and finally getting my foot in the door with the FBI."

Lu got to her feet and went to the curb, where she sat down again, grunting and groaning with every move. "And then the CIA knocked on my door right when I needed it most," she said, not wanting this inevitable good-bye to drag on for too long. "When I worked for the FBI, I was nothing more than a decorated pencil pusher. No matter how many times I applied for field positions, they kept me on a desk. I never found out why, and to this day, it still drives me crazy. One day, out of nowhere, I get a call from a director in the CIA, saying they had an opportunity within a new division. I was freshly divorced and miserable, so I took it."

"You didn't ask any questions?"

Lu shook her head. "I wanted out," she said with a shrug. "It gave me a reason to move out of New York and dive into something new. This was my first assignment after training. I was briefed on the case and told there were reports of supernatural activity in Bender. Did I believe any of it? Not really. But I was out in the field, and this boring post felt like the beginning of something big."

"Hunting Inhumans."

"No, at least that's not what I was told. My new boss told me we were a surveillance team. That's it. Make sure there were no threats."

"Threats to *humans*," Isla said. The more she heard, the angrier she got. "None of this excuses your keeping the truth from me, and that's all I care about." She stood and looked down at Lu. The hot sun beat on her back, adding to her agitation. "You knew my story, my fears, and why I avoided relationships. You did it anyway." She ignored the tears brimming in her eyes.

"I couldn't tell you until I knew everyone was safe. Until I knew *you* were safe."

"But that didn't stop you from jumping into my bed. You didn't think twice before kissing me and touching me and making—" She stopped herself and looked away from the same damn softness she had seen in Lu's eyes since day one. The softness that fooled her into trusting a stranger. "You fucked me anyway."

Lu struggled to stand, but she got to her feet and looked at Isla with watery eyes. "I'm so sorry. I never meant for this to happen. I never meant to hurt you."

She nodded and swallowed back a scream and a sob. "That's what they all say." She walked around Lu and headed for the apothecary, her safe place. Before opening the door, she looked over her shoulder and said, "I hope you have the decency to warn me if the CIA is going to storm my store. It's the least you can do." The bell fell to the floor from the force of her slam.

Chapter Twenty-nine

L u left and went straight home. Her cell phone was dead, undoubtedly because of an energy surge from whatever the fuck Ronan did to her. She wouldn't be surprised if all of Bender experienced power outages over the next few days. Samson made her smile as usual, and a scalding hot shower helped ease some of her aches and pains.

She grimaced at her reflection in the full body mirror. Bruises were starting to bloom all along her body, and her skin looked burned where Ronan's fist hit her back. She should have gone to the hospital to check for any internal damage, but her brain was too exhausted to deal with intake paperwork, never mind coming up with a believable story. Once her phone charged, it chimed with several missed calls and texts. She ignored them and turned the phone off again. That they were able to bug her greatest addiction felt like yet another defeat. She fell back onto her couch after feeding Samson. Work could wait. Her job was as good as gone anyway, so what if she didn't check in with the boss who was hiding something and possibly trying to harm her.

"I really fucked up this time, Samson." She looked down into his droopy dark eyes and knew he understood her. "I should've told her. I know, I know. I was doing the best I could." Samson whined. "If I had told her, I think *everything* would be different. We'd be together right now, celebrating our win, instead of me talking to you." He shook his head, large floppy ears slapping loudly. "I'm sorry. That wasn't nice. You are a very good listener." Samson hopped up on the couch and wedged himself under her arm. She winced slightly. "I really thought I was protecting her."

A knock at the door made her jump up, tweaking every aching spot along her body. "Ow, ow, ow," she said quietly as she walked to the door. She peeked through the peephole and stepped back in confusion. "Kayla, what are you doing here?" she asked as she swung the door open.

"Where the hell have you been?" she asked, marching straight into Lu's apartment. "I sent you a dozen texts, and when I tried to call, it went right to voice mail. I thought you were dead." Kayla smacked her right arm, and Lu yelped. "Are you okay?"

"Please, do come in, Kayla." Lu shut and locked her door.

"Where's my kid?"

"With her father."

"Good," she said, hobbling back to the couch. "I had the worst day."

Kayla stood over her. "You look like you were hit by a bus. Oh my God, were you hit by a bus?"

She swatted at Kayla's probing fingers before she could hit any bruises. "No." She shook her head for longer than necessary, trying to buy time to come up with a believable story Kayla wouldn't see right through. But what was even the point? "Rough day at work."

Kayla snorted, but Lu kept her face serious. "As a parking lot patrolwoman?"

"Kay, I need a favor. It's a big one."

"Okay. Yeah, sure."

Lu proceeded to give Kayla a list of what she needed from the store. She'd go herself, but she was afraid her body would fall apart halfway there. The list included Bengay, booze, and a burner phone. In exchange, she promised to tell Kayla everything and buy her dinner. In under an hour, they were both on the couch with platefuls of pizza, and Lu was talking around a mouthful of mozzarella stick.

"And I don't even care about the job anymore."

"The CIA job. The *secret* CIA job." Kayla's eyes remained the size of saucers.

"I am really sorry I didn't tell you. I don't ever want another position I have to keep a secret from my family. It sucks."

"And you were beaten up by Thor, essentially."

"Do not flatter this guy," she said, taking another bite. Nearly dying really starved her. "I'm not sure it was lightning anyway. Regardless, I'm fine now. Just a little sore, but I'll recover. I think."

"I'm sorry," Kayla said, placing her plate down on the coffee table. Samson eyed it. "I'm having a little difficulty unpacking this." Kayla relaxed into the couch and laid her head back, staring at the ceiling. "Your girlfriend is a real-life witch."

"She's not my girlfriend. At least, not anymore."

"See? That is the least alarming and interesting part of everything you told me." Kayla wiped her forehead and grabbed her pizza again. "But it's what has *you* so messed up."

Lu took a long drink from her beer bottle. The small, locally brewed IPA delivered on the grapefruit undertones it advertised, but more importantly, its robust alcohol content was getting her buzzed quickly. Lu didn't drink often, but tonight was the kind of night that called for a little help numbing her brain.

"Lu?"

"Yeah, uh. Yes. She's a real-life witch." Talking about Isla was about as fun as being electrocuted. "But she's a lot more than that, you know? She's brilliant and funny and cares deeply about people, even strangers. She puts everyone before herself." She set aside her pizza, her appetite lost. "You should've seen her today."

"I wish I could've seen her at all."

"She didn't care about danger or anything. She stepped right up to the asshole and took him on. Do you know how rare it is to find courage like that? Most men I served with were ready and eager to have other people fight their battles for them, but not Isla. Nope."

"She seems pretty great."

"She *is* great, and did I mention funny?"

Kayla laughed. "You may have."

"And so, so sexy," she said with a smirk.

"Ew. No. I don't want to hear that part." Kayla covered her ears with her hands.

"She's also my biggest regret." She ran her foot back and forth on her area rug and waited for the friction to warm her sole. "I'll never forgive myself for fucking it up."

"Oh, come on," Kayla said. "For real, send her flowers and apologize. Make sure she hears what you have to say."

"I tried." Lu looked at the bottle in her hand and realized she had peeled off half the label without even noticing. "I did the one thing she trusted me not to do."

"So, you kept the truth about your job from her. Big deal."

"It's not just any job, Kay. It's not like she found out I was a stripper on the weekends. Which I wish was the case because I'd be able to afford something nicer than this condo." She waved her hands around. "But my job was to investigate *her*, to watch others like her.

The first three months were painfully boring. My boss wanted to pull me from the area, and I should've let him. But I fought him every time he mentioned it."

"Why?"

She looked at Kayla guiltily. "You know why."

"Because you had a crush."

"If I'd told him there was nothing going on, he would've pulled me and sent me on to the next case. Who knows where I'd end up?"

"Far away from your booty call."

She eyed Kayla and wondered, not for the first or hundredth time in their lives, what was actually wrong with her. "And possibly farther away from you and Lilly. I didn't want that. I'm happy here in Bender. It's a small town, but the people are nice, and I like how close I am to a city and the water. It's a good home for this stage of my life."

Kayla appeared to be listening thoughtfully. "But mostly for the booty call." Guess not.

"You're terrible. Do you want more pizza?"

"Listen, I know I'm not an authority on relationships, but I think you can repair this."

"I can't."

"So you believe you can come up with a plan that'll take down your boss with the CIA and allow all the unhumans—"

"Inhumans."

"*In*humans," Kayla said, rolling her eyes, "live their lives safe from investigators like you, but you don't believe you can mend your relationship with Isla?"

"I don't."

"That's a crock of shit, and I'll tell you why. One," Kayla said, holding up her index finger, "you're a fighter. Two, you're loyal to a fault. You defend and fight for any ship you're on, even if you know it's sinking."

She immediately thought of the horrendous job she'd had at a Big & Tall store senior year of high school. Management was a joke, and the company was going bankrupt, but she still showed up for her shift and offered ideas to drive business. She shot Kayla a weak shrug because it was better than agreeing.

"Furthermore, everything you've told me about Isla and how she made you feel seriously clues me in to how much she cared for you. I'm guessing it was as much as you care for her."

"I love her," she admitted for the first time aloud. "It's not like any love I've known. It doesn't feel forced or artificial. Just two people who fell together."

Kayla stayed quiet for a moment, a dangerous occurrence most days, and then she very slowly lifted her foot to poke Lu with her toes. "You love her."

She felt her face flush. "I do."

"And she loves you."

She shook her head too hard and aggravated the headache she had been fighting off. "There's no way that's true."

"How are you so sure?"

"Because she would've seen more when she read me."

"What?"

"If she really loved me the way I love her, when she did her reading of me, she wouldn't have seen only the stupid things I've done. She would've seen and felt my love, and that would've triggered her love." She explained it like it was the most obvious thing.

"Lu, I love you, and you're usually the more logical one between us, but you realize she was in a very high-stress situation being threatened by her uncle who appeared out of nowhere. You can't judge her reaction, nor can you assume to understand how the power of *reading people* is affected by that kind of stress."

She blew out a huff. "I didn't think of it that way."

"Of course you didn't. Looks like I'm the smart and logical one now."

"Let's not get ahead of ourselves." She gave Samson a piece of crust. "Do you think I have a shot, Samson?"

"Yes, Mom," Kayla said in her best Samson impression, sounding more like an eighty-year-old chain-smoker.

Lu laughed and didn't even care about the pain in her back. She finally felt a sliver of hope when it came to her relationship with Isla. All she had to do was make everything else right and convince Isla to read her one more time. No problem.

CHAPTER THIRTY

L u didn't think silence was bad. Silence generally brought peace and relaxation, or at least the confirmation that turmoil was done. However, deafening silence in the wake of Langdon reading her report was decidedly not a good thing. She shifted in her seat and continued to wait. Her gray dress pants and white Oxford button-down felt uncomfortably tight in comparison to the security uniform she had gotten used to.

"Cadman," Director Langdon said, tossing her report onto his desk and leaning back against the front. He crossed his feet at the ankles, and she wished for more distance between them than the scant two feet from toe to toe. "You disappear for two days, and when you finally call, you explain you're physically unwell, but you'll have a report for me." He stopped talking, and even though his statement wasn't open-ended, she felt like he was expecting her to respond.

"That's correct, and I gave you my report."

"I did a lot of thinking when you disappeared because I thought you were dead, naturally."

"Naturally," she grumbled.

"And I didn't feel good about our last interaction. This is my fault, after all. I do believe you have the makings of the perfect agent. You're smart, strong, experienced, and unquestioningly loyal. I think I put you in the wrong assignment out of the gate, and I made a promise to myself that if you were alive—which I really didn't believe," he said with a chuckle, scrunching his long, skinny nose, "I'd find the perfect job where you'd be the most useful."

She took practiced, steady breaths. She couldn't let Director Langdon know how much he was pissing her off. She needed to stay employed if she wanted to find out exactly what her department was up to and stop it. She hummed along in agreement.

"But then you hand me that report, and I got to say, it sounds a little bizarre."

She cleared her throat, ridding her tone of the attitude she so badly wanted to give him. "We're a department that specializes in monitoring supernatural occurrences. I don't see how any of my experience sounds bizarre."

"Oh no, not your experience. I believe what you put on paper, but what's bizarre to me is you had this major event and still came back empty-handed."

"Sir, you need to tell me the whole truth here." Lu had never been an actor, but she put as much emotion into her words as possible. "I nearly died, and my report gives strong evidence to everything we're tasked with investigating, but you're looking me in the eye and telling me it doesn't matter because I didn't return with an Inhuman. How could I when I was unconscious, barely breathing, and left for dead?"

"I understand." Director Langdon checked his watch. "I want you to take the next week off to recover." He walked back around his desk and took a seat.

"Sir?"

"Starting next Monday I'll have you assigned to a different case. Expect the details within the next few days."

"What about Bender?" She swallowed back her desperation. "That place is crawling with Inhumans."

"I'll send someone new."

"You *can't*," she said a little too loudly. "You thought I'd make a good addition to the department for many reasons, but the one you forgot was how I do not walk away from a mission unless it's complete. I have to finish what I started in Bender. There's no one better for the job."

Director Langdon picked up his pen and tapped it three times. He pursed his lips. "I don't think it's smart. You're personally invested."

"You're right, I am." She cracked her knuckles. "They almost killed me, and I want revenge."

"You're too close to the target."

"Our relationship has been terminated." She remained neutral, but her heart ached. "It's detailed in my report. Isla Hoffman sided with Ronan, subsequently becoming a greater threat."

"And she has no idea of your identity?"

She shook her head. "She didn't even question my firearm because she knew I was in the service."

"And you don't know her whereabouts?"

"When I came to, Hoffman's Apothecary and the surrounding areas were empty," she said, quoting her report verbatim. "It was like a ghost town." She could tell she was finally getting through to him, but he still looked skeptical.

"Does Isla know your relationship is terminated?" He raised one eyebrow, and Lu knew she was going to have to stoop much lower than she'd like.

"You know how women are," she said with as much fabricated bro-talk as possible. "If you don't call right away, they assume they're dumped, or they're already fucking someone else." She wasn't sure he'd go for it, but he cracked a smile. "Not to mention any rational human would be running for the hills right about now."

"You're not wrong."

She put up her palms up and shrugged. "But I can still use it as an excuse to get close enough to bring her in, if she's even there anymore. She may be hitting the road with the gaggle of freaks." She felt shame for using the F word.

"I hope that's not the case. We would need to assemble a task force to track them down before they did anything, and we're not a big enough department for that yet. I'd have to call in a lot of favors to get enough agents over here."

"Give me one more chance. I know I've had too many already, but what happened to me the other day..." She covered her eyes for a dramatic pause. "It changed the way I see these *things*. They don't care who they hurt, as long as it's not one of them. Ronan had a blank, soulless look in his eyes as he tortured me. I'll never forget it."

"Because they don't have souls." Director Langdon scratched at his chin. "You'll bring her right in?"

"As long as she's there, I don't need more than one day. If I fail, I'll pack my bags for my next case."

"Backup?"

"Won't need it."

"What's your plan?"

"I'll go to work in the morning like nothing happened and make sure she's around. Once I make contact, I'll invite her back to my place to talk. You know how much women love to talk." She got a laugh out of him. *Hook, line, and...* "Then I'll tranquilize her the moment she's in my condo, triple dose to make sure she stays down. Who knows how strong she is? And then I'll bring her here." She waited with bated breath as he visibly worked through her plan in his head. "If she doesn't want to meet me, I'll march into Hoffman's and get her myself."

"Okay." *Sinker.* "But you better have your phone on you at all times and give me updates constantly. I can't have it go awry like last time."

"Of course," she said, hating how she had to keep playing stupid about her phone being bugged. "You'll know every in and out."

"All right, Cadman," he said, moving to stand, "you have your last chance."

Lu stood up and looked him in the eyes. She might have needed Langdon to believe she was on his side now, but she wasn't willing to let herself appear small. "That's all I'll need."

"You better get out of here and rest up. Tomorrow's a big day, and you're not quite a hundred percent."

"But, sir, where will I bring Isla? As far as I know, we don't have formal suspect holding in this building." She sat back on the edge of the seat but tried not to look too eager for information. "And Isla isn't just any suspect. She could probably abracadabra her way out of here if she wants."

His eyes went wide. "She can do that?"

"She told me some witches can teleport. Ronan could."

"Understood." He seemed seriously deep in thought. "Give me your badge."

She scrunched her face. "Excuse me?"

"Give me your badge." He held out his hand.

She had to play along. Even if she thought he was about to fire her, she had to hand over her badge with the confidence of someone who trusted their superior officer implicitly.

"Here you go." She stood back and watched as he opened his desk and unlocked a hidden box. She couldn't make out many of the contents beyond envelopes and an SD card. Lu jumped when he slammed it shut.

He slid a black square, no bigger or thicker than a stamp, behind her ID photo. "Take this. When you bring Isla Hoffman in, take her straight to the elevators. The people working on ground level will be aware of what's going on, so don't think twice about dragging her body if that's what you have to do." She felt nauseous at the thought. "Hold your badge over the button for the sixteenth floor. It'll read the key I put in there."

She turned the bifold over in her hand. "And what'll that do?"

"It'll take you to the basement."

"We have a basement?" She really ought to look into an acting gig once this was all over and done with.

"Containment and testing. They have chambers that can subdue a creature's powers. It should work on Isla."

"Testing?"

"I can't discuss those details with you, but I'm sure you can imagine why a government-funded agency would want to perform testing on specimens with powers beyond anything humans can come up with on our own."

She hummed and nodded, because all she could muster up was a hum and a nod. Lu felt sick.

"I have a meeting to get to now," Langdon said, "but don't forget to update me every step of the way tomorrow."

"Will do." She followed him out into the hallway and waited until he was a safe distance away before releasing a long breath. "Fuck, fuck, fuck," she mumbled, unbuttoning the cuffs of her shirt. She felt suffocated and trapped. She shook out her hands and tried to focus on the facts. All signs pointed clearly to her next move. She looked at the elevators and approached them like they were on fire. She didn't want to see it, but she knew she had to.

Lu sucked in a breath and exhaled through tight lips. She held up her badge to the sixteen button and flinched when it turned green. The door slid shut, and her anxiety rose. In mere seconds, the elevator dipped and came to a stop. The doors slid open to reveal a long bright hallway, and a strange noise caused her to cringe. At first, she thought it was the elevator doors, but they wouldn't make that noise even on their rustiest day. She looked down the hallway and swallowed hard. The next time she heard the noise she knew what it was.

A scream.

CHAPTER THIRTY-ONE

W e need a refresh. Everything needs to move, prices need to change, and we need more variety. This store has been the same since I opened it, and it can be better. We need more merchandise, more art, more tonics, and more things." Isla put her hands on her hips and looked around. Daria stared at her wide-eyed, and Christopher kept looking at the floor. "What?"

"You good?"

"I'm fine."

Daria sighed heavily. "Isla, girl, please. It's been three days, and you haven't even mentioned what happened with Ronan and Lu. You're acting like it never even happened." Daria's face was softer than it had ever been. "I'm worried about you."

"We're worried about you," Christopher said, still looking at the floor.

She was pretty sure she'd scared them with her powers. Or her silence. She pulled at the sleeves of her sheer black shirt and covered her hands. "There's nothing to talk about, and it's better for me if I can just move on and focus on something bigger. Like this stagnant store." She blew a few strands of hair from her face.

"Not to be *that* guy," Daria said with a raised hand, "but we are trending upward. Really upward. Hoffman's Apothecary is having its best year yet. It's anything but stagnant. So you'll need a better excuse than that."

"It still needs my focus and a refresh for autumn."

Christopher straightened their suspenders before walking out from behind the counter. "Okay so, like, you know how after a breakup we sometimes do drastic things? Like color our hair or cut bangs?" They spun a ring on their index finger. Daria looked at Isla with raised brows. "That's what this feels like."

She dropped her mouth open. "I'm not cutting my bangs."

"But you're looking for a big change," Christopher said, looking at Isla for the first time, "and I back you, but when it comes to forcing change on a masterpiece like this store…"

"Christopher's right, sweetie."

"*I* need a refresh. Fine. We don't have to do anything crazy, but something needs to change." She felt her sturdy walls start to shake. "I need something, okay?"

"Of course," Daria cooed, coming out from behind the counter and wrapping her arm around Isla's shoulders. "We really do support you in anything you want to do, but we don't want you regretting it in the end." Daria squeezed her shoulder and gently rubbed her back. "There's an art show downtown this weekend. Why don't we all go and grab dinner? Maybe something will catch your eye, and we can bring in some local artists like they do at the coffee shop you love so."

"Fine." She wanted to act like a petulant child, but Daria's idea was exactly what she needed. "Sure."

"Good." Daria patted her back a little too firmly and left to prepare a cup of tea. "Until then, why don't you try talking about it?" The doorbell chimed. "Saved by the bell."

"I love that show," Christopher said with a smirk.

"Were you even born in time for that show?"

"I catch reruns."

Isla started to laugh, feeling minutely lighter since putting at least one step of a new plan into action, but her smile fell the moment she turned toward the door. "Maribel."

"Hello, Isla."

"What do you want?" she said curtly. Even though she knew Henry had a mind of his own, Isla still begrudged Maribel for not doing more. That was unfair, but she couldn't control it.

Maribel lowered her head. "I understand why you may be upset with me—"

"With Henry," Daria said. "You didn't know."

"I should've figured it out. I shouldn't have been such a coward. If your husband is acting peculiar, you confront him, right?" Maribel's dark eyes hung with sadness and obvious fatigue. "I was just as surprised as you all. Imagine assuming your husband is cheating on you and finding out he's actually planning a revolution with some stranger he met at McColligan's Pub?"

Isla was still capable of sympathy and care, but she was also jaded and hesitant to trust. *So sue me.* "Why are you here?"

"I was hoping we could talk."

She looked in Maribel's eyes, and it didn't take witchcraft or intuition to see the bare honesty in them. "We can talk in my office." She held out her arm, an invitation for Maribel to go first.

"Be nice," Daria whispered. Isla ignored her.

Once in her office, Isla sat behind her desk and Maribel in the big purple chair across from her. "What can I do for you?"

"I'm sorry." Maribel started to tear up immediately. "I know it may not be much coming from me, but I really am so sorry. I know Henry feels ashamed, too."

"I'm sure he can speak for himself."

"He can and he will, but I need you to know he's been going on about you since the whole thing happened."

"The *whole thing*?" She had a flashback to her store in shambles and Lu writhing in pain on the ground. "When you say *the whole thing*, you mean when Henry stood here trying to intimidate me into joining a ridiculous cause I'd never align with? And when his boss, the guy he was mindlessly following, almost killed someone on my welcome mat?" She swallowed hard, her mouth suddenly dry. "Why would he ever join Ronan? You're both smart, good people."

"Because we're werewolves, Isla," Maribel said in a burst. "You don't know what it's like. Sure, you can listen to our experiences and you can assume, but you'll never really know. Your powers? No one would ever know. We have to be extra careful. One stupid wrong move, like taking the garbage out at the wrong time, and someone could kill us."

"That's what *I'm* here for," she said passionately. "I wouldn't let anything happen to you guys."

Maribel nodded sadly but still smiled. "It's nice to imagine, you know? Living free? I understand why Henry was swayed. I could never be, because I'm not that spontaneous."

Isla let out a long, relieved breath. "Good to know. For a second I thought this was another ambush, and honestly, I don't think I would've had it in me to fight again."

"I really am sorry that happened to you."

"I'm not going to lie and say it's okay, but I'm not mad at you. I understand the appeal of being able to live free, but I do think living in harmony with humans is the most beneficial way to live. My grandmother believed it," she said, pausing to hear Ronan's scathing voice in her head. "Even if her beliefs came late in life. It feels like the right journey for me." She reached out and placed her hand on the desk, palm up. Maribel took it. "I also believe a lot more humans are aware of our existence, but it's easier for them to ignore us."

"Especially you witches. You guys are trendy now." They laughed, and the easiness began to return.

"May I read you?" Isla said before she could talk herself out of it. She wanted change so badly—maybe she really did need to start with herself.

Maribel turned shy. "Of course."

Isla closed her eyes and opened what she liked to call her third eye, but she believed it was really a combination of her heart and mind. She could see darkness and Henry, the tension palpable, and she felt a rush of remorse and sadness. Isla released Maribel's hand and sat back. She had seen enough. She opened her eyes before too much could seep in, and she smiled, meaning it. "I forgive you, and I forgive Henry. One of the reasons I believe we're meant to live in harmony with humans is that the majority of us desire the same things. Freedom, companionship, and success." She bit her lip and looked out the small window in her office. Two birds hopped along the curb. "And love."

"I think you're right." Maribel stood. "And I always have." She turned to leave, but Isla stopped her.

"Maribel?"

"Yes?"

"Please tell Henry he's welcome here anytime."

Maribel stood up taller and grinned. "I will. Thank you." Maribel left the office, and the silence was deafening.

Isla supposed she should follow up and make amends with the others from Ronan's clan, but not today. She was tired from sleepless nights and drained from using her powers at their maximum. She had never acted out like that, and if she could admit it to herself, she was a little scary. At least she knew she wouldn't be tempted to go all-out like that again anytime soon. The hangover wasn't worth it. A quiet knock sounded.

"You doing okay, boss?" Daria said from the doorway.

She considered the question, really allowing her heart to answer this time. "I'm not good, but I'll get there."

"Maybe call her."

Her chair wouldn't allow her to pull back as far as she wanted to. "Excuse me?"

"Maybe I'm playing devil's advocate here, but I think you should talk to her."

"Maybe you're just the devil."

"Don't you want a real final conversation with her? You were obviously crazy about her, and she was in love—"

"Don't," she said, raising her index finger. "Don't you *dare* say she loved me. Everything Lu did was for the job. It was all an act to get closer to me."

"Do you really believe that? In your heart? Listen to that stubborn thing you've got beating in your chest. Do you *really* think Lu faked everything for her job?"

Isla wanted to shut her heart up. "Regardless, she lied in a big way."

"I know I don't have the best history with relationships," Daria said, weighing the air with her hands, "but I think you should give her another shot."

"No thanks," she said with a huff and sat. Daria wasn't going away, and that irritated her even more. "Do you know how upsetting it is to fall for the same bullshit twice?"

"What do you mean?"

"I fall in love twice, and both times I was distracted by the rainbows and unicorns and I missed the obvious. I should've never let Lu in. I fell for her lies the moment I looked in her stupid beautiful eyes. How many women do you think look in her blue eyes and say, *She's so dreamy.* They don't notice anything else." She bit on her thumbnail. "I bet she's a serial cheater and gets away with it."

"Isla—"

"She says she hasn't been in a relationship, but how do I know that?" A light bulb went off. "Oh my God, I bet the whole Tinder story was a crock. I bet she hooks up all the time."

"I think you may be taking it too far."

"Why are you defending her? Did she get to you, too? Are you sleeping with Lu now?"

"Are you for real?" Daria said. "Of course I'm not. Jesus." She covered her face with her hands and stepped aside. "Lu's here." The words were muffled by her hands, but still crystal clear to Isla.

Lu stepped around Daria into Isla's office, but she stayed very

close to the door. She raised her right hand in a meek wave. "Hey."
Why did Lu have to look perfect in dark jeans and a baby-blue short-
sleeved button-up?

"I don't want to see you."

"Look, I completely understand, and usually I would respect that,
but we have a big situation on our hands, and I need your help."

"No."

Lu looked at her, surprised. "No? What do you mean *no*?"

"I'm not helping you."

"It's to protect your people."

"I'm supposed to believe you care about my people?"

"Isla, we do not have time for me to grovel and beg forgiveness.
I can do that *after* we save a bunch of lives." Lu walked right up to
Isla's desk and emptied her pockets. "I'm literally laying it all on the
table. Here's my wallet with my driver's license. Please don't judge the
hair—I needed a cut. This is my CIA badge." Lu opened the bifold. "It
tells you all of my official information, and there's a special key in it
that lets me into the secret basement of my building."

Isla leaned forward to look at the badge. Lu's license photo might
have been lacking, but her official government photo was very sexy.
She tamped down her attraction. "Very official." She scanned the rest
of the ID and noticed Lu's full name.

"The basement where they're testing on supernatural beings."

Isla froze.

CHAPTER THIRTY-TWO

L u was ready to shake Isla out of whatever stupor had suddenly seized her. "I get it. I really do. I was shocked when I saw it, but I did see it, and now we need to do something about it. I need you to pull it together—"

"Your name is Luna?"

She dropped her shoulders and looked at Isla like she had lost her damn mind. "Remember when I said we need to focus on a plan? I meant starting now."

Isla kept looking at Lu's ID.

"Yes, my name is Luna, but I *never* go by Luna. I don't even think I'd answer to the name."

"The moon…"

"Yes, it means moon," she said, trying to follow. Concern replaced annoyance. "Did you hit your head or something the other day?"

Isla crossed her arms. "No, my head is fine. I clearly remember everything, including all the ways you lied to me."

Lu pressed her palms together but didn't know if she was about to pray or beg. "Isla, please, put all of that aside for right now. This is so much bigger than you and me. Even if I wanted to ask for a second chance…" She fought hard against the sudden sadness and fear she felt, almost as if the full gravity of the situation landed on her shoulders at once. "It won't be possible if we don't do something."

"Just give me the directions to headquarters or whatever you call it. I'll take care of it myself."

"You can't!" Lu clenched her jaw and sucked a harsh breath in through her nose. Her patience was fading as Isla's stubbornness reached an all-time high. "You need me to gain access. Unless your plan is to go rogue and blow a hole in the side of the building."

"It's not a bad idea."

"Yes, Isla, it is a really bad idea."

"I think we should listen to her," Daria said.

Lu had no idea Daria was still standing there. She pointed to Daria and said, "See? Daria is being reasonable. Shockingly."

"Hey, buddy, watch it. I think I'm the only one on your side here."

"Yeah. Right. Sorry." She mirrored Isla's stance and cleared her throat. "We need to work together on this. Despite our personal issues, we know we work well as a team." She held her breath and watched as Isla worked through the options in her head.

"What will you need me to do?"

Relieved, but not getting cocky, she looked at Daria and then Isla. "We'll need a team."

"More than us?"

"Yes, and I have a few people in mind already."

"I won't push anyone to do anything they're not comfortable with," Isla said firmly.

"Absolutely."

"And I expect you to be upfront about the level of danger involved, too. I don't want my people going into this without all the intelligence or being misled by lies."

Lu narrowed her eyes. "I deserved that, but can we curb the sarcastic comments for right now?"

Isla bobbed her head from side to side. "I'll try."

Daria tapped Lu's shoulder. "Does that rule apply to me as well?"

"No, Daria, it doesn't," Lu whispered, but her eyes stayed on Isla. "Can you get in touch with the shapeshifter?"

"We have names, you know."

"I *do* know, but the only time I ever saw her was when I was very much focused on other things." She knew the innuendo was obvious, which meant Daria's low whistle was completely unnecessary.

"Daria, can you leave us to talk?"

This was the first time since entering Hoffman's that Lu started to relax. She sat down and said, "We can't mess this up. We have to get in and get out."

"What exactly are we going to do once we get in?"

Lu was hesitant about this part of her plan. "Gather evidence. I find it hard to believe this testing is fully supported by my superiors outside the department. I want to take pictures, take files…" She looked at Isla seriously. "And I want to cause a big enough commotion to get as many detainees out of there as possible."

"We'll be caught if there's a commotion," Isla said matter-of-factly.

"A *subtle* commotion," Lu said. "We have to try. I can't leave them there."

"And what if someone or something as dangerous as Ronan is being held there? We can't let everyone go and hope for the best. We may not be like you average humans, but we should still be held accountable for our actions."

"Good point," she said, rubbing at a sudden discomfort in her chest—something about Isla calling her an average human hurt.

"Do you think there's files or a roster of names? Like an intake report or something?"

"Possibly, maybe in my boss's office."

"Then we get into the basement and the office."

"You make it sound easy." Lu smirked, but Isla remained stoic.

"What's your plan?" Isla asked.

"I bring you and, if you can get some volunteers, some bonus Inhumans in. I'll have you all act sedated, and you'll be handcuffed."

"I can get out of handcuffs," Isla stated simply.

"We have specially designed handcuffs." Pregnant silence fell. "Anyway, that's what the sedation is for, except it's fake. This is where we'll need the shapeshifter."

"Her name is Amanda."

"We'll need Amanda for any of this to work. She'll need to impersonate an agent and then you."

"I don't know if she can shapeshift into other people."

"What do you mean you don't know? You treat her—aren't you supposed to know this stuff?"

Isla began rubbing her temples. "I only know what they tell me."

"I need you to find out if she can, and if she'll help us."

"Amanda is very timid."

"The timid ones are usually the most dangerous." She immediately thought of the Isla she'd met over four months ago. Timid, yet sweet and friendly. What Lu wouldn't give to go back to the days of morning tea from a pretty girl. She might even drink the tea this time if she thought it meant a happily-ever-after was in store for them. "I trust your judgment," she said, knowing that any dwindling hope she held on to for their relationship had to be shown in ways that mattered to Isla. And trust mattered. "I'm just the way to get in and the directions. You're in charge of how this all goes down."

"You know I see right through you, right?" Isla said with a furrowed brow.

"Is that part of your witch powers?" She looked over both shoulders. "Can you see the chair or straight through to the wall?"

"Very funny." Isla wasn't laughing. "I know you're trying to make me feel better about working with you."

"Is it working?"

Isla hesitated. "No, but I'm not helping you for the reasons you may think."

"I know," she said, shocking Isla. "I also know you're not helping *me*. You're helping *them*." Silence stretched on between them, and she knew it was time for her to go. "Here's my new number. My cell was bugged, which is how my boss found out about our relationship."

Isla's expression stuttered. "He *knows*? How much does he know?"

Lu thought of all the places her phone went. "He knows everything, but don't worry. I have him thinking you joined Ronan, and you absolutely hate my guts."

"Only a partial lie."

Her fractured heart finally shattered. "I, um, I'll keep in touch. Let me know who you can get on our team. We need to meet tomorrow around sundown." She ran into the chair on her way out. Her emotions were making her dizzy and oblivious to anything but her exit. She waved and all but ran from Isla's office.

Isla relaxed into her chair and rested her head back. She felt awful for that last dig. She wasn't happy with Lu and might never forgive her, but she didn't hate her guts. She could never hate her guts.

"Luna," she whispered.

Chapter Thirty-three

Isla washed her hands and left the apothecary bathroom with her head held high. Her grandmother always told her leading a coven was a challenge because you had to be the strongest one at all times. When she turned the corner to the main sales floor, she froze at all the eyes on her. "I—" she said, her voice crackling and forcing her to clear her throat. "I really appreciate you all coming today."

"Of course," Maribel said quickly, looking around at the small group. "You've helped us more times than we can count. This is the least we can do." A wave of nodding heads followed.

"And some of us have stupid deeds to atone for." Henry stood meekly at Maribel's side. He had always been a slight man, nothing like the wolf he had inside, which was one of Isla's favorite things about him. "Sometimes it's easy to lose your head and think you have to be the big, bad monster in order to feel like you really belong somewhere."

Her heart hurt. "Henry, you've always—"

"I know. I've always belonged right here with all of you."

"We are a community," she said, holding her hands out for Daria and Christopher to take. They stood at her sides, and she felt the warmth of their power and their friendship. "We're a family here." She locked eyes with Amanda, who was very hesitant to join them but understood it needed to be done. "We're all here for each other, and that means we have each other's backs. I understand if any of you are scared. *I'm* scared, but I know we'll win tonight." She gave Christopher's and Daria's hands a squeeze. "You two stay here."

"I don't like this," Daria said.

"I know. Divide and conquer isn't really our thing, but I need to know you'll both be here protecting the apothecary and ready for anything we may return with." Isla's mind raced. "Or without."

A knock on the front window made everyone jump. Lu stood waving on the other side, showing a thumbs-up.

"Just remember Lu's phone is bugged. From here on out we're all playing parts. Lu is playing a part." *I hope.* Isla surveyed her team one more time before nodding.

Lu slammed her fist harder. "Isla Hoffman, open the door!" Henry unlocked the door and stared Lu down for a moment. Lu kept her distance as she walked around him and up to Isla. Lu handed her an envelope with something hard inside. The outside had instructions to use if needed. "You didn't answer my calls, and now I have no choice. Your time is up."

"What are you talking about?" she said, reciting the script they'd practiced earlier in the day.

"You think I'm some useless security guard, don't you. A rent-a-cop paid to flirt with you."

"Lu, I—"

Lu opened her badge, needing any sound picked up by her phone to be authentic. "I've been watching you. I know what you do here, and I know you're working with Ronan. We're unaware of his whereabouts as yet, but once I get you down to headquarters, I'm sure it'll be easy to get it out of you."

"CIA?" She hoped she sounded natural and channeled her real shock from just days ago. "You work for the CIA?"

"And my job is to protect the world from *things* like you."

Even though they'd gone over what they'd say, she still flinched. "I thought I could trust you. I'm not going with you."

Lu looked at her, her soft blue eyes heavy with sadness, and she mouthed *You can.* "Yes, you are."

Not one to miss a cue, Isla made a small smacking noise against her cheek and then pointed to Henry.

He opened the door to make the bell chime again and said, "What the hell is going on in here?" He added a very impressive growl. "Maribel! Isla needs our help."

"Great, a three-for-one deal." Lu tossed around a few designated items Isla set aside that would make the most noise. Along with the acted-out scuffle, Lu then pretended to drag Isla to her car. Isla's job was to let out incoherent mumbles of protest. In no time, they were in the car on the way to headquarters. Isla, Henry, and Maribel sat in the back, while Amanda rode next to Lu. Their complete silence added to the palpable anxiety. At a red light, Lu took something out of the inside pocket of her suit jacket and handed it to Amanda. Amanda held up a thin syringe, which matched what Isla felt in her envelope. Lu looked back at Isla and nodded. Isla appreciated Lu checking in, and she gave her a subtle nod in return. The only comfort came from knowing the act would be up soon enough.

After a thirty-minute mostly silent drive punctuated by their pretend groans and Lu yelling at them for groaning, they exited the parkway.

Lu said, "And if you even think about using your powers or morphing into the monsters you really are, remember those handcuffs are designed to combat your powers, rendering you all weaker than an average human."

Isla groaned, but this time it was genuine as she recalled labeling Lu an average human.

"Here we are," Lu said as they pulled into an underground garage and stopped at a large glass entrance. It reminded Isla of an emergency room, but she knew no one was coming here for help. "Wakey, wake." Lu reached back, and Henry grabbed her arm. She shouted out and pushed him back.

Isla was seriously impressed by Henry's acting skills. Then a thought hit her like a fist to the gut: What if Lu really was bringing them in to the CIA? What if she had been lying all along again? She began to shake.

Lu dialed her phone and held it to her ear. "McCafferty, I need you to come down to intake and help me out. I have a live one down here." She hung up and dropped her phone between the seat and the console. "Son of a bitch, come on. You're gonna pay for that." Lu got out of the car and opened the back door. She led Isla, Henry, and Maribel to stand together by the entrance. Amanda stood off in a shadowy corner by the door. Lu nodded to her.

Isla let out a shuddering breath. "Are you going to hurt us?" Henry started to growl again.

"It's okay," Lu whispered. "There's only cameras now so they can't hear us. We're going to walk through this door, and I'm going to lead the three of you to the elevators. Look as drugged up as possible. Henry, try to run away. We need to buy enough time to make sure Amanda drugs McCafferty and takes his place. If I know the asshole as well as I think I do, he should be down here any second, ready to take credit for this." The automatic doors slid open, and Lu huddled them farther into the corner as a man Isla recognized rushed past them to the car. "There goes McCafferty," Lu said. "Let's go to the elevators, and Amanda will catch up after she knocks him out."

Isla followed Lu's lead without another word. She'd come this far, and if she wanted to make it out without risking the lives of those around her, she had to believe Lu. She stumbled and barely kept her eyes open. Henry veered off to the side, and Lu made a show of corralling him back. For only having a day of preparation, Isla was proud of their choreography.

Lu waited only seconds before hitting the button for the elevators. Isla heard footsteps. "'Bout damn time, McCafferty," Lu said.

Amanda looked exactly like him. Isla had known many shape-shifters, but she was amazed every time.

All five of them stepped onto the elevator, and Lu selected the basement with her badge. She found the corner with the camera. Isla stood against the button panel and touched it with two fingertips. Once the elevator came to a stop, she gave enough of a little electrical jolt for the cameras to stutter for a few seconds. She removed her handcuffs and handed them to Amanda, who now stood before her as another Isla.

"You got this," Isla said quietly, only mildly freaked out by looking into her very own hazel eyes. She looked at Lu and noticed she was a little pale. Isla chuckled and hid herself in the corner.

"Fourteenth floor. Walk straight until you hit a wall, then turn right. Langdon's office will be straight ahead," Lu said, speaking as quickly as she could. "I don't know what or if you'll find anything in there, but I'll come up to get you when we're done."

"And Director Langdon?"

"Is waiting to meet me and the Inhuman he thinks is the witch, Isla Hoffman."

"Be careful," Isla said.

"I'll see you soon." Lu stepped off the elevator with her prisoners in tow.

Isla waited for the elevator doors to shut before worrying. What if she never saw Lu again?

❖

Lu had never seen the inner workings of the basement, but she tried to appear confident for the sake of Henry, Maribel, and Amanda. These people had volunteered to risk everything, and Lu couldn't let them down. "Remember," she said quietly enough for the others to hear, "stay safe and collect anything you can. The moment you feel like you're in danger, we'll pull out. I can't have any of you get hurt." Her surroundings were eerily quiet.

"We won't leave empty-handed," Henry said.

"Here we go." Lu approached the young agent working the intake desk. He was visibly more concerned with his word-find puzzle than his surroundings. "Hello?"

"Yeah?" he said, not looking up from the paper.

"Agent Cadman with three Inhumans for processing." She didn't see Director Langdon anywhere, which worried her. She had calculated every move of this plan, and his tendency to operate like clockwork was one of the most important details. If he was still in his office...

He finally looked up from his puzzle. "Who are you?"

She squinted to see this agent's name badge. "Lu Cadman, and you are Agent Chris Evans?"

"Like Captain America himself," he said with a wink to Amanda, well, Isla. Which somehow still ruffled Lu's feathers.

"Is Director Langdon around? He wanted to be here for processing." And like magic, the mention of the director's name got Evans moving. "I brought in three. Two werewolves and a witch."

"Yeah, okay," he chortled.

"I'm sorry, do you not believe me?"

"Look, I've seen a lot of things come in and out of here, but werewolves? How are you going to prove that one when it's not a full moon?"

She blew out a long breath. "Where's Director Langdon?"

"Why are they all so calm?"

"Because I drugged them, a lot, and it was great fun. Where's Langdon?"

"He's around here somewhere..." Evans spun around in his chair, acting more like a bored child than an actual adult working for the CIA. Lu didn't understand how she worked with this many boneheads at a top-notch government agency.

"Cadman," Director Langdon said from behind her. "I'm very pleased to see you actually delivered this time." Instead of his usual navy-blue suit and tie, he wore a black tactical uniform.

"With a bonus," she said, making her voice sound as pleased as possible. She needed to be a believable government robot.

"Yeah, two *werewolves*." Evans snorted.

"You managed to get the werewolves. Very impressive, Cadman." His eyes were on Amanda/Isla the entire time. "Go ahead and get them processed. I'll handle Isla Hoffman."

"Sir?"

Splitting up was not part of the plan.

CHAPTER THIRTY-FOUR

Sweat trickled down the center of Lu's back, making her more uncomfortable than ever. It had been nearly twenty minutes since Director Langdon had led fake Isla down a corridor out of sight, and too many people were hanging around while Henry and Maribel were being processed. She should've left her jacket in the car.

"Why is it so hot in here?" She removed her top layer and tossed it over a nearby chair, rolling her sleeves up to her elbows.

"We have a yeti in the back. They don't like the warmth." Evans continued typing away.

Lu had worked in this building for almost a year, and she'd had no idea what horrific torture had been going on below ground. Her mind was blown, and she knew this was no longer a place she fit in. "What's the point of making it uncomfortable?"

"What's the point of keeping it comfortable?" He scanned two bracelets that looked like standard hospital issue and handed them to her. "Put these on them and take them down the hall. The red room is waiting for them."

She read the bracelets: *Werewolf RED ROOM EXP 48HRS.* "What does this mean?"

Evans rolled his eyes. "You're clearly new here," he said with a huff. "We label the creature, where they belong, and when they expire."

"Expire?"

"Exactly what it sounds like. We get what we need and then *pffft.*" He gave a thumbs-down.

She felt Henry go rigid. "Makes sense," she said, hating the two words as they came out. She hated every minute of pretending to be like these people. "Let's go." She tugged Henry and Maribel down the hall. She lowered her voice and said, "Once we're right outside the red room, I need you both to go wolf."

"You think we can just turn it on like that?"

"You can't?" she said almost too loudly thanks to the sheer stab of panic she felt.

"Just kidding. Of course we can." Maribel laughed. "Sorry. I make jokes when I'm nervous."

"I'm nervous, too, but we'll be okay." Lu slowed them down a step and looked around. No one else was in the area. "You don't have to do anything more than make a scene. You don't have to interact with anyone."

"Except maybe Evans," Henry said with a sneer.

Lu nodded emphatically. "You can absolutely interact with him if you want, and Director Langdon if he shows his face again." She placed her hand on her holster, knowing her firearm was there by the weight on her belt but needing to feel it. "Okay, ready?"

❖

Isla jumped when the alarms started to blare. She took them as a sign Lu's part of the plan was moving forward seamlessly, while she had just entered Director Langdon's office. She had no idea what she was looking for. Anything and everything could be evidence. Isla was more of a black-and-white, cut-and-dried woman when it came to directions.

She rushed over to a filing cabinet and yanked it open. Every single drawer had employee folders, user manuals, and enough files on policy and procedures to put Isla to sleep for good. She started to get nervous and anxious, the alarms only adding to her agitation. She focused on Langdon's desk. It was large and wooden, either really expensive or really old. She ran her hand along the smooth edge and felt decades of energy coming from it. Definitely old. The first drawer she opened held office supplies, and the one below it was filled with snacks. For a CIA director, Langdon sure loved his Nerds.

"Never judge a book by its cover," she said. The bottom drawer was locked, but that was no real challenge for Isla, who gave it a little tap and jolt. She found more files, but their labels were cryptic, with numbers and abbreviations that meant nothing to her. She pulled out a handful and started flipping through them, taking pictures of what she could. Lu could decipher the information later. But something caught her eye as she went to return the files.

She saw a small lockbox hidden at the bottom of the drawer. She pulled it out and set it on the desk with a few files she planned on taking. She rushed through the three drawers on the other side and grabbed anything that appeared important or was labeled top secret. Lu could sort through it later.

She pushed away from the desk and noticed one more drawer in the center. It wasn't deep, and Isla almost brushed it off as unimportant, but something told her to open it. Her hand began shaking as she touched the wood. Again, the lock barely delayed her, but she pulled the drawer open with too much force, causing it and its contents to fall and fan out across the floor. They were countless photos of her at various ages, memorializing events from her life, the most recent being a shot of her and Daria from Daria's sister's wedding last October.

Realizing she was being followed or stalked was a bizarre feeling. She first felt the shock, and then the fear set in, quickly coupled with shame. How could she, with all of her intuitive strengths, not have known? She picked up another picture, this one from the day she went to live with her grandmother. She recognized the heartbreak across her tired face, the memory of the day still feeling fresh and raw.

"Fun fact," an unrecognized deep voice said. Isla didn't look up instantly. She kept her head down and felt a chill run across her skin, leaving goose bumps in its wake. "Even the most intuitive witches won't sense something if it isn't immediately recognized as a threat."

She stayed frozen, trying her best to think rationally and act smart. *What would Lu do?* She remained as still as possible while trying to pull her phone from the side pocket of her tight cargo pants. She only had seconds before her stillness and silence would work against her. Slowly and shakily, she looked up. She'd never met the man leaning against the doorway, but something about him seemed familiar.

"Who are you?" She stood up and placed her phone beneath the stack of photos and papers she had in her hands. Going by spatial memory, she tried to access the voice recorder app and hoped she did so properly.

"You should know."

"Should I?" His plain black clothes gave nothing away.

"You're in my office."

She noticed several framed pictures on the wall of Director

Langdon shaking hands with many esteemed politicians. As intuitive as she was, Isla could sometimes be oblivious to her surroundings.

"The shapeshifter was a cute idea, but I know you too well to fall for a cheap trick like that."

Her stomach turned. "I don't know you."

"You can call me William." He stepped farther into the office, both of his hands in his pockets. He looked like a stereotypical CIA agent—tall, thin, and white with no eye-catching or worrisome traits—and yet, Isla was terrified. He placed his hands on the back of the chair across from her. "Did you know that intuition, no matter how strong or otherworldly it may be, won't immediately sense danger from anyone sharing your blood? It's like your default is to assume family is safe."

"That's why I couldn't see Ronan's face." It all made sense.

"We both know blood relations mean nothing. Isn't that right, sis?"

"Sis? I don't have—"

"Do not finish that sentence." His grip on the chair visibly tightened. "I'm not sure what Mom and Dad told you. Even in the last moments of their life, they wouldn't give that up, but here I am," he said, holding up his arms, "your brother."

"Mom and Dad..." Isla felt faint. To learn her brother was still alive after all these years and hearing him say her parents were dead was emotional overload. How many more family members were going to come back to haunt her?

"We got what we could from them and disposed of them, much like they did to me—and *you*, for that matter. Except you got to have Grandma Celeste because you weren't like me." He pulled out the chair and sat, his nonchalance only adding to her discontent. "When they realized I was a boring, useless human, it was a catalyst for many decisions. But the biggest was putting me up for adoption and making sure any trace of my relationship to them and you was destroyed. Our father showed minimal remorse when I reunited with them. Mother, on the other hand, was very moved."

"She was half human," she said.

"Huh. That explains why she cried and kept apologizing. Anyway, when I got older, I went into law enforcement, probably to prove my worth or some other deep psychological reason, and I decided to use my training and resources to find them and you."

"Should I be flattered?" She winced at her choice of words. She needed to abide by the no-sarcasm rule.

His thin lips twitched. "I was long gone by the time you came along, but I needed to know if you had suffered the same fate. Was there someone out there who would understand what I had gone through? I'd finally have family."

"We are *not* family."

"Aren't you mad? Aren't you disgusted by what they did to us?"

"Yes," she said loudly, feeling some of her tension leave as she spoke, "I hate them for it, and they were clearly never meant to have children. But I couldn't, I wouldn't—"

"Kill them? Well, neither could I, but we have a brilliant team of scientists that handled the task." He picked fuzz off his sweater. "Uncle Ronan was a surprise, though. I was worried he'd steal my thunder for the most shocking return, but he was just as pathetic as the rest of you. It does make you wonder how many people father lied about."

Tears rolled down her cheeks. She wasn't crying for the parents who left her behind—she was crying for the mother who baked cookies with her and the father who explained the rules of football on Sundays. She mourned the childhood of whimsy and magic that wasn't too much for a child to understand. She cried for the Christmas mornings past and for lighting the menorah, for the memories she clung to so she could keep her head above the deep waters of despair.

"I'm sorry they abandoned you," she said.

"It's okay—look where I am today." He pointed to the photos on the wall. "I'm the youngest director to ever run a department, never mind it being a department proposed and created from the ground up by me." He seemed positively giddy. "When I first explained what I wanted to do, everyone thought I was crazy, but then I brought them actual proof. The fear in their eyes told me the department was as good as mine before their stamp of approval ever did."

"But why? If you know I'm one of them?"

"Good ol' Mom and Dad didn't teach me much, but they did teach me that creatures, monsters, Inhumans, whatever you want to call them, do not have a place here. They're all dangerous and selfish."

"No, we're not."

"Tell me this, Isla, did you really join Ronan's crusade, or was that all part of Cadman's ruse to get in here?"

She looked away from William. If he knew this was planned, Lu was in danger. If her theory about Lu was correct, she should be able to feel Lu. The moment the alarms stopped, as soon as she closed her eyes, Isla tuned in to her surroundings, the building buzzing with anxiety and fear. Nearly everyone but William was scared. In a fraction of a second, she felt Lu's heartbeat in her own. Lu was alive and full of adrenaline. She took an easy breath.

"The only crusade I'll ever join is ours." She looked back up at William and smiled.

William placed his hand on his chest and said, "I'm happy to hear you say that."

"I think she was talking about me." Lu stood behind William with her gun held up.

CHAPTER THIRTY-FIVE

A re you okay?" Lu tried her best to assess the situation. Both Isla and Director Langdon appeared at ease and unharmed. Most importantly, Langdon was unarmed. But she couldn't assume that meant he was weapon-free.

"Oh, hi Lu, I'm glad you could join us," Isla said. Her voice had a small tremor. "My brother and I were catching up."

"Your brother?" she squeaked. "How did you go from no family to family everywhere?"

"Believe me, I'm just as surprised."

She knew Isla must've been shocked, because she'd never sit afraid in a situation she could easily power her way out of. Isla's confidence was gone. "Well, I'm sorry to cut this reunion short, but I think it's time to get out of here. Henry really went to town on the lab."

"You know I can't let you two leave," he said, standing and turning to Lu. "Agent Cadman, I'm so disappointed in you. You could've been the perfect agent."

"Debatable."

"And Isla," he said over his shoulder. "I was willing to spare you because you're my sister." He reached into his pocket.

"Don't even think about it," Lu shouted.

"Relax," he said with a smile, pulling his keys from his pocket. "You're going to shoot your boss over a set of keys? How would that look when the agency reviews this case?"

She noticed Isla shaking her head, silently telling her not to engage, but who was this asshole to threaten her? "You think I care what the agency will do to me after I shoot someone who used his position for his own gain?"

"I also know you won't shoot me."

"You seem to think reading a file about me means you know me."
She stepped closer. "You don't know anything about me or the lengths
I'll go to protect the people I love."

"You're right, I don't," William said, pressing a button on his key
fob. "I guess it's a good thing I had those new ultrasonic dampeners
we've been working on installed in here." He must have seen the
confusion on her face. He leaned in and whispered, "Let me put it into
terms you can understand. She can't use her powers in here."

Lu drew back her pistol and whipped it across his face. As William
stumbled, she held out her hand to Isla. "Come on, we gotta hurry."

Isla's quick movements came to a sudden halt, and her eyes went
wide. "I..." Her face twisted. "I can't move," she said, forcing the
words through her clenched jaw.

"Jesus Christ, that hurt!" William touched his cheek where a smear
of blood covered the swelling skin. "What aren't you understanding?"
he shouted. "I'm ten steps ahead of you all." He held up his key fob,
and the keys jingled loudly. "What do you think I've been preparing
for? All of the data I've collected and the creatures I've dissected."
Lu swallowed back her nausea and forced her expression to remain
neutral. "I may be human, but to them I am God."

"You're not *my* God." Lu pulled the trigger.

The time shift was subtle, but Lu first felt it in the slow movement
of her trigger finger. The bullet lagged, moving in slow motion. *What
the hell?* She stood by watching the bullet travel toward his body
slowly, like it had been shot through water. His eyes started to widen in
recognition of what was about to happen.

Isla stepped up between them and looked at the bullet before
turning to Lu. "I'm sorry," she said as she reached out and picked the
bullet out of the air. "I know you understand."

No. She wished she could speak and protest. She understood how
difficult it must be for Isla, but Lu struggled to accept this decision. She
could hear Isla's voice in her head. *What if it was Kayla?* She could tell
time was returning to normal by the way the blood rushed to her head.

"Kayla would never..." she said as she fell to her knees, dizzy and
queasy. She took a deep breath and looked up at Isla. "He hurt living
beings."

"And he will be punished, but death is not right."

William leaned back against the chair and gripped his chest as he
heaved for breath. "That was close." He started laughing maniacally.
"I can't believe it. How did you do that? You're more powerful than I

thought, and yet you seem to be the weakest of us all." Lu went to raise her gun again, but Isla stopped her.

"Not wanting you dead is hardly a weakness. If anything, it's a strength. I don't know you, though I may share your blood, and I don't owe you anything. I can't gain anything from your survival, but I still know when it's not my call to end a life."

Lu looked at Isla and saw beyond the beautiful exterior and kind personality she'd grown to love. She saw Isla with her heart, felt her deep in her bones. She saw her for the brilliant soul she was, and something deep within her own self felt whole. She'd finally found her place and her role. She had always been meant to find Isla and help protect the safe haven she'd worked so hard to keep and build.

"Leave him then," Lu found herself saying. She extended her hand to Isla. "He'll get his, but we should go." She waited and watched.

The gunshot popped loudly in the small space.

She watched in terror as Isla's body crumbled to the ground. Tears instantly obstructed her vision, but that didn't stop her from screaming and charging forward. She landed her first punch against the side of his head and the second in his solar plexus. Anger from deep within came rushing to the surface, like a solar flare burning hot for the years of being forced into roles she didn't want and following rules she disagreed with. She grabbed his collar and threw him into a large wooden bookcase. Not until he was motionless on the ground did she come back to herself and rush to Isla's side. Isla lay unconscious and bleeding.

"Isla? Hey." She tapped Isla's cold cheek. "Please wake up. You can't go. Not like this and not now." She took a shaky breath and held Isla's hand against her chest. "We have too much left to do, you and me. Your shop and my boring condo. You haven't even argued with Kayla yet, and that's one of the most fun parts of life. Please," she said through a sob. She tried her best to compose herself, but she had nothing inside but panic and tears. "I need help in here," she yelled and covered the bullet wound with her hand to stop the bleeding. Lu wiped her nose and lowered her face, pressing her forehead to Isla's. "Please. I never got to tell you how sorry I am, how I took a job I would take a hundred times if it meant meeting you." She felt for a pulse, but the thump was weak against her fingertips. "Come back to me. Whatever magic you have left in you, use it to come back to me."

"Come on."

She jumped when a hand landed on her shoulder. She turned to find Henry behind her. "I can't leave her." She looked back at Isla's lifeless body, her linen top bloodstained and torn. She shook her head and cried. "She never even met Samson."

Henry's eyes were glassy. "Get to the car. I'll bring her."

"I love you," she whispered one last time, kissing Isla's parted lips.

❖

The scent of iron, no, blood filled the air. Isla ached but couldn't move. She felt heavy, but light. The contradictory sensations triggered panic, but she could not move. She could hear muffled sounds around her as a chill crept up from her stomach to her chest. Isla realized what was happening. She was dying.

"Isla?"

She heard the deep timbre of Henry's voice, but she couldn't answer him. No matter how hard she tried to speak, no voice came. Pressure brought immense pain, and Isla whimpered.

"It's time, Isla," Henry said.

Isla fought to open her eyes, using what little life she had left to do so. "Hen—please." Breathing grew harder. She watched Henry smile, a bright grin that seemed so opposite from the tears in his dark eyes.

"I always wanted Maribel to be proud of me, to be with me. I knew we were meant to love each other until the end of time. Eighty-four years is a crazy long time." His laugh turned into a short sob. "You've found that now with Lu—everyone can see it." Henry took her hand.

Isla tried to speak, tried to put the visions of Lu into words, but nothing came out. She gripped Henry's hand with all she had.

"I want you to take my life force."

Isla widened her eyes. "No," she said weakly.

"I know you can. I remember Celeste telling us about how witches take another's life force to save themselves, and you need to save yourself. Our community needs you."

"Maribel…"

"Maribel," he said, pausing to take a deep breath, "will be fine, but this fight is not over, and you are our leader. Please." He lowered his head and pressed his forehead against Isla's. "Accept my offering."

Isla closed her eyes again and tried to focus on all the reasons why she shouldn't accept Henry's life, but she knew she'd be dead within minutes if she refused. Her life with Lu, her coven, and the deep love she felt for the small town her grandmother had raised her to protect would all be gone. Isla struggled to breathe, struggled to think, and struggled to listen as Henry begged for her to stay.

❖

The way back to the car was a daze. Agents rushed around Lu and cried out about one emergency or another. The elevators were inoperable, and the stairwell was hot. By the time she stepped out into the garage, her legs ached and her fingers were tacky with blood. She looked at the car where Amanda and Maribel waited anxiously. Amanda fell to her knees the moment they locked eyes, and Maribel covered her mouth to stifle a cry.

"I tried." She slumped against the car. "I tried," she said again, trying to convince herself. She heard sirens in the distance, undoubtedly belonging to the police officers and first responders lining up at the main entrance. "We have to get out of here before anyone comes down."

"What about Isla?" Maribel choked on a sob.

"Henry was going to bring her down." She turned her back to the door, unable to watch as he carried Isla out. She heard the door swing open, and a louder cry erupted from Maribel. It wasn't until Amanda gasped that Lu turned back. Isla stood before them, disheveled and bloody but alive, tears in her hazel eyes. Isla fell into her arms, and she held her tightly.

She looked at Isla in wonder. "How?"

Isla stepped back and looked at Maribel. "Henry gave his life force to save mine," she said. "I'm sorry. I was so weak that I couldn't refuse him," Isla said, her voice thick with emotion.

Lu watched as Maribel broke down in mourning. Henry had sacrificed his life and the love he had for nearly a century to save Isla.

Isla spoke quietly. "I heard him in the last seconds before I woke up. He kept saying how much he loved you and will always be with you. He wanted you to be proud of him."

Maribel cried out. "I was always proud of him."

Isla ran to Maribel to comfort her. "We all know that, and so did he."

"Henry was a hero," Lu said. Maribel cried harder into Isla's shoulder. Lu looked away, struggling with her own warring emotions. She was grateful and sad, devastated this night came down to a sacrifice everyone in the community would feel deeply for a long time to come.

But she couldn't stop the relief from rushing to the surface. Her Isla was still alive, *they* were alive. Sirens grew closer. "Let's go." They got in the car.

"What about his body?" Maribel asked.

"I have this for you," Isla said, holding out a silver ring in the palm of her open hand. "I know it's not the same."

Maribel took the ring and held it to her heart. "Thank you." Lu watched her smile in the rearview window. "He made this ring when we got married. We'd be celebrating eighty-five years next year."

Lu looked ahead at the dark road. "I'm sorry I got you all mixed up in this. If I had thought—"

"No. This was the only way. You wouldn't have been able to stop them on your own." Isla reached across the console and squeezed Lu's forearm.

"We all knew the risks," Maribel said flatly. After another few minutes of silence, Maribel spoke again. "I saw the director guy run out of your room, Amanda. I know you distracted him as long as you could, but how did he know you weren't the real Isla?" Lu had been wondering the same.

"He talked about Isla's parents a lot," Amanda said. Lu couldn't see her face. "I don't know anything about them, and I guess he got suspicious. This is all my fault."

"We need to stop blaming ourselves," Lu said firmly. "It's not going to change anything. We did the best we could with the information we had. Maybe we'll be able to stop him, maybe we won't. What I do know is I won't stop." She tightened her grip on the steering wheel until her palms burned. "Henry's death will not be in vain."

"No, it won't. We grabbed a bunch of files and all the paperwork from that Evans guy's desk." Maribel pointed to a stack of folders on her lap.

"That's not all," Isla said, handing over her phone. "I recorded him admitting his personal agenda. It may not be worth much, but it should be enough to dismantle whatever William put into action."

Lu held up the phone. "I think we just saved your people."

CHAPTER THIRTY-SIX

Isla couldn't even look Daria and Christopher in the eye when they arrived back at the apothecary. She'd insisted they stay back to make sure there'd be a coven to continue her work, but she couldn't imagine losing more of her family. Now, she had to say good-bye to Maribel, who'd go home to an empty house.

"Come by anytime for anything. I mean it." She held on to Maribel, hesitant to let her go for fear of her falling apart.

"Thank you. I just want to go home, even though I know it'll hurt. I'll at least be surrounded by his things."

"We couldn't have succeeded without you two. I'll be forever indebted."

Maribel shook her head sadly and walked away.

She felt Daria and Christopher step up to stand at her sides on the sidewalk. The night was dark and humid, the air still and quiet. The earth's atmosphere matched their melancholy. Lu sat in her car and idled, and Isla felt overwhelmed.

"So that's it?" Christopher said, breaking the thick silence. "We won?"

"Maybe." She crossed her arms and winced at the soreness that lingered near her shoulder. Traumas like a gunshot wound took longer than regular wounds to heal completely. Apparently. "Lu has to submit our findings to someone who will listen and someone she can trust, but as far as our role goes, we're done."

Christopher looked at her with desperate, hopeful eyes. "Do you think we won?"

She thought of Lu's reaction to her recording. "I think so."

"I hope so," Daria said. "For Henry's sake." They bowed their heads and shared a moment of silence for their fallen family. "What's next?"

"We get back to work. If I've learned anything over the past couple of weeks, it's that this community needs us, and we need them."

"I wasn't really talking about that." Some spunk returned to Daria's tone. She nudged Isla and nodded toward Lu. "I'm talking about you two."

"It's complicated."

"You're gonna tell me after all of this, after she stepped up and risked everything to help us, well, to help you, you're gonna give her a hard time? We all make mistakes, Isla. You can't be this stubborn and expect to get anything you want in life. It doesn't work like that, and from where I'm standing, she's a good person with a good heart, and she's madly in love with you."

Isla waited. "Are you done?"

"May I say something?" Christopher said.

"Is it in Lu's defense?"

"Yes."

"Then no."

"Isla, you're being too—"

"Stop," she said with a raised hand. "Lu doesn't need anyone to state her case for her." She gave Daria a brief but meaningful look. "The universe has already shown me how important Luna Cadman is to me."

"Luna?" Daria said in a scoff. "Lu is short for Luna?"

"Yup."

"I thought it was short for Louise," Christopher said.

Isla didn't say a word—she didn't give a hint. She knew it would sink in eventually, even as she listened to Daria go on and on about having a hard time seeing Lu as a Luna because it was a feminine name and Lu was such a handsome butch.

"She'd never be a Louise. Come on," Daria said, ready to argue with Christopher.

"Daria?" she said, needing the chatter to stop. "When I say Luna, what comes to mind?"

"That chiseled hottie," Daria said, pointing to Lu with zero discretion.

Isla closed her eyes. "What else?"

"The moon," Christopher said, their tone hinting they had caught on.

"The moon." Daria slapped her arm, and Isla yelped.

"I got shot tonight," she said between clenched teeth.

"Oh shit. I'm sorry." Daria tried to soothe the spot she had already assaulted. "Lu is the moon, and you're Isla, the island. Did you lose your mind when she told you her name?"

"She didn't tell me." She recalled the feeling of reading *Luna Cadman* in black and white. "She laid her credentials in front of me, showing me who she really was, and I read it."

"Wow. Grandma Celeste always knew."

"She did," she said, nodding. She took a deep breath and continued to watch Lu through the windshield. "She really did." Clarity felt good, but Isla had a mess to clean up, and the night was not getting younger. "Head home, guys, and take the day off tomorrow."

"You can't work alone after the night you had."

"We're closing tomorrow. I think we all deserve it, and I'd like a dark day in remembrance." She looked up at the stars and made a promise to live the life Henry gave her for more than service. He lived to love Maribel and devoted himself to the life they built together, and Isla would honor that. She smiled and pulled her two friends into a hug. "Good night, witches."

"Good night," Christopher said.

"Go get your woman." Daria gave her a gentle nudge.

Isla started to walk over to Lu's car but stopped and looked over her shoulder and said, "I love you both very much. I'm lucky you're my family."

"We love you, too," Daria said. She put her arm around Christopher's shoulders. "We're the lucky ones."

With a reassuring nod, she turned back and kept walking to Lu. Out of everything she had been through, she was most scared of this. She opened the passenger side door and got in the car. She didn't say anything at first, unsure of what exactly would fit in the moment. She could apologize or explain herself. She could even break down all the reasons she could be so hardheaded, but nothing felt right.

"Did you listen to the recording?" she said, wanting to smack herself immediately for being so basic.

"I did. It's great—I mean, sad and awful, but it'll help us a lot."

Isla bit the free edge of her painfully short thumbnail. "I need to apologize—"

"Can we talk?" Lu said, cutting Isla off, then laughed. "You don't—"

"Let's talk," Isla said, interrupting Lu. She pointed to Lu, signaling for her to go first, and was not at all surprised Lu said no.

Isla opened her mouth but promptly closed it. Even her ability to reconcile was tainted by her stubbornness. She looked out the window, and the moon looked back. "When I was little, my grandmother would tell me the same story every night. I don't even know if it was her favorite or my favorite, but she would tell it every night until I was maybe ten or eleven." She looked at her reflection in the window, too nervous and too shy to look at Lu. "Then when my parents left," she said, a swell of emotion catching her off guard, "she started telling it to me again. I was sixteen and dependent on my grandmother's bedtime story." She laughed now at the absurdity of it all.

"My family was never warm like that. I blame the military mentality."

She wanted to ask Lu more about her childhood and her life in New York, but there'd be time for that later. Hopefully. "The story was about the Island and the Moon." She finally risked looking at Lu, and she swallowed hard at the tired blue eyes looking back. "You see, the Island was all alone in the middle of the ocean but never felt lonely because a whole world lived on her that she was responsible for. As long as they were thriving, she believed she was thriving, too. Until one night when she looked up and saw the Moon." She tried to control the tremor of her voice and the tears she knew were ready to fall. "The Island was so absorbed in her own little world, she never noticed the Moon shining every night, watching over her and waiting on the horizon to steal a moment."

"Was this from a children's book?" Lu said thickly, with a laugh meant to cover her emotional state.

She laughed through her nose. "No. She said it was my story."

"How does it end?"

She put out her hand, palm up, and waited for Lu to take it. When she did, Isla finally felt her heart, mind, and magic align. "Even on the cloudiest nights, the Island would search the sky for the brightest clouds and wait until the Moon came close enough to kiss. It was a long wait, but it was worth it to hear the Moon whisper to her."

"What did the Moon say?"

She hesitated before saying, "*I have always loved you.* So even though the Island didn't see it at first, she finally understood the universe created them together, to be together."

"Wow," Lu said as she traced the back of Isla's hand and up to the inside of her wrist. "The picture in your shop?"

"My grandmother had it commissioned for my thirteenth birthday.

I was always the Island—my parents made me an only child and then left me, my grandmother passed, and I had this community to care for."

Lu reached out and caressed her cheek. "But then you finally looked up."

"The Moon had been waiting there all along." She started to feel drowsy at Lu's touch. "Luna."

"No," Lu said, placing her fingertip on Isla's lips. "We don't use that name."

She giggled against Lu's finger before kissing it gently. "Thank you."

"For what?"

"For not going away, for always being in my sky, even when I told you to go."

"That was just a really cloudy day," Lu said, tucking Isla's hair behind her ear. Lu lightly touched her cheek and then the mole next to her eye. "You are the most extraordinary woman I have ever met, and I realized tonight that I was put on this earth to protect and serve *with* you." Lu took Isla's hands and guided them to her face. "I want you to read me again."

She was tired and weak. "I can't—"

"Please. I want you to know the truth, I want you to know *everything*."

She ran the pad of her thumbs along Lu's defined cheeks. The temptation to kiss Lu was much greater than her desire to read her, but she would do anything Lu asked of her. She pressed her forehead to Lu's and closed her eyes. Everything rushed forward. She felt Lu's regret and remorse. She felt the sadness and loss and especially the self-blame. What shone brightest, what warmed over the other darker feelings, was her love for Isla.

She saw the moment Lu met Samson as a puppy and felt the fear from that night in the desert. She watched as Lu spun her niece on a playground, and she experienced the chill of Lu's father's disappointment the night Lu told him about her discharge. Isla followed the flashes of Lu's timeline up until the moment she listened to Director Langdon condemn creatures like Isla. She couldn't stand the sight of William and pulled away to focus only on the details that mattered here and now. Love was never to blame—it had never obscured her vision. Love was clarity.

"I think we're made of the same soul."

"Like twin flames?" Lu said, laughing at Isla's audible gasp of shock. "I do actually know about that. I'm a romantic, even if I don't look like one."

"I love you," Isla blurted out. "I have loved you for a while now, even before we, you know…" Her ears warmed and suddenly her body was alive with desire. She had a lot of emotional baggage to unpack after everything that had happened, but tomorrow was a new day to tackle all that. Right now, she focused on life and love. "And I'd like it if you let me love you for a really, really long time."

Lu started leaning in. "Under one condition."

"Anything."

"You let me love you back." Lu kissed her, and she readily accepted Lu's soft lips against hers. Silently, she was telling her she'd accept anything Lu was willing to give.

After years of living and loving with restrictions, her heart bloomed, and her outlook on life completely changed. Her soul broke free and finally reunited with Lu's. Isla felt whole and loved and more powerful than she ever had.

EPILOGUE

Two years later

Lu stared, overwhelmed, at the full room before her. Sure, she had mentioned a party to celebrate the opening of Cadman Security, but she didn't expect the hoopla Isla had put together. All of Bender seemed to have turned out to congratulate her.

"Wipe that look off your face, babe. You deserve this," Isla said, kissing Lu on the cheek.

"I didn't expect this many people." She removed her thick wool coat and tossed it on a nearby chair. The home they had purchased was the perfect balance of modern and bohemian, a true combination of them both. She grinned as Lilly came bounding toward her. "Hey, kiddo," she said, grunting as she lifted her growing niece.

"Can I play with Samson?"

She laughed. "Of course. I'm sure he's around here somewhere, waiting for food."

"Mom said I wasn't allowed until you got here."

"I'm sorry your mom is mean." She set Lilly down and ruffled her dark hair. Lilly sped off immediately. "You know, I liked her better when she liked me better."

"She still loves her Lulu," Isla said, wrapping her arm around Lu's. "Now go mingle while I get the rest of the food out."

She pulled Isla back to her and kissed her. She couldn't come home and *not* give Isla a proper kiss, not on a night like this. "Hurry up. I miss you." Isla gave her a wink and then left.

She stepped farther into the open living room, the exposed beams offering a sense of warmth incomparable on cold winter nights. She shook her head as she approached Kayla and Ken. "I'm glad you two made it."

"Like I'd miss celebrating my sister opening her own business?" Kayla took a sip of her drink. "Or a chance to get myself some of Isla's magical drinks? Whatever abracadabra she does to keep me from getting a hangover, she better never stop."

"It's not that kind of magic." She watched Kayla gulp the rest and turned her attention to Ken. "Thank you for coming. I know it was probably tempting to stay home," she said with a sideways glance at Kayla. Ken snorted.

"Excuse me?" Kayla looked at them.

"Is that Daria and Christopher? Gotta go." She snuck away as Kayla started calling her some extra-cute nicknames.

Daria rubbed her hands together before throwing her arms around Lu. Christopher soon joined in the hug. "I'm really happy for you," Daria said. "For both of you. First, Hoffman's finally got its Ocean Avenue location, and now this."

"Thank you, thank you." Lu took a deep breath. "Is it weird that I'm nervous?" She tugged at the collar of her violet sweater.

"Absolutely not. This is big."

"It's huge," Christopher said. "And speaking of huge, my boyfriend is coming by later, and we've been fighting a lot lately. So if you sense some tension, just ignore it."

"What are you fighting over?" Lu asked, mostly paying attention to Isla as she laughed with Lu's parents. She'd never grow tired of the sparkle in Isla's eyes or the way her throat sloped when she threw her head back.

"Hello?" Daria waved a hand in front of Lu's face. "Earth to Lu."

"Sorry, I...um, yeah." She knew her smile was goofy, but she never took her eyes off Isla.

Daria dismissed her with a quick gesture. "Just go. It was very nice you tried to talk to us."

Lu kissed Isla's temple and said, "What's got everyone laughing over here?" She touched Isla's lower back and then up to the nape of her neck. She had to touch her. It had been a long day of finalizing paperwork and building walk-throughs. She needed the physical confirmation she was home.

Her father wiped a tear from his matching blue eyes. "Isla was telling us about your latest interviewee."

She groaned. "Can you believe that guy? I haven't heard from McCafferty since we dismantled the department, except for a few very colorful voice mails about how I ruined his life for a witch, and then his résumé pops up in my email the day I posted the job listings." She recalled her own disbelief and shook her head. "He misspelled two words on his cover letter."

"What were they?" her mother said, still laughing slightly.

"Probability and necessary. Oh, and he wrote *inhumane* every time I know he meant Inhuman."

"Why bring him in for an interview then?"

"Payback for the voice mails," she said with a shrug. She should have felt shame, but she felt nothing but satisfaction. She listened as Isla retold her favorite parts of the story and counted her blessings. Thanks to Isla's encouragement, she'd reached out to her parents to try to rebuild a better relationship, one that fit the person she had grown into. They weren't able to erase the past, but everyone was trying for a better present and future.

"Champagne," Amanda announced as she walked into the room carrying more full flutes than Lu's naked eye could count. Lu took one, and one for Isla, and couldn't help but steal another kiss when she handed it over.

Maribel tapped her glass and held it up to get everyone's attention. "I think it's time for a speech," Maribel said, looking at Lu with a raised eyebrow. Lu's heart started to pound. "I am so proud and happy. Bender is in the best hands with you two. Get up here, Lu!"

She took a quick sip of champagne to battle her dry mouth and took Maribel's place at the front of the room. I—" Her voice cracked. After clearing her throat, she continued. "I came to Bender about three years ago with a job to do and zero expectations. Little by little, I started to fall in love," she said, looking only at Isla, "and it became clear to me this was my home. This is where I'm meant to be, and these are the people I'm meant to serve and protect."

She placed her champagne on a nearby table and held out her hand. "Isla?" Isla joined her at her side, and she turned to face her fully. "Falling in love with you and getting to love you every day has been the greatest joy of my life. I not only found my place in this world, but I also found myself. You push me and you challenge me to question the world and grow continuously as a person, and you have me eating healthier than I ever cared to." Everyone in the room laughed. "I am the person I am today because my soul found yours." Lu took the velvet box out of her pocket and got down on one knee.

No other reaction in the room compared to Isla's wide eyes. "Oh my God. What is…?" Isla covered her mouth with her hand. "What is happening?"

She loved Isla even more right then. For all the powers Isla had and all the ways this surprise could've been discovered and ruined, she still managed to pull it off. "Isla, I'm lucky to have found you early in this lifetime, and I'd like to spend the rest of it at your side. Will you marry me?" She opened the box and presented Isla with an engagement ring she'd designed herself. The pear-shaped diamond sat on a platinum band and was surrounded by colorful tourmaline.

Isla looked like she was about to faint. "Yes," she said with a forceful nod. "Yes, of course, a million times yes." Isla practically clawed at Lu to get her to stand.

Lu wrapped her arms around Isla and lifted her gently to spin her. Finally, after setting her down, she placed the ring on Isla's finger and kissed her. Sweetly and softly, she used the kiss to promise a forever full of love and safety. Everyone around them was clapping and hollering their congratulations, but they were lost in each other.

Lu brought Isla's hand to her lips and kissed the ring symbolizing their forever. Looking into Isla's eyes told Lu everything she needed to know. She smiled before leaning in to whisper in Isla's ear, "I have always loved you."

About the Author

M. Ullrich is a four-time Goldie Award finalist and a two-time Lambda Literary Award finalist, and she has been featured in *The Advocate* magazine. She currently resides by the New Jersey Shore with the love of her life and their three furry children, but dreams of living someplace with a lot less road rage. When she's not writing or working her full-time job, M. Ullrich appreciates the simple pleasures in life like breakfast foods and sweet treats, working on her artistic skills, and using her ridiculous humor to make people laugh.

Books Available From Bold Strokes Books

A Cutting Deceit by Cathy Dunnell. Undercover cop Athena takes a job at Valeria's hair salon to gather evidence to prove her husband's connections to organized crime. What starts as a tentative friendship quickly turns into a dangerous affair. (978-1-63679-208-8)

As Seen on TV! by CF Frizzell. Despite their objections, TV hosts Ronnie Sharp, a laid-back chef, and paranormal investigator Peyton Stanford have to work together. The public is watching. But joining forces is risky, contemptuous, unnerving, provocative—and ridiculously perfect. (978-1-63679-272-9)

Blood Memory by Sandra Barret. Can vampire Jade Murphy protect her friend from a human stalker and keep her dates with the gorgeous Beth Jenssen without revealing her secrets? (978-1-63679-307-8)

Foolproof by Leigh Hays. For Martine Roberts and Elliot Tillman, friends with benefits isn't a foolproof way to hide from the truth at the heart of an affair. (978-1-63679-184-5)

Glass and Stone by Renee Roman. Jordan must accept that she can't control everything that happens in life, and that includes her wayward heart. (978-1-63679-162-3)

Hard Pressed by Aurora Rey. When rivals Mira Lavigne and Dylan Miller are tapped to co-chair Finger Lakes Cider Week, competition gives way to compromise. But will their sexual chemistry lead to love? (978-1-63679-210-1)

The Laws of Magic by M. Ullrich. Nothing is ever what it seems, especially not in the small town of Bender, Massachusetts, where a witch lives to save lives and avoid love. (978-1-63679-222-4)

The Lonely Hearts Rescue by Morgan Lee Miller, Nell Stark & Missouri Vaun. In this novella collection, a hurricane hits the Gulf Coast, and the animals at the Lonely Hearts Rescue Shelter need love—and so do the humans who adopt them. (978-1-63679-231-6)

The Mage and the Monster by Barbara Ann Wright. Two powerful mages, one committed to magic and one controlled by it, strive to free each other and be together while the countries they serve descend into war. (978-1-63679-190-6)

Truly Wanted by J.J. Hale. Sam must decide if she's willing to risk losing her found family to find her happily ever after. (978-1-63679-333-7)

A Good Chance by Ali Vali. Harry, Desi, and Desi's sister Rachel are so close to getting everything they've ever wanted, but Desi's ex-husband is coming back to get his revenge and rip apart their chance at happiness. (978-1-63679-023-7)

A Perfect Fifth by Jaycie Morrison. Streetwise pianist Zara Keller and Lady Jillian Stansfield couldn't be more different, yet their connection brings a new awareness of who they are and what they truly want in their lives—including each other. (978-1-63679-132-6)

Catching Feelings by Ana Hartnett Reichardt. Andrea Foster expected to catch a lot of pitches from the Alder Lions' star pitcher, Maya, but she didn't expect to catch feelings. (978-1-63679-227-9)

Defiant Hearts by Lee Lynch. In these stories, you'll find your lovers, friends, and lesbians you wish you knew—maybe even yourself. (978-1-63679-237-8)

Love and Duty by Catherine Young. All Princess Roseli wants is to marry her three lovers, but with war looming, she must instead marry Princess Lucia to establish a military alliance between their planets. (978-1-63679-256-9)

Serendipity by Kris Bryant. Serendipity brings jingle writer Annie Foster and celebrity pop star Bristol Baines together, and their undeniable attraction keeps them close, but will their different paths drive them apart? (978-1-63679-224-8)

The Haunted Heart by Jane Kolven. A ghost, a ring, and a quest to find a missing psychic—it's a spell for love. (978-1-63679-245-3)

The Rules of Forever by Nan Campbell. After reconnecting at their high school reunion, Cara and Lauren agree to embark on a textbook definition friends-with-benefits relationship, but trying to keep it uncomplicated is harder than it seems. (978-1-63679-248-4)

Vision of Virtue by Brey Willows. When virtue and desire come together, be prepared for sparks in this next installment of the Memory's Muses series. (978-1-63679-118-0)

The Artist by Sheri Lewis Wohl. Detective Casey Wilson and reclusive artist Tula Crane are drawn together in a web of passion, intrigue, and art that might just hold the key to stopping a killer. (978-1-63679-150-0)

Cherry on Top by Georgia Beers. A chance meeting leaves Cherry and Ellis longing for a different life, but when Ellis's search for truth crashes into Cherry's insta-filter world, do they have any hope at all of a happily ever after? (978-1-63679-158-6)

Love and Other Rare Birds by Angie Williams. Ornithologist Dr. Jamie Martin and park ranger Rowan Fleming are searching the Alaskan wilderness for a bird thought to be extinct, and they're about to discover opposites really do attract. (978-1-63679-108-1)

Parallel Paradise by Mayapee Chowdhury. When their love affair is put to the test by the homophobia of their family, community, and culture, Bindi and Rimli will need to fight for a chance at love. (978-1-63679-203-3)

Perfectly Matched by Toni Logan. A beautiful Cupid named Hannah, a runaway arrow, and just seventy-two hours to fix a mishap that could be the best mistake she has ever made. (978-1-63679-120-3)

Slow Burn by Missouri Vaun. A wounded wildland firefighter from California and a struggling artist find solace and love in a small southern town. (978-1-63679-098-5)

The Inconvenient Heiress by Jane Walsh. An unlikely heiress and a spinster evade the Marriage Mart only to discover true love together. (978-1-63679-173-9)

The Value of Sylver and Gold by Michelle Larkin. When word gets out that former Boston Homicide Detective Reid Sylver can talk to the dead, the FBI solicits her help on a serial murder case, prompting Reid to assemble forces once again with Detective London Gold. (978-1-63679-093-0)

Wildflower by Cathleen Collins. When a plane crash leaves seven-year-old Lily Andrews stranded in the vast wilderness of Arkansas, will she be able to overcome the odds and make it back to civilization and the one person who holds the key to her future? (978-1-63679-244-6

BOLDSTROKESBOOKS.COM

Looking for your next great read?

Visit BOLDSTROKESBOOKS.COM
to browse our entire catalog of paperbacks, ebooks,
and audiobooks.

Want the first word on what's new?
Visit our website for event info,
author interviews, and blogs.

Subscribe to our free newsletter for sneak peeks,
new releases, plus first notice of promos
and daily bargains.

SIGN UP AT
BOLDSTROKESBOOKS.COM/signup

Bold Strokes Books
Quality and Diversity in LGBTQ Literature

*Bold Strokes Books is an award-winning publisher
committed to quality and diversity in LGBTQ fiction.*